Dimwater's Dagger

By

Sam Ferguson

Dimwater's Dagger

Text Copyright © 2016 Sam Ferguson

Artwork © 2016 Dragon Scale Publishing

All Rights Reserved

ISBN: 1-943183-24-4
ISBN-13: 978-1-943183-2-41

Front cover art by Bob Kehl

To R.F. and H.I.

Table of Contents

Chapter 1

Kyra stepped through her portal into the aspen grove, but sighed when she saw Leatherback was not there. It had been several days since she last saw him. The breaks she had between lessons with Cyrus never seemed to coincide with Leatherback actually being where he was supposed to be.

She assumed he was out hunting. He had told her that his appetite had been growing much larger since the fight with the shade. Not that he had needed to tell her. She could plainly see the pile of bones heaped up in the far corner of the grove.

"Leatherback," she huffed. "You have to get rid of these piles," she chastised. If the dragon slayers ever came through this area, one look at the pile of bones would have them setting up an ambush, for only a dragon could eat so much.

Kyra moved to the large pile, holding her nose against the foul odor. She looked down and noticed one particular skull that looked unfamiliar. Most of the bones belonged to moose or elk, but there was one that looked to be a long-horned cow. She would have to ask him about that the next time she saw him. No matter how large his appetite became, he had to stay away from cattle and other domesticated animals.

She summoned a large fire and let the magical flames consume the bones, all the while controlling the smoke with her magic. When the pile was gone, she tried to make new grass sprout over the scorched earth.

Unfortunately, despite her many talents, she never seemed able to get the grass to grow over the burned spots. She made a note to learn a more efficient spell to rid the area of bones without leaving any trace.

She then and sat upon the rock in the middle of the clearing and pulled out a book that she had intended to read to Leatherback. Instead, she sat by herself and read the book alone until it was time for her to return to the academy. Kyra sighed disappointedly, but there wasn't much she could do.

"At least he is taking the staff," she noted as she pulled at a pile of branches and debris to look around next to the saddle she used to ride him. The saddle was undisturbed, but the staff was not in its place.

She wondered what the dragon might be up to, but decided she would figure it out another time. She wasn't overly worried about him, for he had never shown any sign of being tainted by the blight before. She decided to check the pond they made the next time she came to call upon him. Maybe he was swimming more. He was awfully fond of that.

Kyra bent down and picked a small daisy and then set it upon the stone, and then she went back to the academy.

She went to her classroom where Cyrus was waiting for her.

"Did you find him yet?" Cyrus asked.

"Nope," Kyra huffed.

Cyrus nodded. "Headmaster Herion is returning tomorrow," he said.

A wave of dread rolled over her and Kyra suddenly found her throat dry and her face warm and flush. "He's done?" she asked.

"Master Fenn said he would come to your room tomorrow morning. Herion wants to speak with you."

Kyra groaned.

She had not been looking forward to this. It had been two weeks since she had slain the shade. There had been a flurry of commotion the day after, and Headmaster Herion had rushed out of the academy on foot, without a driver or any sort of escort. Cyrus had informed her afterward that Feberik Orres had already been sent to the battle site to secure it. Herion was determined to get rid of any evidence of the recent battles and then go through the nearby countryside looking for any possible witnesses.

Kyra hadn't understood the reason for all the upheaval, but she had taken comfort in knowing that her punishment would be delayed until Herion's return. Now that he was done and on his way back, she wished she could find a very large rock to crawl under.

Cyrus must have sensed her trepidation. He approached her and offered a reassuring smile. "How about we skip the rest of the lessons for today and you can go and relax, or maybe go out and get into more trouble with Linny. Just don't get caught stealing more biscuits from the kitchen, all right?"

Kyra laughed, but her uneasiness didn't diminish. She shook her head. At this point, the only thing that might help to clear her head was focusing on her lessons. "Actually, let's practice," she said in a mousy tone.

Cyrus shrugged. "Very well. Let's go through some warm up fights first." He turned around and walked toward the front of the room as he pushed the desks and chairs up to the side walls with his magic. "Shall we start with imps?"

Kyra groaned. She hated imps.

*****

Leatherback soared high in the air, circling in and out of the clouds and scanning the seas below. His sharp eyes ensured there were no ships or boats anywhere around what he had claimed as his island.

It wasn't large by dragon standards, but it was large enough. There were two smaller foothills budding from a larger mountain that rose high enough into the sky that it still had snow upon the peak. The lush forest was like a verdant carpet stretching out to each sandy beach surrounding the entire island. The ample vegetation was perfect, for it helped several herds of wild pigs and miniature deer thrive upon the island. There were even two herds of wild cows that roamed the southern portion of the island.

More than that though, there was the song.

A melody called out to him from under the mountain, stronger than anything he had ever experienced anywhere else. Even as he flew high above the island, the music filled his mind and invigorated his heart.

Now that he knew the area was clear, he dropped down through the warm, moist air and set upon the western side of the mountain. He had formed a kind of landing pad there, having cleared out the trees over the last several days. He folded his wings and forced his way through the forest as he followed the music to its source.

As the melody grew loud and vibrations coursed through his bones he stopped and looked down at the ground. He had come here several times, hunting and resting in his makeshift clearing while he listened to the music coming from the ground, but he had never felt the call as intensely as he did today.

He reached out with his right foreleg and stabbed his talons deep into the dirt. He raked a gash in the ground, tearing loose plants, dirt, and rocks. The music increased, as if shouting out for him to uncover the source.

Leatherback set himself to work, tearing and ripping at the ground. Soon he had a large pit nearly as deep as he was tall. He heaped up the mounds of fresh dirt behind him and kept working and digging earnestly until the day was nearly spent.

Then, as the sun began to hang low in the horizon, Leatherback smiled. The music was so loud that it was almost all he could hear. He looked down and saw dirt caked onto a nugget of yellow.

"Hello there," Leatherback said with a grin.

He continued to widen and deepen his mine until the moon was nearly up in the middle of the sky, and then he begrudgingly peeled himself away to return to the grove.

Chapter 2

Kyra stood in a strange room. People were gathered all around her. Some she knew, like Feberik and Janik Orres, and others she didn't. They all watched her with wide smiles painted across their faces. She smiled back, and only then realized that she was in the north parlor of her home.

No, that couldn't be right. Her father had disowned her. She lived at Kuldiga Academy now.

Yet, here she was.

Kyra spun around and saw that she was indeed in her home. In the center of the north parlor stood a round table, the wood concealed beneath a cloth of white. Atop the cloth were platters of breads, fruits, and cakes of all kinds.

"Happy birthday, Kyra," one of the unfamiliar nobles called out as she raised a glass of wine into the air.

"Happy birthday," echoed a chorus of people that Kyra swore she had never met in her life.

Feberik Orres bent low in a kind bow, while Janik only tilted his head downward, though that was to be expected since his left leg was crippled and hardly capable of allowing the man to bow properly.

Kyra absently nodded to both of them and found herself walking through the room toward the table. As she did so, music began playing from some unseen band of strings and the nobles began to dance around her. They twirled in their fine dresses and suits, but none of them seemed to pay her any mind now.

Where am I? Kyra wondered.

"Here, my darling, have a bit of cake, it is most delicious," a voice called out.

Kyra looked up and saw her father, or at least she saw the man that she knew as her father, standing before her and smiling as he held out a piece of white cake for her.

"But you disowned me," Kyra whispered.

Her father pursed his lips and cocked his head to the side. "A new arrangement has been made," he said.

Kyra shook her head and gently pushed the offered cake away. Her father's eyes turned sad, and then he disappeared back into the twirling and dancing crowd.

"You really should have some of the cake. Aren't you hungry?" another voice called out. This one was very low, and seemed somewhat familiar. "It will sate your hunger."

Kyra looked to her right and saw a man standing with his back to her, facing the table and fiddling with a pair of wine glasses. He had silver hair that hung down to the middle of his back. He wore a leather jerkin over a green silk shirt tucked into black wool trousers that were in turn tucked into mid-length leather boots that had been polished to a high sheen.

Kyra's heart skipped in her chest. She had seen this man before.

He turned slowly, a glass of wine in each hand and a wicked, slick smile stretching his thin, gray lips over his pale face. He winked at her with dark eyes and then held out his left hand toward her.

"You!" Kyra exclaimed.

"Me," the vampire said as he nodded and his smile grew wider to reveal the pointed teeth.

Kyra wheeled around. "Feberik, this man is a vampire, he killed Master Baird and Lady Stirling!"

The crowd of twirling nobles danced around her in such a thick throng that Kyra could not find the large man, even when she hopped up to look over the crowd.

"FEBERIK!" Kyra screamed.

At the sound of her scream, the music stopped and all of the nobles seemed to freeze in place, as if they were nothing more than painted statues.

"He can't help you now," the vampire said softly. "He is dead."

Kyra spun back around to look at the vampire, and then gasped when she saw Feberik's body lying on the floor at the vampire's feet.

Kyra lifted her hand, ready to call a spell, but then stopped short as the light was sucked from the room. A cold air rushed around her.

Laughing voices taunted her as she flung fireballs in every direction.

Then, a great, blue flame shot up in a ring around her. She was now standing upon unpolished stone. Great walls arced above her, and a large hole in the rock ceiling let in the silvery light of the moon.

"You are one of us now, Kyra," the vampire said as he appeared beyond the ring of blue fire. "You are the daughter of a vampire, and destined to live among us."

The table from her home was still there, but now there was only a bubbling fountain of wine in the center of the table. It was overflowing, staining the white table cloth and running out onto the floor.

A great puddle stretched out toward her, and then she realized that the liquid was not wine. It was blood.

"No, I am nothing like you!" Kyra shouted. She hurled a bolt of lightning out at the vampire, but it was blocked by the ever growing ring of blue fire.

"Drink from the fountain, and take your place as my queen," the voice commanded.

Kyra snarled and shook her head. She could never join with such a monster. She gathered her courage and sent her magic at the table in the center of the ring of fire. It took the hit, trembling under the tremendous energy, but it remained intact.

The vampire laughed at her.

"You cannot fight it forever," the vampire said. "The darkness is inside of you. It lurks just beneath the surface, waiting for you to loosen your grip and let it run free."

"No!" Kyra shouted.

The blue flames rose high around her as the vampire laughed. Then, the flames lurched inward and she found herself bathed in azure flames.

Kyra opened her eyes, sucking in a terrified breath and glancing around the room. Now she knew where she was. She was in the same small room she had been brought to by Master Fenn about an hour ago. She must have dozed off for a few moments. She breathed a sigh of relief. *Just a nightmare*, she thought. *Just a nightmare, that's all.*

Kyra rubbed her right arm, working furiously at the goosebumps prickling up her skin in response to the deathly cold room. Headmaster Herion had not yet arrived, so she waited in the wooden chair and stared across the small, wooden table at the door.

There was nothing else to look at anyway, for the walls were bare, dreary stone, and there were no windows. She had never been in the basement of Kuldiga Academy before, but she found this room more like a cell in a dungeon than any chamber she would have expected to meet with Herion in.

Her stomach writhed and twisted in knots, partly from nerves and partly because she had missed breakfast and lunch today. When she had been brought down here to meet with Herion, the sun was already dropping low into the sky.

It was never pleasant to be as nervous as she was now, but it was even worse with a grumbling stomach that did nothing but churn acid inside of her. Adding to that the nightmare she had just woken from made for a miserable mix.

The door opened, stealing any opportunity she might have otherwise had to process the meaning of her terrible dream.

Headmaster Herion walked in. From behind his gold-rimmed glasses he peered at her with mean, blue eyes. A flick of his wrist and the door closed behind him. Then the metal bolt scraped into place.

"We can dispense with the pleasantries," Herion announced in his gravelly voice as he pulled his spectacles down to clean the lenses on his brown shirt. "You know why you are here."

Kyra nodded. News of her dealings with the shade had not taken long to ripple through the hierarchy of the school. From what Cyrus had told her, it had taken great effort for the higher ranking masters to keep the news from spreading beyond the academy.

"Fortunately, most of the students have not returned yet, as it is still the summer holiday, so it has been somewhat of a manageable task to keep your *activities* quiet, but that does not excuse what you have done," Herion said.

Kyra shook her head. The snakes squirming in her stomach faded, and she found courage she had not previously expected. She stood up, placed her hands on the table, and looked Herion dead in his icy blue eyes.

"What I did, was avenge my mother's murder. When was the last time you have slain a garunda beast? When was the last time you stepped out from the protection of these walls and fought the darkness that encircles this realm?"

"SILENCE!" Herion boomed with surprising force.

Kyra backed away from the table, but she did not sit back down. She folded her arms and glared at the wizard.

"I have not come to be chastised by a youngling who has no comprehension of the ramifications of her actions." Herion huffed and shook his head as he cleared his throat and pointed to the chair. "Sit."

Kyra shook her head. "No."

Herion raised a snowy eyebrow over his right eye and then he snapped his fingers. Some unseen force pushed Kyra into the chair and then held her there. Kyra fought against it at first, but only when she gave in did the force pull back from her.

"You are a talented apprentice, maybe the best we have ever had, but that does not mean that I have no tricks left to teach you. Nor does it mean that I am not worthy of your respect." Herion snapped his fingers once more and a chair appeared across the table from Kyra. The old wizard sat down and then sighed as he stroked his right hand through his white hair.

Kyra's anger left her then, for now it was Herion who was acting strangely. If she didn't know any better, she would have sworn that he was sad when he looked up at her next. There were slight tears in the bottom of his eyes, though they did not fully form. The man's chin quivered ever so slightly, and his voice cracked when he opened his mouth next.

"Kyra, your actions have brought the academy under scrutiny that has brought about terrible things."

Kyra guessed that Herion was either talking about the king, or perhaps more likely, he was referring to the deaths of Master Baird and Lady Stirling. She had been concealed in a crawl space next to a secret chamber where Headmaster Herion had used magic to watch their battle with a vampire, a vampire whom Kyra now understood to be the master of the shade, and the true cause of her mother's murder.

"Two of our masters have died in battle," Herion said flatly. "They died fighting a vampire."

Kyra perked up once she realized that Herion was opening up to her. Despite the respect she knew she should show for the fallen, inside her heart she couldn't help but hope for some declaration of war against the vampire. If any of the other masters would ally with her in hunting him, then her mission would be so much simpler.

"The vampire is not near to our location here, but now that we have attacked him in the open, he has sent his servants to us," Herion continued.

Kyra nodded. "The garunda, and the shade," she said.

Herion sighed. "The attack at Caspen Manor was no accident," Herion continued. "I suspect there is something the vampire wants, and he is not going to stop until he gets it."

Kyra balked and her throat seized. All of a sudden her dream came back to her in terrible detail. Had she and Headmaster Herion had this conversation yesterday, she would have sworn that the vampire sought a dagger. But now, after the dream, she was not so sure.

"There is something I need to ask you before I continue," Herion said abruptly. "Was anyone else with you? Did anyone else help you fight the shade?"

Kyra's mind raced to Lepkin. Kathair Lepkin had been indispensable during the fight, but she doubted that he would receive any accolades for his work. More likely Herion would expel any other student involved. Even if the headmaster chose mercy, Lepkin would be dealt with by the Dragon Slayers. After all, he was apprenticed to them, and he was withholding information about a very large dragon.

On the other hand, Herion already knew about Leatherback, so there would be no harm in disclosing the dragon's involvement. Kyra hoped that that bit of information would suffice.

"Leatherback was with me, of course," she said. "He was with me when I hunted the garunda as well."

"The two of you make for a deadly pair," Herion replied evenly. "The summer is not yet over and the two of you have slain wylkins, garunda, and a shade." Headmaster Herion sat back in his chair and whistled through his teeth. "On the subject of your dragon, the priests from Valtuu temple have informed me that the animal is not yet turning."

The animal? Kyra repeated in her mind. Leatherback was her friend, and her most trusted ally. If not for him, she would have died before finishing her first year at Kuldiga Academy, let alone the most recent encounter with the shade.

"I have offended you?" Herion asked with a suddenly softer tone.

Kyra nodded her head.

11

Herion smiled. "Well, I appreciate your honesty," he replied. "I am sure you understand my prejudice toward the creature. His proximity to the school, and a knowledge the things he would be capable of if he succumbed to Nagar's Blight leave me feeling most uneasy."

"He would not harm anyone," Kyra replied.

Herion nodded, but she could tell that he was not agreeing with her, he was simply acknowledging her statement.

A tap came at the door.

Herion looked to Kyra and placed a finger up to his lips, his eyes stern and cold. Kyra nodded and remained quiet.

Headmaster Herion turned and waved his arm at the door. All at once, the color faded from the portal and it almost appeared as though there was no door at all, except for the faintest of haze clouding the doorway.

Master Fenn was standing outside the door.

Janik was limping into view, carrying a bucket in his good hand. He looked up and nodded to Master Fenn. "Herion has you down in the basement guarding closets now, eh?"

Master Fenn shrugged and shook his head. "I was told there were rats down here, I came to investigate."

"Rats? Down here?" Janik spat. "There are no rats down here, believe you me. If there were, I would set traps before anyone else found out."

Janik set the bucket down and reached into his pocket for his ring of keys. He pulled it out and then slid a key into the now invisible door.

Herion waved his hand once more, but Kyra didn't see the effects of this spell.

Janik pushed on the invisible door and then he moved in to set the bucket down inside. "No rats in here," Janik said as he started kicking around at things.

Kyra was most confused. It appeared that Janik was grabbing at things that weren't there and moving them around. She couldn't see what Janik must have been able to see, but every time Janik moved, there were sounds like sliding wooden legs on stone, or

12

drawers opening and closing. Then there was a rustling of metal and Janik hopped backward on his good leg.

"Ah, Icadion's beard!" Janik swore.

"Find a rat?" Master Fenn called out from the corridor.

Janik nodded. "I'll go and get the traps," he said.

"Go ahead," Fenn said. "I'll pull the door behind you and ensure it doesn't escape."

Kyra watched until the invisible door was closed again and then it reappeared right after Master Fenn took up position outside once more.

Herion turned back around with a wink. "Thank you for remaining quiet. It would have been harder to keep up the illusion if I had to mask sounds as well."

"Illusion?" Kyra asked.

Herion smiled mischievously. "We sit in a small room, but Janik saw nothing more than an equipment closet, complete with gardening tools, old chains, desks and other things stored here for years with a thick layer of dust."

"And a rat," Kyra added once she caught on.

"Yes, well, better to have him chase an imaginary rat than to interrupt our conversation. It will take him some time to get the traps and return."

"Is it easy to create an illusion for others to see and fully believe?" Kyra asked.

Herion shook his head. "Illusions are difficult to master, but I will give you a tip. If you create an illusion based off of an emotion, and give people what they already expect to see, then it is much easier."

"That's why Master Fenn told Janik about the rats," Kyra said with an understanding nod. "Then, already angered by the possibility of rats, he opened what he expected to be a janitorial closet and was confronted with the very rat that Master Fenn had already said was there."

"Precisely," Herion said. Headmaster Herion cleared his throat and then began drumming the table for a moment. If Kyra hadn't known better, she would have thought that *he* was nervous to talk to *her!*

"I know your type," Herion began. "No, that doesn't sound right." The old wizard sighed, shook his head, and then began again. "What I mean is, I understand your motivations. I understand why you feel as though you must do the things you are doing. So, I won't try to stop you, because I know to attempt such a feat would be foolish. However, I cannot officially condone your actions either. I would be lying if I said I wasn't truly impressed, and proud, of your conquest over the shade and his ilk, but as Kuldiga Academy's headmaster, I cannot give you permission to continue on this way."

What? Now she was entirely confused.

"If word got out to the nobles that a young apprentice was out hunting demons and monsters, there would be all sorts of havoc at my door within a week's time. We would lose patrons, you know. Nobles all talk big about war, chivalry, and honor, but few ever really put their own flesh on the line." Herion sighed and shook his head as his eyes seemed to look off to a distant point in the past. "It wasn't always this way, the academy was once fully self-sustaining, but now we depend upon the donations of our benefactors." He smiled then and his focus came back to the present as he looked back to Kyra. "Do you understand?"

Kyra nodded. "I understand that others wouldn't like it if someone discovered Leatherback."

"Not like it?" Herion echoed sarcastically. "It is categorically illegal. It would be a disaster for the school if anyone every found out about the dragon."

Kyra swallowed down the way he said the words 'that dragon' and continued on with her question. "But why would people be mad about what I am doing? Why would my activities cause you to lose patrons?"

"The nobles like to believe that evil does not exist in the Middle Kingdom. They make a big show of sending their children here out of tradition, but only a handful of families truly understand that the school exists to fulfill the same goals it always has." Herion sucked on his teeth and made a sour face. "If it was widely known that you were fighting creatures that most nobles pretend don't exist in the Middle Kingdom anymore, then it would likely scare them to their soft cores."

Kyra nodded. She understood now. "Then there is the matter of my real father. I guess that would likely cause some problems." She had a hard enough time being accepted at school as it was.

Herion nodded. "Brave and smart; a good combination for a sorceress!" He flashed a toothy smile and then he leaned in and his voice grew quiet, almost like a whisper. "There is another side to the coin as well, my young friend. Not all nobles are as they would appear on the outside."

Kyra snorted knowingly. She had only to think of Lord Caspen, the man she had once called father, to understand what Herion was getting at.

"There are some houses in the Middle Kingdom that seek the darker powers. To be sure, some of them do it only to obtain influence over their corner of the realm, but others have more nefarious alliances. This brings me back to where we started a few minutes ago. Your actions, though noble and heroic they may be, have brought upon us more open scrutiny from these other houses. There are enemies that lurk in the shadows. They will send their spies, their agents, and their assassins against you should they ever discover your role in recent events. If they can, they will use information and blackmail, as extortion has always been the game nobles play in their bids for power. However, if they fail to break your spirit, they will come for your heart. They will seek to kill you, your dragon, and anyone you hold dear."

Kyra sat for a moment, taking in the warnings and listening carefully.

"So, I must ask you again, was anyone else with you when you fought the shade? I need to know."

She answered more quickly this time, still deciding to keep Kathair Lepkin's involvement a secret. "No, Headmaster Herion. There was only myself and Leatherback. Njar knew of it, of

15

course, but he was injured in a previous battle and did not fight the shade with me."

Herion nodded and stroked his smooth chin. "Very well. As I said before, I cannot condone your hunting activities, but let me offer you a word of caution. Do not pull anyone else into this. If you do, there will be repercussions far beyond what you can imagine. You have talent, skill, and courage, but the enemies are many. Do you understand?"

Kyra nodded.

Herion rose to leave, but Kyra stood and felt the urge to make sure that he understood her as well before the meeting was over.

"I won't stop," she blurted out.

Headmaster Herion turned a stern eye on her.

"I mean, I can't stop. The vampire is the reason my mother is dead. Even if I were to give up, I feel that he will come after me anyway. I have to find him."

Herion smiled and nodded. "And you had better be prepared for that moment," he said. "As I said, I cannot condone this quest of yours. However, if Cyrus were inclined to teach you various types of advanced spells and wards that would be useful in a battle against a vampire, then he would be free to teach such lessons, as part of your total curriculum of course."

Kyra smiled wide. She had finally made friends with Headmaster Herion.

Chapter 3

Two days later, Kyra walked into the classroom, a sly smile on her face and an enthusiastic bounce in her step. She and Linny had spent the weekend playing star-flies with each other. It was a kind of game they had invented where they would sneak out into the fields to the south and try to zap each other in the darkness with little yellow balls of magic. Kyra was winning the ongoing match, with one hundred and four points to twenty five. It was fun, and helped take her mind off of everything that had happened over the last few weeks, but it also cost her some much needed sleep. Still, even with the lack of sleep, she had been so relieved with how everything had gone with Headmaster Herion that she couldn't hide how she felt. She opened the door and nearly skipped to her assigned desk, which still sat in the middle of the front row of desks in the room.

"You're in a cheerful mood," Cyrus noted as he set down a thin, tan leather book he was reading.

"Headmaster Herion has given us permission to train," she said, purposefully leaving out the part about the vampire to make Cyrus guess.

Cyrus sighed and folded his arms. "We already have permission to train, that is what the academy is for," Cyrus said, refusing to get pulled into her game.

Kyra huffed, relenting as she swept a hand up to her hair and brushing a stray lock out of her face. "I am ready for the vampire," she said bluntly.

Cyrus shook his head. "No you aren't," he replied.

"Yes I am!" Kyra shouted back, forgetting her place. She stood up and glowered at the old wizard. "I defeated the shade this time. I'm a lot closer than I was before. All I need to do is prepare for the final battle."

"You'll never win a battle of magic with a vampire," Cyrus said. He reached over and picked up the book and opened it. "I doubt you understand just how dangerous a vampire can be." The wizard raised the book to cover his face from her.

Kyra walked around to the front of Cyrus' desk and reached out defiantly to take his book. "You deny me now!"

"Oh but I can," Cyrus said.

Kyra paused. His voice had not come from in front of her. She turned around to see Cyrus stepping away from the wall at the back of the classroom. Confused, she pulled the book down and saw another Cyrus smiling up at her. "An illusion," she guessed.

"One of a vampire's most basic tricks, however, he will have mastered illusions far better than I," Cyrus replied. "Tell me which is the real me, if you are as ready as you say."

Kyra raised her right hand and focused on an incantation her mother had taught her once that dispelled magic. As she spoke the words, she felt a small portion of energy leave her body, as she did any time she worked a spell. However, this was the first time she felt a kind of resistance to the energy itself.

"Ah, another weapon that a vampire will have in his arsenal," Cyrus said. "Right now you are wondering how I am blocking your magic, are you not?"

Kyra could feel her cheeks grow warm and flushed. She had come in happy, eager to learn. Leave it to Cyrus to deflate her confidence and zeal. She concentrated harder and repeated the spell.

This time the resistance pushed back and then wrapped around her. She could still move physically, but her mouth failed to utter any words when she opened it, and her magic was stunted, stopped somehow at the very source.

"This is why I say you are not ready," Cyrus said. "You are now faced with the challenge of uncovering which is the real me, but you have no magic to aid you in your plight."

Kyra shook her head, determined not to let the old wizard beat her so badly. She turned to the Cyrus sitting at the desk, and then her stomach flipped when a third Cyrus emerged from the wall behind the desk. She glanced back to the other side of the room and noted that a fourth had appeared next to the second.

"Your odds of winning are becoming slimmer," Cyrus said. "Imagine you have a weapon in your hand. You must choose now which of us to kill. Choose wisely, for if you fail, you are dead."

Kyra made what seemed to her the logical choice. Cyrus always sat at his desk during the beginning of class. She first saw him there, and she didn't sense any teleportation magic being used since she entered the room. It had to be the wizard sitting at the desk with the book.

Then again, Cyrus would know that she would come to that conclusion, so he must be one of the others.

"Time's up, you hesitated, you're dead," Cyrus said. A bolt of blue lightning shot out from each of the Cyrus forms and zapped her body. It wasn't a particularly harmful spell, Cyrus had given her only a mild shock, something to help the lesson sink in, but it stung and made her even angrier.

She rubbed her arm and grunted.

"Round two, choose one, now," Cyrus commanded.

Kyra turned to the form at the desk and pointed. "You."

"I am a real person," the Cyrus at the desk said with a nod as he rose to his feet. "But I am not Cyrus." The magic melted away and Janik stood where Cyrus had once been.

"Oops," said the three remaining Cyrus forms. "It appears you have chosen to kill a friend."

Kyra turned to the second Cyrus at the back of the class. "You!"

That form melted away, as did the other two, leaving only Kyra and Janik in the classroom.

"I don't understand," Kyra said.

Janik snorted derisively and pointed to the shadows near a book case by the window. "He's over there."

"Ah, now where is the fun in that?" Cyrus said as he appeared from the darkness. "I would have liked to give her a chance to find me herself."

Janik shook his head. "I fought a vampire before," Janik said as he offered Kyra a half smile. "And I have fought with demons," he added.

Kyra missed the deathly glance Cyrus shot at Janik.

"You aren't ready," Janik finished as he rubbed at a sudden pain in his chest. "Trust me. I would never steer you wrong."

"That will be all, Janik," Cyrus said abruptly. "I'll take the lesson from here. Thank you."

Janik bowed his head and turned to limp out of the room, dragging his maimed leg behind him with each step.

"So teach me to break the vampire's charms," Kyra said, undaunted by her failure. "This is what classes are for, right? You show me my weaknesses and then we work on them together. I can do this."

Cyrus shook his head and walked to the desk. "You know I admire your courage..."

"Don't do that," Kyra said, anger threatening to flare up. "Don't give me the speech about trying hard and impressing you by making it this far. *This* isn't enough. The vampire must die, not only for my mother, but for me. It's the only way I will ever be safe."

"Or, we could arrange a deal with him and let him retrieve the dagger," Cyrus offered.

Kyra balked and her mouth hung open.

"You might trip on that," Cyrus commented with a gesture to her hanging jaw. "You know I don't want to stop any more than you do. I think the fact that I have helped you this far should prove that."

"No," Kyra said. "I can beat the vampire too."

Cyrus rubbed a weary hand over his face. "I had a daughter like you once," he said truthfully. "Impetuous and headstrong, always jumping before stopping to look." He sat back in his chair and a soft smile pulled at the corners of his mouth. His demeanor shifted then, and Kyra found herself waiting, not knowing how to respond.

After a few moments, Cyrus cleared his throat and his usual, stern expression was back upon his face. He turned and pointed a finger at the book case. A thick book bound in black leather with red trim floated over to the desk and fell gently to rest upon it. The old wizard opened the tome and then turned it around and pushed it toward her.

"Another reading assignment?" Kyra guessed.

Cyrus shrugged. "If you won't listen to me, then perhaps you will listen to Archmage Durit."

Kyra's hand paused on its way to the book. She knew the name well. "What is this?" she asked, nodding to the book.

"It is a rare treasure of knowledge. A book that required much sacrifice to acquire."

"Arts of the Soul Thief," Kyra said in a whisper.

Cyrus nodded. "Archmage Durit is renowned as the foremost expert on these matters. It is by reading this book, and studying the methods therein, that I have become the demon-hunter I am today. Though I dare say it has taken more than a fair toll on me in exchange."

"My mother used to look for this book," Kyra said. "She never spoke about it in front of me, but there were a few times I would sneak to the library, or I would hear things I shouldn't..."

"It's called being a snoop," Cyrus said with a nod. "Most children do that, though some appear to never shake the habit."

Kyra felt his eye linger upon her, but she didn't care. She was busy piecing together a puzzle in her mind. Her mother had always sent discrete servants to look for the book, or exchanged letters with various scholars about it. Not until Kyra was twelve had she ever asked about the book. Her mother had nearly frozen stiff she had been so taken aback by Kyra's mention of the title.

Of course, all her mother had said then was that it was a special book about magic, written by a powerful wizard, Archmage Durit.

Now she understood. Kyra's mother had been searching for a way to defeat her vampire father all that time.

"Well," Cyrus said, shaking her from her thoughts. "Are you going to read it, or are you going to stare at it?" He shook his head. "The words won't jump off the page and come to you, you must engage your brain."

Kyra reached out and took the book in hand. She pulled it up to her face and studied the picture drawn upon the left page. There was a man standing before a mirror, reaching out to touch the glass with his left hand. In the mirror's reflection, a sharp-fanged vampire reached back for him. Under the illustration she saw a single phrase.

"When one reaches out to fight the darkness, it reaches back to ensnare the warrior," she read aloud.

Suddenly the book became very heavy. Her head began to throb. She lurched forward and fumbled the book onto the desk.

"Careful!" Cyrus bellowed.

She tried to say she was sorry, but her vision darkened and her knees slackened. She was only vaguely aware of the fact that someone had caught her before she hit the floor.

When Kyra next opened her eyes, she was in her room, lying upon her bed. Cyrus was there as well, watching her and smoking from a long, curved pipe. As her vision cleared, she realized he was not actually smoking at all. He was holding a thin, curved stick that was burning on one end.

"When did the nightmares start?" Cyrus asked when she woke.

Kyra sat up, putting a hand to her head. It was still sore from before. She closed her eyes and took in a deep breath. Along with the air came the scent of the smoke from the stick, it was like rotting eggs mixed with the soggy black mud from a marsh. Her nose tried to fight the odor and she coughed against it.

"Breathe it in," Cyrus said. "It is a special root that helps clear the mind."

"It's awful," she replied.

Cyrus nodded. "Not everything that is good for a person is pleasant," he replied evenly. "Now, about the nightmares, when did they start?"

Kyra instantly recalled the terrible dream she'd had a couple days before while waiting for Headmaster Herion. "A few days ago," she said.

"One time, or many times?" Cyrus pressed.

Kyra pulled her arms into a hug around her own shoulders and frowned. The prying question shouldn't have made her feel uncomfortable, but it did. "Every night," she admitted. "Since the first time it has been every night."

"Then he is already here," Cyrus said with a shake of his head. "He is coming for you."

"He is coming here?" Kyra asked, a tinge of fear in her voice for the first time since encountering the shade.

Cyrus nodded. "And we will have to do whatever we can to ensure you stay safe."

Kyra put on a smile, forcing bravado. "I thought you wanted him to have the dagger."

Cyrus shook his head. "I said I would bargain for the dagger, but not for you." His eyes turned dark and he grumbled something that she couldn't quite hear. "Get up, I will teach you a few wards that will help block the nightmares. Tomorrow, we will begin training like you have never trained before. We will start with illusions, and work on them until you can discern the truth no matter what I throw at you."

"How did you know of my nightmares?" Kyra asked.

"You have been unconscious for two days," he replied. "Ever since taking the book in hand, you have been ill. As I tried to ward off the evil, I could hear your moans and screams as the terrors set in."

"Why did I react that way to the book?" she asked.

Cyrus shook his head. "That, I don't know. If I didn't know better, I would have thought someone had put a spell upon it, a magical trap if you will, but that can't be the case. That is my book. I have had it for years."

"Maybe it is my heritage," Kyra said. "I have seen magic designed to hurt monsters and demons." She was speaking of the charms that Al the dwarf had given to her and Lepkin only a short while ago in preparation for their fight against the shade. Even though she was not a full vampire, they had worked against her as well.

"No, that isn't it," Cyrus said. His voice seemed sure and resolute. "I would have caught something like that," he added. He turned and smiled at her once more. "Linny has been assisting with you, and she has kept this incident quiet. Extend to her my gratitude."

Kyra nodded. "Where are you going?" she asked.

Cyrus sighed and set the smoldering root on the chair as he stood up from it. "I have someone I need to visit. Linny is here if you need food or water. Janik is posted outside the door for added measure."

"If the vampire is coming, shouldn't you alert Headmaster Herion?"

Cyrus shook his head. "A vampire who attacks in dreams is a patient hunter. It is not yet time to alert the entire academy. However, rest assured that Herion is a great wizard as well. He may have earned his position through a bit of politics and back-scratching, but he is not without merit. I would wager he is already preparing as well. I assume he started after your first encounter with the shade." Cyrus smiled then and nodded. "Go back to sleep. The smudging root will keep your dreams clear. We'll resume training in the morning."

Cyrus walked toward the door as Kyra was dropping back down to rest. Her eyes closed before the wizard reached the hallway.

"How is she?" Janik asked.

Cyrus nodded and closed the door. "She is all right. Where is Linny?"

"Getting some soup from the kitchen," Janik replied.

Cyrus nodded. "Wait for my return," he said. "When Linny returns, tell her to wait out here. Under no circumstances is anyone to enter that room until I am back. Understand?"

Janik nodded.

"And don't think for one second that I failed to notice your quip about dealing with demons," Cyrus put in. "The next time you tread close to the edge of revealing my identity, I will give you more than chest pain, are we clear?"

Janik looked to the floor.

The old wizard knew he had made his point. Normally he would have reprimanded the crippled warrior immediately, but he had needed to work fast against the spell that had caught Kyra. A simple threat would have to do, for now.

Cyrus glanced down the hall and then he opened a rift in the very air before him. Static pops of electricity sparked into life around the opening, and then he slipped into darkness and disappeared from the hallway.

Cyrus had lied to Kyra. The burning root was not there to clear her mind of nightmares. Quite the opposite, it was going to strengthen the nightmare, prolong it, and induce a deep sleep.

But then, that is what he required if he was to find the dreamwalker.

It took great skill to lay a trap that Cyrus would fail to detect. Great skill, and not a little power and experience. Cyrus knew there were only two possibilities. The first was the vampire, but that was unlikely, for the trap would have to be placed upon the book while the caster was in the immediate physical vicinity of the book. The second possibility carried far greater implications.

The wizard focused his mind as he walked through the swirling darkness. This portal was not like most. Instead of carrying him to a new physical location, he was traveling to a realm only few could enter, and fewer still ever survived.

Light began to break through the darkness, and Cyrus took in a deep breath as a rush of air, like that of a great tempest, blew the darkness apart and left him standing upon a deeply rutted dirt road that was busy collecting puddles.

A moment after he noticed the puddles, Cyrus saw the droplets of water falling from the sky and sighed when the light rain turned into a heavy downpour.

Why must nightmares and storms always be connected? In his experience, the light hid nearly as many monsters as the darkness. Still, there was no reason to fight against the rain here. It wasn't real, although he could feel every droplet of cold liquid strike him with the force of a small bee, stinging his face and hands.

The light then turned gray as the clouds rolled through the sky and lightning flashed around him. That was the way with dreams. Natural laws were only obeyed if the dreamer realized that the laws should apply. In this case, the rain had followed the puddles, and the clouds had come after the rain. It was something Cyrus found quite curious, but now was not the time to contemplate the threads that wove the strange tapestry of Kyra's nightmare.

He looked up and walked toward Kyra's manor, or at least something that approximately resembled her home. This image of the house was much darker, with windows that appeared angular and sharp, as if the house itself was taking on a life of its own.

Cyrus walked up the steps and pushed the front doors open. He saw Kyra walking into a group of people. She walked as if hypnotized, stiff and unblinking. Cyrus was careful to mask himself as a nondescript nobleman, that way he would match the others in the nightmare and not draw any undue attention to himself.

He walked around the left to gain a better vantage of the party. It wasn't long before he spotted the vampire. He was startled at first by the details. The wizard realized that in order for Kyra to have such a clear picture in her mind of the vampire, she must have already seen him at some point. The only question now was whether she had seen him recently, or if this was some subconscious construct formed by a memory created when she was a baby, or perhaps a very young child.

Then something caught his eye. A movement at the top of the stairs.

It was like a shadow, but somehow it didn't match the other shadows in this surreal place that existed in the recesses of Kyra's unconscious mind.

Cyrus left the party, along with poor Kyra's tormented soul, down on the first floor. He wasn't interested in the nightmare's progression. He could deal with dreams easily enough once he had finished the task at hand. For now, she would have to endure her suffering until he had completed what he needed to do.

In the end, his success would mean safety for *both* of them.

Cyrus stalked up the stairs and turned to his right. The hallway here was deformed, with slightly bent walls and doors made in irregular shapes. He made his way down the corridor as best he could, careful not to trip and fall as the very floor seemed to shift beneath his feet for a time. Then, he slipped into a familiar room. He had been here before, in the real world, and so he recognized the place as Kyra's mother's library. Even with the distorted light and the skewed window and books that seemed to open and close on their own, he recognized it well enough.

He stepped into the room and then he closed the door.

The sound of the metal latch catching as it clicked into place startled the other intruder. A warlock turned and pulled his hood back. There was no reason for pretense now. Both of them knew the other.

Cyrus let his disguise melt away and he stared at Bothias, one of the warlocks he was currently working for.

"I should have known," Bothias said. "I could tell she had woken up, but I was trapped inside." He folded his arms and sat upon a rectangular desk that began to float into the air just a bit, swaying back and forth as it hovered over the floor. "You woke her," he said with a wag of his finger. "I didn't think you would be able to do that."

"I suspected you could dreamwalk," Cyrus said, ignoring Bothias' comment, "but I did not think you would be so foolish as to come here."

Bothias held his arms out to the side. "It was too easy not to do," he replied. "The enemy already has a hold on her fears. It was simple to bring them out to the forefront of her mind."

"So you planted the nightmares?" Cyrus asked. "I had thought that perhaps the vampire had done that."

Bothias shook his head. "I took the form of a raven," he said. "I found her in the woods, on her way to see that dragon of hers. I planted the nightmare a few days ago."

"And then you put a curse upon my book," Cyrus accused.

"Well, in my defense, you normally hand your student the books to read and then send her on her way. I had assumed she would read it while out in the forest, giving me more than enough time to slip in and out before you would find out about it."

"How did you know which book I would give her?" Cyrus asked.

"Come, come," Bothias replied with a smirk. "What other book would you give to her?"

"You should have left me alone to my task," Cyrus said, his voice turning cold.

Bothias' smile turned into a confused expression, as if he was unsure what to make of the statement. "Surely you don't mean to attack me here, do you? If we duel, then either she will wake, or she will discover us. Either way, we will end up trapped in her mind, or she will falter if her mind is weak, and then she will die. You know how delicate a thing it is to walk in the dreams of others."

Cyrus nodded. "So what, then, shall we do?"

"Help me find the dagger," Bothias replied with a nonchalant shrug. "I am certain the girl knows where it is. You risk too much in letting her run around the countryside."

"The dagger is for me," Cyrus replied evenly. "I have a bargain with the patriarch of your order."

"Ah yes, well the truth is we have been using you, my friend. You have been our... shall we use the word 'scout' to describe you?"

"I thought you wanted the girl," Cyrus said.

Bothias nodded. "We'll take the girl, *and* the dagger."

Cyrus nodded. "And what of me?"

"You think we *don't* know about your secrets?" Bothias asked. "Once we have what we need, we will offer you two choices. The first option will be to serve our order."

"And the second?" Cyrus asked.

"The second option is death."

"You have the consensus of your brothers then?" Cyrus pressed.

Bothias shook his head. "Not yet, but they will come around to my way once they see I have produced the dagger quicker than you ever could."

"The girl doesn't know where it is," Cyrus said. "If she did, she would have told me by now."

"Bah," Bothias said with a dismissive wave. "She saw where her mother put it, of that I am sure."

Cyrus doubted very much that Kyra had any notion, subconscious or otherwise, where the dagger might be. From everything he had learned about the family, if Kyra was cunning and smart, then the mother was doubly so. He studied Bothias as the dreamwalker moved. Cyrus noted the man's fingers twitching, possibly drawing runes in what he thought was a discreet ruse while trying to distract Cyrus with conversation.

Bothias was not a large man by any means, but his powers were not to be taken lightly. Cyrus had heard of several of Bothias' conquests, and even he had to admit the dreamwalker had talent. Then there was the fact that Bothias had managed to magically trap Cyrus' own book.

Fortunately, Cyrus was far more powerful than the dreamwalker could ever have imagined. That was why Cyrus didn't counter the spell that came racing toward him then. A blue tendril of light stretched out from Bothias' hand and slapped Cyrus in the face, knocking him to the ground. A second later, it was coiling around him, squeezing and sizzling as wisps of smoke rose from Cyrus' clothes.

"You're losing your touch, Cyrus," Bothias exclaimed triumphantly. The wizard rose from the desk and then resumed his search through the many shelves that lined the walls.

Cyrus watched, now suspended in the air as if the magical coil was a great fist clenched around him and holding him in place. He was waiting for the right moment to strike. Until then, he would let Bothias believe he had won. One quick counterattack, and it would be over without so much as causing Kyra to stir in her sleep.

Bothias tore books from shelves, wrenched open drawers on the desk, but he found nothing. Then, almost inexplicably he turned to one of the empty book cases and grabbed it, tipping it away from the wall. The dreamwalker laughed then and he waved his hand and muttered a spell that levitated the book case away without dropping it to crash on the floor.

There, nestled in a hole in the wall, was a brown box.

"Poor Cyrus, it seems you have failed, my friend." Bothias took the box, opened it, and held the dagger up in his right hand. He examined it carefully, noting the details and studying each portion of the handle and blade. "This is it!" Bothias turned and opened a portal. "I think I will leave you in here," Bothias told Cyrus. "Wouldn't want you escaping before the others are ready for you."

The magical bindings constricted tighter, holding Cyrus rigid. Now was the time to strike.

Cyrus focused his power and a great wave of heat flowed out from him, dissolving the blue bands and spreading through the room faster than a flood of water. Bothias looked up with a confused look and opened his mouth, probably to counter the spell, but no words came out. He clutched at his throat with his left hand and then the sphere of heat engulfed him inside of it.

Suddenly there was no sound at all except for Cyrus' footsteps as he marched toward the bewildered dreamwalker.

"Don't look so shocked," Cyrus said. "I have tangled with demons. What made you think I couldn't handle a dreamwalker?" Cyrus snapped his fingers and the dagger plunged into Bothias' heart. The dagger wasn't exactly real. It was a magical construct, an illusion much like the extra copies of himself he had shown to Kyra in the classroom. Cyrus had planted it behind the book case in order to break Bothias' focus. Still, in the realm of dreams it was not an entirely impossible thing to turn an illusion into something almost real.

The pain Bothias felt was real to him, and therefore it was real.

A stronger mind might have dispelled the charade, but Bothias had not Cyrus' experience.

The dreamwalker collapsed on the ground and stretched a hand for the portal he had opened. Cyrus knew that Bothias was trying to close it, but it was too late. The magical sphere Cyrus had cast not only protected the immediate area from Kyra's subconscious, it also muted all of Bothias' magical powers. Cyrus was able to freeze the portal open, which meant he was going to use it as his own exit. But first, he had to dispose of Bothias so as not to do any harm to Kyra.

Cyrus bent down to Bothias and smiled at him. He placed a hand on the dying dreamwalker's head. "A dreamwalker is rare. It is a shame that I must remove one from the world of the living," Cyrus said.

Bothias shook his head. "Mercy," he squeaked. His body convulsed and his hands pulled at the dagger, trying to pull it from his body.

Cyrus shook his head. "Mercy is not one of my defining traits," he said. Cyrus turned to the portal and spoke an incantation that would hold it open a few moments longer. Next, he focused on the sphere of magic, which was now glowing a soft red around them. He caused it to shrink, and then stepped out of it as the sphere continued to diminish until it was no larger than a marble. He picked up the sphere and whispered a final incantation, one that would keep it intact through the portal, and then he stepped through Bothias' planned exit.

This portal was not like the one he had used to enter Kyra's nightmare. It was short, and filled with gray light. The dreamwalkers were not all accustomed to traveling through utter darkness as Cyrus was. Most dreamwalkers required some sort of light to guide their way into a person's mind. It was an easy thing to misdirect such a spell, and that would result in a lifetime of being stuck in limbo.

A dreamwalker could only cast one portal at a time. Either to or from a dream. One could never cast an exit portal until they had completed their travel into a dream, and likewise, one could never return to the dream if a dreamwalker was lost along the way once they initiated their exit.

This was the delicious irony Cyrus was about to employ.

As soon as he saw the end of the portal, Cyrus threw the sphere out to the side and gave it a magical nudge with a force like a gale that sent it hurtling across the great, gray nothing.

Cyrus then called upon the shadows he so loved, and covered all of the light. The sphere would likely hold for a century at least, ensuring Bothias' entrapment in limbo even if the dreamwalker somehow managed to overcome the dagger illusion, which Cyrus doubted he could. In any case, Cyrus only needed a few more seconds, and then he would exit the portal, and it would close behind him.

There would never be an escape for Bothias.

Cyrus was almost sad he couldn't hear Bothias scream as the realization dawned on him. It would have been all the sweeter to hear the man's terror. A fitting punishment for one who used nightmares to overpower his enemies, Cyrus thought. The wizard stepped out through the opening and then looked around.

As he had suspected, Bothias had been lying. The dreamwalker did not have the approval of the other warlocks. If he had, then he would not have connected the portal to a small cabin at the top of some mountain. Had this been a sanctioned mission, the dreamwalker would have been planning to return to the coven.

Still, Cyrus was never one to leave loose ends. He turned about, orienting him to what he very soon realized was Mount Lark, a great mountain in the northern reaches of the Middle Kingdom overlooking the sea to the west.

This was far away from the coven.

Cyrus put on another illusion, disguising himself to appear as Bothias, and then he trudged through the ankle-deep snow toward the cabin. It was a small, shabbily constructed building. Perhaps it had once been a trapper's cabin, but now the signs of disrepair were painfully obvious. Gaps appeared between some of the logs, and the door hung askew even when shut.

A form moved by the window and Cyrus smiled, wondering to himself who the partner may have been.

He stepped into the cabin and removed a cloak, folding it over his left arm.

"Did you find it?" a raspy voice asked.

It was not a voice that Cyrus recognized. That was good. It meant that there were no other warlocks involved. Bothias had betrayed them as well as him. That would make things simpler.

Cyrus turned and caused a great light to shine in the cabin.

A silver-haired man dressed in black robes stood in the far corner. He winced, shutting his purple eyes from the sudden light. That was when Cyrus realized it was not a man in the cabin, but a drow, a dark elf. Cyrus seized upon the moment of the elf's blindness and reached out with a powerful spell that grabbed the drow and slammed him into the wall.

The drow grunted and struggled to fight back, but even for an elf this particular drow was old. His strength was long gone from his body and his meager fireballs that appeared in the air were easy enough for Cyrus to dodge.

"I think you and I need to have a chat," Cyrus said as his lips curled up into a sinister sneer.

It was nearly midnight before Cyrus appeared back in the hallway. Janik, the ever watchful cripple, was still where he had left him. The wizard dismissed Janik with a wave of his hand, and then he went into Kyra's room. He didn't bother knocking. He knew she would still be asleep.

Cyrus picked up the remainder of the root, which was now barely more than a finger's length, and magically snuffed the fire. He then created a vortex that pulled the smoke out from the room and he banished it to another plane.

He bent low to the girl's ear and whispered softly the words of an incantation that would remove the remainder of Bothias' poisonous spells from her mind, and then he let her sleep.

They had a lot of work to do in the morning.

Chapter 4

Janik rolled onto his left side as sleep struggled to keep hold over him. A sudden pain ripped through his left wrist that shot up through his arm and caused his shoulder to ache. No matter how many times it happened, Janik had never gotten used to the random pains that coursed through his body. More than a few times, he cursed his weakness and wished he could recall the oath he had given to Cyrus.

There was no going back now, though. He could never go back.

The only way out for him was death, although it did occur to him that even then he might not find rest. Could it be possible that Cyrus was powerful enough to reanimate him from the plane of the dead? In any case, it wasn't a solution he was willing to contemplate.

He sat up, wondering whether he might ever please Cyrus enough that the old codger might help relieve the pain in his mangled limbs.

The warrior-turned-janitor swung his legs over the side of the bed and down to the floor. His left foot tingled, asleep from being pinched in the night. He winced slightly as he put pressure upon his feet and the tingling turned to burning needles, but it was better this than the aches and pains he normally felt upon waking.

His body was stiff, tight, and unyielding in the morning's cool air. Living in the basement didn't help either. He needed one of the better rooms that could be had in the upper levels. The extra warmth would at least lessen his stiffness and help ease his twisted muscles.

Unfortunately, the good rooms were reserved for the masters who taught at Kuldiga Academy. Servants and other employees such as cooks, stable hands, and others, all lived downstairs in the basement.

Had Janik not been crippled, he could have easily taken up a teaching position at the academy. After all, he was the eldest son of a nobleman, and he had many conquests under his belt, not that any of them did him good now. These days no one remembered anything of his victories, only that he had been crippled fighting a vampire.

Kyra was the only one who seemed to ever look at him with the respect a warrior like him deserved. That was because she knew what he had done. She did not see a crippled has-been. No, Kyra saw the warrior within him.

Janik scratched his chest with his good hand and then gently shook out his left arm. The pain subsided enough that he was able to change into his daytime clothes without pausing to catch his breath, but it did not entirely subside.

After he pulled on his clothes, he glanced toward the broom he had brought back to his room last night. He shook his head, grimacing at the tool as if it was responsible for his lot in life.

"I used to wield axes," Janik told the broom. "But now, here I am, swinging a broom from side to side like a dunderhead." He clenched his right fist and closed his eyes. "Better to return home and live out my days in the family manor. At least there I could do as I choose."

He had only barely said the words when a slight twinge of hot pain came into his chest. He sighed and rubbed until the sensation left. A subtle reminder of his oath. His life was no longer his own to do with as he saw fit. He was Cyrus' slave.

Perhaps if he served well enough, then Cyrus would one day release him, or at the very least the wizard might elevate Janik's brother Feberik to become the next Headmaster. At least then

Janik would have a bit more freedom and status, even if only vicariously.

Then again, now that he thought of it, he wasn't entirely sure what else Cyrus wanted from him. He had already addled his brother's mind with charm potions and other magical devices to keep Feberik in line, not to mention the betrothal to Kyra, which Feberik never would have agreed to otherwise. Other than that, Cyrus had only asked Janik to help by gaining Kyra's trust. Now with the wizard teaching at the school, it was a bit of an added burden.

Cyrus was constantly checking up on Janik's efforts to keep Kyra close to him. The girl was not an easy one to sway. He had to draw upon his nicest, most charming behavior to keep her feeling like he was a friend. It was a shame she wasn't susceptible to the same sort of magic that kept Feberik in line. Even a charmed amulet he had given her last year had had no effect. Perhaps her strength could be used to his advantage. If she truly saw him as a friend, someday she might be strong enough to help rid him of Cyrus, and then he would be free to do as he pleased. It was definitely a good move to have let a few key teachers know about her parentage. That had certainly done wonders to keep her isolated from the rest of the faculty and students. Yes, someday she might be the perfect ally…

But that was just a dream, and Janik knew it.

Janik had managed to earn a bit of the girl's trust, but lately she was nearly entirely consumed with her training, as well as the recent fights with creatures that Janik himself would have hunted had he not been crippled those many years ago. He heard little from her anymore, and he saw even less. The priests from Valtuu Temple didn't make it easy either. Their strange breed of magic helped them see through a person and discover their true intent. Janik could never approach Kyra whilst the priests were nearby.

Even Cyrus avoided the priests.

Janik shook his head and turned to the door as he heard the faint scrape of paper sliding across the stone floor.

A small envelope came to rest a couple of feet inside the chamber.

"You could knock!" Janik called out after the steward. There was no answer. There never was. The steward, unlike Janik, was not of noble birth. Therefore, he took every opportunity he had to rub Janik's face in the fact that he now held a position higher than the noble-born janitor. Making Janik stoop over, a painful struggle in the mornings with his body still tight and achy, had become a common occurrence.

Janik bent low, his right leg wavering slightly as he let his crooked left leg hang out behind him as a kind of mangled counterweight. He snatched the envelope and moved to the small table he used as a desk.

As he looked over his list of tasks for the day, he frowned and his brow crinkled. "At least during the school year I can get help from students given demerits." He shook his head. There were no demerits given during the summer holiday. This list of chores was his and his alone.

It was going to be a long day.

His eyes lifted from the paper to see the green bottle hidden behind one of his books. A sly smile curled the left corner of his mouth and he laughed to himself. Perhaps he would mention it to Feberik the next time he administered Cyrus' drink, and see whether he could have some of the apprentices of the sword filtered over to him somehow. Surely someone must be in need of punishing for something done during the summer?

He folded the list and placed it into his pocket. Then, grabbing the green bottle and hiding it in a different pocket, he left his room and entered the well-lit, yet dank corridor. Before starting any of the tasks on the list from the steward, Janik had to check Feberik's journal.

Feberik was a peculiar individual. A great, muscled oaf, deft with a sword and barely able to control his own temper. Yet, he was religious about writing in his journal every day. It was a habit that he had picked up from their father.

Janik shook his head as a memory shot through his mind of the time he had first read of his father's infidelity. Fortunately, he had taken and burned any journal that spoke of the young daughter Janik's father had sired. He had hoped that would be the end of it, but now the girl was here, masquerading as a noble's child.

He would have to deal with that later.

For now, he was concerned with Feberik's diary.

There was a mark made on each page in the journal since Janik had begun administering the powders Cyrus had given him. It was almost imperceptible to anyone but Janik, for Janik had chosen the symbol himself and told Feberik to write it every day in his journal. It was his way of ensuring the powder wasn't wearing off.

Everything would be ruined if Feberik somehow became immune to the powder.

Soon he was climbing the stairs and found himself in the main audience hall. The empty pews stood quiet, though a few could use a good dusting to be sure. The podium upon the dais in the front of the hall was covered with a green and gold cloth. It was customary to keep it hidden until the beginning of each year when the new students had been welcomed.

Above the dais were the banners of each school found in Kuldiga Academy. Each of them were made with a forest green background encircled by a thin ridge of gold trim. In the centers of each banner he saw the symbols of each school. The first one on the right was a hand, palm facing outward with a spark representing healing. The second was an image of a path leading between two mountains and leading toward a sunrise; that was the symbol of the priests. The third flag had the symbol of an unblinking eye; the symbol of the scholars. The left side of the hall was adorned with a flag that had an arrow, for the rangers, another that displayed a sword, for the future knights, and a third that showed a snake coiled upon a set of scales for the alchemy school. Those six flags all narrowed in to point at the single flag at the back of the hall, which prominently displayed a staff, the symbol of the wizards in training at Kuldiga Academy.

Now that he knew Cyrus, the great hall had a quite different meaning for Janik. Most of the nobles knew that Kuldiga had once been a stronghold for shadowfiends, and that once they had been eradicated, Kuldiga Academy had been founded upon the same stones painted with their own blood. To most others it seemed a noble triumph, a symbol of the Middle Kingdom's power and resolution to abolish necromancy and the shadowfiends, as well as any other demon that plagued the nation. Kuldiga Academy stood as a testament to the fact that nobles and their snot-nosed brats had brought down, and kept down, one of the strongest, most powerful orders that had ever lived upon the face of the Middle Kingdom.

To Janik, it seemed little more than a hollow victory. The very stones of the building seemed to laugh at him now that he knew the truth. If the others knew what he knew about Cyrus, the school would rip itself apart in a new war. The darkness had never been defeated entirely, it had only been pushed out to hide under new rocks. Hiding, waiting, biding its time until it snaked back into its rightful home.

He glanced up to the nearest banner, studying the marks of dust accumulating upon the fabric. The stinking banners would have to be taken down and cleaned before the last day of summer term in preparation for the masses of students and parents who would descend on the school for the orientation ceremonies in August. That was a task that could wait for a couple of months though.

According to his list of chores, today he would need to meet in the steward's quarters with the kitchen head, the stable master, and the grounds keeper to listen to the steward deliver the monthly demands from the headmaster. These demands would be in addition to the normal chores doled out by the steward. Janik was certain he would receive more than his fair share too. The steward would ensure that.

At least one benefit to Feberik being such a wunderkind was that Janik had great hopes that one day Feberik would become headmaster. Then perhaps Janik could have this steward retired, and he wouldn't have to answer to him anymore.

Cyrus had told him he would look into that. Janik would have to remind him of this the next time he saw the wizard.

Within a few more minutes he was in Feberik's office. It was much nicer than the man deserved. After all, Feberik had never slain a vampire. As it was, he was barely known as a warrior outside of his home lands.

Sure, he had accomplished a few things, and he certainly had the *talent* for more, but Feberik had not actually attained any sort of real success that one would expect from a master at Kuldiga Academy. Had Cyrus not been pulling several strings, and throwing in gold through various channels, Headmaster Herion never would have agreed to take on Feberik and Janik.

As Janik limped toward the desk, he had to wonder if Kyra was worth all of this trouble.

He opened the book to the most recent page. There, in the middle of the page, between two sentences, was the mark. It was simple really, but a foolproof mechanism for ensuring Feberik's pliability. The mark consisted of a capital letter 'T' with a hook drawn on either side of the cross line, and a heavy, sharp point at the bottom so that it almost resembled a sword without a proper handle. If Feberik was fully under the influence of Cyrus' magic powder, then the mark would be complete. If the influence was waning, then the letter would look like all the other capital Ts that Feberik wrote, and that would be the signal to add another drink to the regimen.

Janik left the bottle in his pocket today. The mark was complete.

Now off to meet Cyrus before the morning training began.

Chapter 5

Kyra walked in that night, exhausted from her hours-long training session of trying to dispel illusions with Cyrus, to find Linny standing in the middle of the bedroom. All the furniture had been cleared from the floor, pushed up against the walls as much as possible. Linny's ebony wand was held firm in hand, and she was aiming at a drawing of some sort of strange creature that was tacked to the wall.

"What are you doing?" Kyra asked.

Linny nearly jumped, her sandy hair bouncing into her freckled face. "Oh, I was just practicing my homework." She pointed to the paper on the wall. "I am supposed to hit it with a fireball."

Kyra nodded with a smile. She remembered doing similar drills with her mother when she was younger, only the spells she was taught to throw were more akin to darts made from magic than large fireballs of any sort. She walked into the room and lazily flung herself onto her bed, keeping her eyes on Linny and watching the young girl practice.

"Am I doing it right?" Linny asked as she flicked her wrist toward the paper.

"What spell are you trying to cast?" Kyra asked in turn. There were numerous ways to conjure a fireball, and it wasn't as if knowing one of them instantly gave the caster access to each of the others. Each spell required mastery.

"The book is on the bed," Linny said as she pointed to her bed.

Kyra, despite the fact that her body wanted to slump into the mattress and remain there, rolled off her bed and went to pick up Linny's book. She smiled when she read the instructions. It was a spell specifically suited for wand users. Kyra hadn't used a wand for some time now, but she understood what to do. She turned to Linny and reached out for the wand.

Linny hesitated for a brief moment, as if the wand was all she had left in the world, but then she gently placed it into Kyra's hand. Kyra looked and found a brown spot on the wall. She pointed to it.

"I'll hit that mark there, so as not to destroy your paper." Kyra gripped the wand in her left hand and set her left foot forward. "Stance is key. When you use magic, you are calling upon the essence of Terramyr. You can control it, and even amplify it with your own energy. Feel the power coming up into you. As you focus on the spell, imagine that force is going through your body and into your wand. Then, you simply give the wand a single shake, like so, and release the energy." Kyra sent a single fireball out to the wall. It crashed into the stone with a noisy *pop!* Then it faded away.

Linny reached over and took the wand back. She planted her right foot as she held the wand in her left hand.

"No, no, whichever hand you hold the wand in, your lead foot should match," Kyra said quickly, pointing to Linny's left foot.

"Right," Linny said as she shifted around. When she was set in place, she turned back to Kyra for an approving nod. "Like this?" she asked when Kyra was half a second too slow to approve.

"Like that," she replied. "Now, call the essence up into your body and let it gather into the wand."

Kyra watched as Linny poised herself. A few seconds passed and then Linny flicked her wand. It wasn't as refined a technique as Kyra's, but it did the job. A yellow mass of flame shot out and devoured the paper.

"I did it!" Linny exclaimed. "Again!" She turned and pulled another paper out, hastily tacking it to the wall without bothering to draw an imaginary enemy this time. She got into position, and then closed her eyes as she drew in a loud breath, holding it for just a few seconds before exhaling.

Kyra noted something different about Linny this time. Somehow, she seemed larger, or perhaps stronger. Kyra wasn't quite sure, but something was different.

Linny mouthed something and then flicked her wand, much more controlled this time. A great, green light rose from the base of the wand and a massive mess of golden flames erupted from the end of it. The air around the girls crackled with energy and the room turned hot as the fireball expanded to twice the size of a man's head before slamming into the wall.

Kyra gasped when the stones in the wall relented under the spell's force, and shattered outward. As Kyra was housed in a tower, this part of the wall actually separated her room from the outside.

The two girls stood there, too stunned to move until they heard the crunching and cracking below.

Kyra ran to the hole in the wall and poked her head out just in time to see a few of the shattered stone bricks slide off the lower roof and thump into the grass below.

"I think we had better not practice in here anymore," Kyra said. She pulled her head back in and turned to see that Linny was as flabbergasted as she was. The young girl panicked and threw her wand onto Kyra's bed as if it had been responsible for the mishap.

"I didn't mean to do that!" Linny said as she backed into the opposite wall and held her arms down at her sides.

Kyra smiled. "It's all right, it just means that you have more talent than you thought," she said softly. "Come on, let's see if we can fix the wall before someone notices," she added.

"How are we going to fix the hole?" Linny asked. "It's a hole that is at least two feet wide and almost the same height."

A puff of gray smoke erupted in the room followed by yellow sparks that flowed outward.

Linny screamed and fell back, Kyra instinctively prepared a spell to attack with. Fortunately, it was Headmaster Herion.

"Are you all right?" the old, beardless wizard asked.

Linny nodded, but her words had not yet returned to her.

"We were working on an assignment she had," Kyra replied.

Herion turned around and inspected the hole in the wall. Kyra wasn't entirely sure if he was admiring it, or disappointed by it. "Which one of you did this?" Herion asked.

"I was trying to help her focus," Kyra said quickly. "Perhaps I…"

"I did it, Headmaster," Linny said as she regained her composure. "I didn't mean to do it, but I am the one who did it."

Herion's eyebrows shot up at that and he glanced between the two young ladies. "Well, isn't that interesting," he said with a slight frown. "Well then, let me just…" Herion's words trailed off and his eyes caught sight of the black wand on the bed. "Kyra, is that yours?" he asked.

"It's mine, sir," Linny replied.

Herion walked over to the wand and picked it up in his hands. "Well," he started as he turned it over and inspected it, "I would appreciate it if you are a little more cautious in the future." He turned and handed the wand back to Linny. "I'll have to ask you both to sleep somewhere else tonight. It is already too late to have the hole repaired. I'll have it fixed by tomorrow."

"Can't you put it back with magic?" Linny asked in a mousy tone. Her eyes shifted to the floor when Herion gave her a quizzical look.

"I could indeed," Herion replied evenly. "However, *I* am not the one who caused the damage. The two of you will fix it tomorrow, with your hands. Janik will show you where the materials are in the morning, and he will supervise your work to ensure it is done properly."

Linny nodded.

Kyra turned back to look at the hole. "We could do it tonight," she said.

Headmaster Herion shook his head. "No, the mortar needs to be set in the daylight, while it is warmer."

"We could use magic to warm the mortar," Kyra replied.

Herion shook his head and then looked to her sternly. "A sorceress should learn that not everything can be undone with magic. No, you will use your hands, and no magic whatsoever. I want you both to appreciate the work that goes into building a wall. That way, you will have all the more respect for something before you destroy it." Herion leaned in to Kyra and then whispered, "I am glad you are all right." Then he straightened up and *poofed* out of the room in an eruption of gray smoke that left the two of them coughing and waving their hands futilely.

*****

Normally, Cyrus would be meeting with one of the warlocks in the outer part of the cave at a stone table. This was the first time he had been brought in through the door from which he had always seen them emerge. Whether that meant they trusted him more, or perhaps suspected his involvement in Bothias' death, he wasn't sure.

He followed the warlock in front of him, trying not to look over his shoulder at the one behind him as they moved through a long hallway hewn and polished from the very mountain they were inside of. Had he not known any better, he might have thought that this lair had been created by the drow tribes that inhabited parts of the Middle Kingdom. They were second only to the dwarves in their ability to create an inhabitable subterranean settlement out of solid stone. However, like the dwarves, the drow also were fond of embellishment. Had this been their handiwork, there would be runes etched into the walls as well as murals painted along the great, straight expanses of tunnel. There was nothing here but smooth, naked stone.

Cyrus assumed that the warlocks had found this place, for he had never known any of them to be fond of working with their hands. Most had neither the temperament nor the skill to do so. More than likely there had been an animal here before them. They had probably either killed it, or enslaved it.

A great worm of some sort, perhaps, or possibly it had even been a naturally occurring network of caves that had formed either with lava or water. Whatever it was, there was no sign of the cause now.

Normally, focusing on such a mundane topic as the original builder and inhabitant of the cave system would have taken his mind off the fact that he was being led somewhere like a slave. It didn't help today.

"Where are we going?" Cyrus asked. He had already asked his guides, but since they had refused to say anything in response, he felt he could press them again.

Unfortunately, his inquiry was met with the same results.

The two warlocks guiding him through the tunnel were silent, and there was nothing to answer his inquiry save for the rustling of cloth as their long robes brushed against the floor with each step, and the soft *pit-pat* of their leather-soled shoes.

He hated not knowing the answer, but he remained calm. The riddle would be solved soon enough. Then, he would not only know their destination, but what they had planned for him. If they were going to betray him, then these two would die first.

They walked for another five minutes through the dark corridor before stopping at a large, wooden door fastened to the stone with great, iron hinges. The door opened and the smell of food tickled Cyrus' nose. His guides led him into the room and then broke off to sit at a large, round table.

Cyrus counted seven chairs around the table, and noted that there was one empty seat after his guides had taken their places at the table.

A warlock stood up on the far side of the table. His hood was overshadowing his face, but Cyrus could feel the man's eyes upon him.

"Come and sit," a raspy voice called out from under the hood. It was not a warlock Cyrus had heard before.

As he moved to take his seat at the empty chair, he realized that upon the wooden table was drawn a seven-pointed star. Each chair was positioned so that each person at the table sat at one of the points.

Am I to be interrogated? Or is this an initiation?

"One of our order has gone missing," the standing warlock said. "It has been made known to me that he is dead."

That was faster than I expected. Cyrus could barely control the smile that wanted to come out onto his face at hearing those words. Fortunately, he had decades of experience in such situations, and was able to stare back at the standing warlock without betraying his satisfaction.

"In seeing your dealings with the girl, we thought we might extend an invitation to you," the warlock said. "What do you say?"

Cyrus shook his head. "Our arrangement remains unchanged," he replied evenly. "I will uphold my end of the bargain, and you will uphold yours. Once our business is concluded, I will travel my own path."

Some of the other seated warlocks murmured or let out sounds like snarling lions, begging to be unleashed upon him for his insult. It was not likely that anyone had ever refused such an offer before, and if they had, they had most certainly not lived to speak of it, but Cyrus was not just any wizard. More than that, the group sitting around the table needed him. He could provide them with something that no one else could.

"Pity," the standing warlock said. "I had hoped that once you saw our trust in you, you would have come to see us as potential brothers."

Cyrus toyed with the idea of asking how many of them knew of Bothias' plot to take the dagger for himself, but he immediately thought better of it. He reached out toward a bowl of fruit and took an apple from it. He raised it to his mouth, but he was already casting spells and counter charms to ensure it wasn't trapped, poisoned, or otherwise tainted by the warlocks. When he took the first bite, he smiled. He loved sour apples the most, and this one was extremely sour, almost like a crab apple, but with just a hint of sweet, instead of the bitter aftertaste left in one's mouth by a crab apple.

His eating insulted the others further.

Good. If any of them were involved with Bothias, they might break their silence if I continue to offend them.

"Will you not reconsider?" the warlock asked.

"No," Cyrus replied. "I will ensure the girl becomes an ally of the coven, or that she is no longer a threat to you. That is the end of our bargain."

"She knows about the dagger," the warlock said. "More than that, others know of the vampire. You were supposed to keep things quiet."

Cyrus stood up from the table and smiled confidently. "No one knows of your dealings. To the world outside of this room, there is no Order of the All-seeing Eye. Don't concern yourself with news of the vampire. Severin is seen as an enemy, but there is no connection back to you."

The warlocks were all quiet then. Cyrus could feel their eyes upon him. He knew most of them were likely trying to calculate their odds of defeating him in a magical firefight. He had already decided to break this order of warlocks when he was done with them. For now, he needed their gift. One thing he was not adept at was seeing into the future. While this coven of warlocks was not infallible with their visions, they did have something to offer him in that area. Still, he saw no harm in poking the bear a bit.

"Besides, why would I join you?" Cyrus asked. "You are supposed to be able to see the future, yet you have lost one of your brothers and you don't know where he went? Sounds to me that either you have killed him, and are trying to hide that fact from me, or that perhaps you were blindsided by the development."

A couple of the warlocks stiffened at that last jab.

"Ah, so that's it, then, isn't it?" Cyrus pressed. "Not one of you soothsayers caught even a glimpse of his departure. Tell me, did he take something from you all then? Is that why you are quick to replace him with another?"

"Enough!" the warlock roared. "We have already demonstrated our ability to see into the future. We have told you where the dagger is."

Cyrus shook his head. "No, that is scrying the location of something. That is not quite the same as telling me the future."

Now the leader stiffened and folded his arms across his chest.

Cyrus smiled wider. It was fun to toy with them. He had not been able to so freely taunt anyone other than Janik in a long time.

"What is it you want?" the warlock said after a while.

"Tell me when and where Severin will strike."

The warlock scoffed. "It doesn't work like that," he admitted. "It is difficult to see the future when dark magic is involved."

Ah, so that was why there had been inconsistencies in the information they had given him about the dagger. The dagger itself was formed with dark magic. Moreover, that would be why they feared Kyra so much. She was quite talented, and they likely wouldn't be able to see her future clearly enough to discern whether she would ultimately become a friend or foe as she had been tainted by her father's blood. Cyrus wondered if that was why the order had failed to catch Bothias' treachery. After all, each of the warlocks depended on dark magic. If Bothias could shroud his intentions for the order, then Cyrus could as well.

"So you were guessing the location of the dagger?" Cyrus asked.

The warlock sighed, the fight seemed to leave with his breath as he sat down. "No," he said with a shake of his head. "We could catch glimpses of the dagger whenever certain people came into contact with it. We gave you the best information we had. When we saw the dagger, we consulted together and sought visions about it. We relayed the information to you."

Cyrus nodded and let out a small chuckle. He should have been angry. Now that he knew how faulty the warlocks' processes were, he should have raged on them, but he didn't. They had given him enough useful information that this revelation was funnier to him than it was insulting.

He tapped a finger to his forehead and then gave a mock salute to the warlock. "I think I will see myself out now." He could feel the daggers being thrown at his back by their gazes, but he was not about to look back now. This meeting had helped him establish his superiority. It would make his final victory over them all the sweeter when the time came.

Chapter 6

A middle aged man sat upon a cold, round boulder as he looked down from the hillside and across the grassy valley where his sheep slept. He wiggled his body a bit, finding the right groove in the rock that was the most comfortable. A depression had formed there which almost perfectly cradled his backside. It was a welcome relief from the day's walking after the sheep.

The night was warm, but the wind carried with it a briskness from the sea just a few miles to the west. Clouds covered the sky like a dimly glowing gray blanket. A few patches of stars could be seen where the clouds had left the sky bare.

The shepherd looked up to find the stars as he pulled an amulet out from under his shirt. He rubbed the polished stone with a dirty, wide thumb and began to say his nightly prayer for the flock. When he had finished, he tucked the amulet back into his shirt and then turned to his satchel. Inside he would find the cornbread his wife had made him earlier that day, along with dried apples and figs. He fumbled around until his fingers gripped a particularly plump apple ring and then he pulled it out and stuffed it into his mouth, sloppily chewing as he then retrieved the cornbread.

He laughed when he found the small clay jar of honey.

"Ah, so she does love me!" he said of his wife as he pulled the wax seal apart and began to drizzle the sticky liquid onto a square of cornbread.

A heavy shadow fell over him then, nearly blocking out the moonlight entirely. He looked up, expecting to see one of the thick clouds moving along the sky, but his eyes spied nothing.

The long-haired dog at his side huffed as it turned to lie on its side.

Seeing that the dog was at ease, the shepherd returned his attention to his cornbread. He took a bite of the crumbly deliciousness and then turned around to reach for his drink. He grabbed his waterskin and lifted it up as he twisted and pulled the stopper free. The sweet aroma of wine wafted out from the container and he smiled. He put the opening to his lips, but then stopped when another shadow threw the surrounding area into total darkness.

He lifted his eyes up and then dropped the wine.

"Kita!" he yelled out for the dog as he rolled to the side and dove to the ground.

The dog lunged up, barking and growling. Down in the valley, the sheep were bleating and screaming. The shepherd heard the sound of hooves tearing the ground and knew that they had seen the danger as well.

Kita let out a sudden yelp and the shepherd peered around the rock just enough to see what had happened.

A warm splotch of liquid struck him in the forehead and he looked up to the sky. His dog was being carried away by a winged beast.

"No!" the shepherd called out. He gathered his courage and reached for his crook and a light, crude crossbow. That courage was drained from him a moment later as the winged beast tossed Kita's body through the night sky and off into the forest. Then it spread its wings, tilted around, and dropped down toward the sheep while spewing fire over the grassy valley. The animals not lucky enough to receive a quick death as the beast gobbled several of them up, were either roasted alive by the fire or slashed with the nasty talons.

The shepherd ran, hoping that his flock would be enough to trade to the beast in exchange for his own life.

*****

Kyra was just wrapping up her training session with Cyrus, which had seemed harder than normal thanks to her bad habit of staying up well beyond midnight playing star-flies or trading fairy tales with Linny. The wizard had need to dismiss the last of the nasty creatures he had conjured up as sparring partners while Kyra dusted herself off. This lesson, she had needed to identify which imps were real, and which were only illusions. The only problem was that all of them attacked her, and illusion or not, the cuts she got were real.

"You were up late again," Cyrus chided.

Kyra nodded. "We had to repair part of the wall in our room, and by the time we were done with that we... well..." she let the words trail off. She felt silly trying to explain that they had felt like they needed to go outside to play star-flies again. Instead, she changed the subject. "You know, Linny should practice with us," she said.

"I think you two spend enough time together. I need you to focus at least *some* of the time."

Kyra smiled at the intended reprimand and shrugged it off. "No, I mean it. She blew a hole in our wall with a simple fireball spell. I've seen that spell, and many spells like it, but I have never seen someone obliterate stone with it before. She has a lot of talent."

Cyrus looked at her curiously for a moment and then nodded. "I will keep that in mind for the future, but the answer is still no. Now go and get some rest."

Kyra shrugged and gathered her things. She turned as the door opened and Lepkin walked in.

"Wrong room," Cyrus called out.

Kyra could see from Lepkin's face that something was wrong.

"I need to speak with you," Lepkin whispered.

Kyra turned to Cyrus. The wizard nodded and waved his goodbye. "We'll resume again tomorrow. Try to concentrate more."

Kyra nodded and rushed out the door. Lepkin grabbed her left wrist and was pulling her down the hallway. "What is it?" she asked.

"There have been some attacks," Lepkin said. "The dragon slayers are preparing to head out in the morning."

"Out where?" Kyra asked. "Is this about Leatherback?"

Lepkin pulled her along through the halls and into the laundry room where the entrance was to their special eavesdropping place. "Come on," Lepkin said as he peered around the room, ensuring they hadn't been followed. "Herion is calling his group together. We need to hurry or we'll miss what they decide."

The laundry room was full of large vats of steaming water and they had to duck under several rows of linens hanging on lines. They snaked around the large tubs and then stopped at a grate that was about three feet long and two feet wide. Kathair bent down and pulled the grate up.

Kyra glanced around to ensure they were not being watched, and then they dropped down. Lepkin went first, so as to offer his assistance to Kyra as she dropped into the tunnel beneath the laundry room. When they were both inside, Lepkin reached back through the opening, grabbed the grate, and pulled it into place.

Lepkin tugged at her arm again. He was more insistent than she had seen him in a long time. "Hurry up, we have to get there before they start."

The two of them hunched low and waddled through the tunnel as quickly as they could.

The light from the laundry room stretched for quite some way into the tunnel. Whenever it appeared to dim significantly, there would be another drain from above that would allow in more light to help them see by. None of the other drains were nearly large enough to crawl through. They were all the normal kind that appeared to be just a few inches across, nothing like the one from the laundry room.

They made their way through a series of turns and twists, and then they emerged from the tunnel to stand in a room that was ten feet across and about fifteen feet long.

The two of them rushed past the table and chairs and went to the book case. Lepkin pivoted the thing out to reveal the small doorway leading to the ladder they used to get into position.

The ladder went up at least two stories before reaching the platform where they could crawl into a small space at the top that led into another tunnel. There were cracks in the wall, spaces where the mortar had fallen out, that let in enough light to see by.

"They've started," Kyra whispered softly as she moved to her preferred spot.

Lepkin nodded and sat close to her, watching through a different space where the mortar had fallen out.

Through the crack she saw the rectangular room where Headmaster Herion held his secret meetings with a few of his favorite instructors at Kuldiga Academy. The sconces along the far wall were brightly burning and a set of braziers was set upon the long table in the center of the room. Wooden, high-backed chairs were situated along the table. A few people were already sitting there, their backs turned to the wall behind which Kathair Lepkin and Kyra hid.

A door on the right, bearing a large engraving of an eagle, opened, and in walked Headmaster Herion. The old wizard was dressed in a black tunic and green trousers. He moved into the room and then stopped at the head of the table.

"Those aren't masters," Kyra said as she noted the forms sitting in the chairs with their backs to the wall.

Lepkin shook his head. "Priests," he confirmed.

"Why aren't they speaking?" Kyra asked.

Her answer came when a strange portal opened on the far left of the room. Kyra had to stifle her surprise as a large painting swung to the side and in walked a large man. He stepped into the room more confidently than any Kyra had seen before. He stood as tall as Feberik, and was heavily muscled as well. His hair was gray along the sides, but the top had not yet fully yielded to age and was still fairly dark. His eyes were stern, but not cold.

He approached the opposite side of the long table and then he drew out his sword. Kyra cocked her head to the side at the sight of the strange, black metal. The sword looked sharp enough, but it looked different somehow. It *felt* different too.

"Telarian Steel," Lepkin said breathlessly. "That sword is legendary," he added. "The runes along the blade are an ancient spell. The metal itself is the toughest in all Terramyr, and capable of withstanding a dragon's flame."

Kyra was about to ask who would have such a weapon, but the meeting started and she fell silent.

"Be seated," the stranger said.

Kyra found it odd that Herion was not leading the meeting himself.

One of the priests turned to the stranger and bowed slightly before standing up to address them all, but from behind all of the priests looked alike to Kyra. She had no way of knowing which one it was.

"It is an honor to have the Keeper of Secrets with us," the priest said. Kyra recognized the voice, it was Warty. Of course, that wasn't the man's real name, but the priests had never offered their names to her, not even after they had begun their examinations of Leatherback. Therefore, she had given them names herself. The priests were known to her as Dumbly, Glumly, and Warty. Warty had a rather large wart on the back of his hand, which was the reason for his name. He was also younger than the other two, and apparently in charge of the trio.

"It is always good to be among friends," the stranger addressed as the Keeper of Secrets replied. "Headmaster Herion, I have heard some rather troubling news of late."

Kyra glanced to the wizard. He nodded and clasped his hands atop the table as he leaned forward. "I have also heard the reports. However, I should like to point out that the priests have had access to the dragon known as Leatherback for some time now.

They have never seen even the slightest evidence of taint within his soul."

"So it is your opinion that the attacks are coincidental?" the Keeper asked.

Warty looked back and forth, and then apparently decided that he was not needed to conduct the meeting and he sat back down and let the Keeper and Herion work things out directly. Kyra couldn't help but smile at that. The snub served the pretentious priests right.

"It is my opinion that the attacks are related to something else entirely," Herion replied.

The Keeper nodded. "Yes, I have heard of the recent attacks by a shade as well."

"It appears you are fairly well up to date, then, Keeper." Herion replied. "Yes, we have had a couple of run-ins with a shade, though he has been slain by one of our very own students, with Leatherback's help I might add."

The Keeper nodded. He then turned to Warty. "This student is the one you spoke of in your letter?"

"What letter?" Kyra asked.

Lepkin nudged her with his elbow and put a finger to his lips.

Kyra nodded and looked back through the hole in the wall.

"It is," Warty replied directly. "Kyra Caspen is her name."

"That's not my name," Kyra growled through gritted teeth.

Headmaster Herion cleared his throat and held up a finger. "She prefers to go by her mother's name, Dimwater."

"Kyra Dimwater," the Keeper said aloud. "I knew her grandfather. He was a good man."

A proud smile appeared on her face.

"What do you think, Herion, is Kyra worth testing?" the Keeper asked.

"Testing?" Headmaster Herion echoed curiously. "I thought you came to discuss the dragon?"

The Keeper nodded. "I did, but now that the topic has been broached, I see no reason we can't decide both questions at once."

Headmaster Herion shook his head and sat back in his chair, folding his arms as his back slapped the wood of the chair. "I have to admit, I have never been a devout follower of any religion. As such, I don't buy into most prophecies, regardless of their source."

"What is he talking about?" Kyra asked.

Lepkin shook his head as if he didn't know, but his eyes were transfixed on the black sword lying atop the table. It was as if he was almost hypnotized by it. Kyra sighed and returned her attention to the room.

"Still, a man of your experience should be aware that prophecies are fulfilled; some of them religious, and others brought about through magical visions. You cannot outright deny this fact."

"It is rare," Herion replied. "Rarer still to have the vision be literal. I find most oracles shroud their prophecy in vague language. It helps them mold it and keep their vision pliable."

The Keeper let out a throaty laugh and tapped the table with his right knuckles. "Then I will posit the question a different way. Do you think that Kyra Dimwater is a capable enough student that we should test her abilities in the hopes that she might one day grow powerful enough to defeat Nagar's Blight?"

Kyra felt her heart stop in her chest. What had that man just said? Nagar's Blight was a terrible curse. One that, for all she knew, was omnipresent throughout the Middle Kingdom and had no single source of power to destroy. Yet, here was this seemingly imposing warrior asking whether *she* might be able to reverse the curse that had been set upon the land for nearly five hundred years.

"She is strong," Herion replied. "She is possibly the greatest student I have ever seen in my lifetime. However, she comes with a curse of her own."

That stung. Kyra had not expected Herion to talk about her as if she was something tainted like that.

"Her mother was a wonderful woman, and a powerful sorceress in her own right, but her real father was a vampire,"

Herion went on. "I would suggest waiting another couple of years to see how her father's blood will affect her."

Kyra pushed away from the wall. She felt angry and sick all at the same time. What had happened to the kind man she had spoken with in the basement? Was everything a ruse set up to use her for her abilities? Her father had seen only the possible future dowry he might win by marrying her off. Was it possible that Herion was only nice to her in order to win her loyalty against Severin the vampire?

Suddenly a hand gripped her shoulder. "Hey, don't let them get to you," Lepkin said. "If your happiness depends on other people never speaking ill about you behind your back, then you will often be sad and let down by those close to you." Kathair Lepkin smiled then and gave a tight squeeze on her shoulder. "Be confident in who you are. *You* are the only person who knows your whole story. You just be sure never to let yourself down. Take pride in your heritage."

Kyra smiled but shook her head. "Take pride in being the daughter of a vampire?" she whispered.

Lepkin nodded. "I'm jealous of it," he said.

"You're jealous?"

Lepkin nodded again and turned fully to face her. "If I had vampire blood in me, then I would be even faster than I am with the sword. My senses would be sharper, and I would have magic."

"But you are the best apprentice of the sword in all of Kuldiga Academy," Kyra replied. "The first time I saw you, you were trouncing many other students with a wooden sword, and even their instructor."

Lepkin nodded with a smile. "And I would have trounced them even better if I had even an ounce of your strength," he said. He then turned back to the wall.

Kyra smiled at that. He always had a way of making her feel better about herself, no matter what others did or what was happening around her. She admired that skill. She turned back to the space and continued watching. She had missed something in the conversation. Now they were talking about Leatherback again.

"We will go in the morning and perform another examination," Warty said.

"I will go with you," the Keeper said. "If there is any taint, we will need to act quickly."

"Might I suggest you inform Kyra?" Headmaster Herion asked. All of the others turned to look at him. "If you intend on making a surprise visit to the only true friend she has, she will want to know about it. To do otherwise is to invoke her wrath, and as we have just discussed, she has already put a shade into the ground."

"Is that a threat?" Dumbly said as he stood up. He never talked much, but when he did, he was usually either grumpy or pessimistic. Kyra could scarcely tolerate looking at Dumbly.

"I am saying she has the right to know about it. She also has the right to go with you."

"I hardly think that is appropriate!" Dumbly said.

Warty turned to say something, but it was the Keeper of Secrets who spoke first.

"I agree with you, Headmaster Herion," he said. "If you would accompany me in the morning, then I would be happy to explain the situation myself. This would also give me a chance to observe her and see if she should be tested."

Herion nodded as Warty and Dumbly sat down. "It should be noted that Kyra is a ward of this academy," he said after a few moments. "The law would require her guardian's permission before she is taken to undergo the Test of Arophim."

The Keeper smiled. "As you know, my position affords me certain permissions beyond the scope of the law."

Herion nodded and Kyra could feel a heavy air settle around the room. Neither of the men were moving, but somehow this conversation had turned into a very real struggle, one as potentially deadly as anything with a sword.

"There are those here in Kuldiga Academy who would not accept the idea of Kyra being taken without permission, regardless of your station."

The room was heavy with tension as the two men stared at each other from across the table. No one moved or spoke a word. Kyra even found herself holding her breath for a while until the Keeper finally spoke.

"I am not in the habit of kidnapping children," he said with a forced smile. "However, if she were to agree to the test, assuming I found her suitable in the first place, then I would hope her legal guardians would see the merit in allowing her to do so."

Herion nodded. "That would be acceptable." Herion seemed to open up then as he shifted forward in his seat and glanced at the priests. "The dragon slayers will be leaving in the morning as well. They will head north to the villages that have reported dragon attacks. Along with a shepherd who lost an entire flock, we have several farmers who have lost cows and horses in villages to the northwest by the sea. While you are conducting your investigation, the dragon slayers will be doing their own. I feel confident that you will see something else at work here."

"I hope so," the Keeper said with a nod. "I would not like to take the life of a dragon, as that would go against everything I am working for."

"Please continue to keep a low profile while you are here," Headmaster Herion said. "If the dragon slayers were to discover Leatherback, they will not hesitate to attack. Their order is very different from yours."

The Keeper nodded. "We shall be discreet. For now, I assume that the stories of the shade are enough to keep the dragon slayers from combing the mountains looking for Dimwater's dragon."

"For now," Herion replied.

As if some unseen signal had called an end to the meeting, all of the people present rose simultaneously. Herion left through the door, while the priests and the Keeper left through the hidden passageway.

Lepkin and Kyra scurried out and down to the chamber below with the table and chairs. Lepkin replaced the bookshelf and Kyra took a seat and conjured a flame to light the candle sitting upon the table.

"I have to go to him," Kyra said.

"What?" Lepkin replied as he finished setting the book case in place. "You heard them, they're just going to examine him."

Kyra shook her head. "I'm not worried about the stupid priests," she said. "I know Leatherback didn't attack the animals. He hunts elk and moose. I know, because I go with him a lot. He wouldn't do this."

"Then why?" Lepkin asked. "Are you going to fight every monster that comes into the Middle Kingdom?"

Kyra stood up and nodded defiantly. "If I have to, then I will. Especially if the dragon slayers are still here. Maybe once they leave, then I can relax, but as long as reports come in of strange attacks that look like a dragon could be involved, then I have to do what I can to protect Leatherback. If that means going and fighting whatever attacked the sheep and cows in the villages, then so be it."

"What if it's another dragon?" Lepkin asked.

Kyra hadn't thought of that, but her courage was not dampened by the thought. "Then that dragon will have to contend with another dragon *and* a sorceress."

"I can go with you," Lepkin offered.

"Can't use swords on a dragon's back," Kyra replied.

"I'm good with a bow, too," Lepkin said with that boyish smile of his. "I just got one from Al as a present when I returned the amulet he let us use."

Just then a pebble skitted across the floor behind her. Kyra wheeled around, hands up and at the ready. Lepkin was rushing around her as well, pulling at the wooden sword he carried.

"Whoa! Stop, it's me!" Linny shrieked as she cowered and put her hands up in the air.

"What are you doing here?" Kyra asked.

"I saw you sneak into the laundry room. I was just… I mean, I…"

"You shouldn't have come down here," Lepkin said.

"How much did you hear?" Kyra asked.

Linny rubbed her hands together and looked to the floor.

"She heard all of it," Lepkin said.

Kyra rushed forward. She didn't mean to frighten Linny, but the young girl shied away from her and closed her eyes. "You shouldn't have come down here!" Kyra said. "Why were you following us?"

Linny slowly opened her eyes and looked back to Kyra. She glanced to Lepkin, and then back to Kyra. Her breathing slowed.

"I didn't mean to pry," Linny said.

"Meh, we're snooping on others," Lepkin said suddenly. "I suppose we can't be too mad if she snoops on us."

Kyra turned an angry glare to Lepkin. "No, it isn't the same."

"It's pretty much the same," Lepkin said with a shrug.

Kyra let out an exasperated sigh and locked eyes with Linny. "You had no right to come here."

"I…I thought we were friends," Linny said.

"We're friends, but we're not sisters or anything like that," Kyra replied sternly. "If anything happens to Leatherback, I swear I will…"

"She didn't mean any harm," Lepkin put in. "Come on, don't be so hard on her."

Kyra heard the words, but she was furious. Sure, she had had fun with Linny staying up late or working on homework projects together, but that didn't mean she would trust her with this secret.

Linny cracked a faint smile and nodded. "I won't tell anybody about him."

"Come on, we should get out of here before all three of us are missed for dinner," Lepkin said.

"You two go, I have to go to Leatherback," Kyra replied.

"Sure you don't want my help?" Lepkin offered.

Kyra shook her head again. "I'll go alone this time. You just get her out of here." Kyra then pointed a finger at Linny. "Not a word to *anyone* about Leatherback, do you understand?"

Linny nodded.

"And don't come back down here snooping on me again." Tears were welling up in Linny's eyes, but Kyra was too mad to care. She opened a portal and then stepped through before another word was said by anyone.

Chapter 7

Kyra stepped into the grove and found Leatherback sleeping on his side in the late afternoon sun.

"There you are!" she shouted angrily.

He opened his eyes and a smile, or at least what passed for a smile upon a dragon's face, appeared. "Where else would I be?" Leatherback asked as he rolled over and looked at her.

"You tell me!" she demanded. "I have come here for days and haven't seen you."

Leatherback's smile disappeared. "I thought you were busy training."

"Uh-uh, don't try to tell me that. Where have you been?"

"Hunting," Leatherback said.

"How many cows have you eaten?"

Leatherback snorted. "Why are you angry with me?"

Kyra strode up to him and poked the end of his snout. "I saw the cow bones here the last time I came. You have been eating cows. Now there is a village somewhere to the north that is complaining about a dragon eating their livestock. Was it you?"

Leatherback shook his head. "No." His tone was final.

Kyra took in a couple of breaths and then clenched a fist as she looked down to her feet. She hadn't really believed he had been responsible, she was just so angry that every time something bad happened it was blamed on a dragon. Worse than that, was that every time a dragon was blamed, Herion had to convene a special meeting to discuss it.

"Sorry," Kyra said. "I worry about you."

"I don't steal," Leatherback said. "The cows are wild cows. I have been hunting out west, but I don't go near any settlements."

Kyra nodded and reached out to pat his snout to make up for poking him. She knew she hadn't hurt him physically, but she still didn't like the idea of being so rough with him. Especially since she hadn't seen him hardly at all since their battle with the shade, it made her feel terrible that she would open a visit by yelling at him.

"How are you feeling?" Kyra asked.

"Tired," Leatherback replied. "Listening," he added as he closed his eyes again and rolled back onto his side.

Kyra heard a strange metallic noise and cocked her head to the side. She walked around to see a small pile of gold and gems tucked under the dragon's back. From her studies of the books her mother had given her about the dragons of Kendualdern, Kyra knew that gold and gems sang to dragons, and had healing properties.

For just a moment, she worried that perhaps Leatherback had raided villages, but then she shook the thought from her head. Villages would not have so much gold to steal, and even if they did, no one had complained about stolen riches, only dead animals.

However, the pile of wealth presented a different problem.

"Where did you get this?" Kyra asked as she moved in and put a hand on the large dragon's wing.

Leatherback rolled back to his stomach and craned his neck around so he could look at her over the pile of treasure. His eye lid cracked open and a throaty rumble came out along with a wisp of smoke as Leatherback spoke. "I found it in the ground. I dug it up."

"No, no no!" Kyra said as she put her hands on her head. "You have to be more careful. First you leave piles of bones in the clearing, which I have been cleaning for you by the way, and now you bring a mound of gold and jewels and plop it on the ground, this is careless."

"No one will look for it," Leatherback said. "I didn't steal it."

Kyra shook her head and moved to the pile. She put a hand out onto the top of the pile and then put the hand to her waist to emphasize how large the pile was. "You don't understand. If the dragon slayers come by here and see a large pile of bones, or a heaping mound of gold and jewels, they are going to know this grove belongs to a dragon. Worse than that, if they pass by the hole where you dug all this up, they will know you are nearby."

Leatherback snorted. "They won't find my treasure mine."

Kyra looked to the sky and cried out, "Ugh!"

"Leatherback rose to his feet. "Come, I will show you."

"Near or far?" Kyra asked.

"In the sea to the west," Leatherback said with a sly smile.

Kyra narrowed her eyes on him and then nodded her head. She moved to the hiding spot and pulled back the branches. This time she found the saddle and the staff. She secured the saddle to Leatherback's neck and then climbed on.

"All right, but let's make this quick. I really need to get some sleep tonight."

Leatherback leapt into the air and went straight into the clouds. He turned and flew due west, flying faster than he had ever gone before. Kyra noted how much stronger he seemed and wondered if that was in part due to the gold and jewels he was now finding and using to heal and strengthen himself.

They flew out over the sea for nearly two hours, and then Leatherback dropped below the clouds and circled a beautiful island. Kyra first scanned the area for any sign of human life, but then she let her eyes take in the breathtaking mountain on the island. Whatever anger she had felt melted away as she saw the large, dark brown pit dug out of the western slope.

"So this is your mine?" Kyra asked.

"This is my *island*," Leatherback stated proudly. "You are my first guest."

Kyra patted him on the neck. "I bet you say that to all the girls you bring here." She laughed, but the joke was lost on the dragon.

He angled his wings and the two of them descended down directly into the pit. Kyra could see the many nuggets of yellow and the several gemstones poking through the sides. More than that, there was a pile of gold along the bottom that was twice as large as the one back in the aspen grove.

"Wow," Kyra said. "With even a portion of this, we could go north and live a comfortable life."

"Can you hear the music?" Leatherback asked with a smile.

Kyra shook her head and frowned. "No," she said.

Leatherback laid down atop the gold and promptly closed his eyes. Kyra clambered down from the saddle and wandered around for a few minutes, using what was left of the late afternoon sunlight to study several different gems.

Then she turned back to Leatherback. "We still need to do something about the attacks."

"Where is the village?" Leatherback asked.

Kyra shrugged. "Somewhere to the north, I think, but I don't know for sure."

"Then why go?" Leatherback asked.

"Because, they say a dragon is killing livestock. We have to make sure that there is nothing that would cause the dragon slayers to make a thorough hunt. They might find you eventually."

"What if it *is* a dragon," Leatherback asked.

Kyra shook her head. She knew from her studies, and from her visit with Njar's Pools of Fate that dragons were a rare sight in the north of the Middle Kingdom. Any rare beasts that were left now were far to the south, which was why the dragon slayers were headquartered in Ten Forts, the southern border along the orc lands.

"It isn't a dragon, but I don't want the dragon slayers to ever find you."

Leatherback stood up and then stretched his wings. "We hunt the culprits so no one hunts me?" he asked.

Kyra nodded. "The dragon slayers will be leaving the academy tomorrow. If we can slay the animal responsible and then leave its body for them to find, then maybe they will leave us alone."

"Or we could fly north," Leatherback said.

Kyra shook her head. "You aren't strong enough yet for that, Njar says it will be some time yet."

"I am stronger than he knows," Leatherback grumbled as he puffed a bit of orange flame through his nostrils.

She was about to argue with him, but stopped short. Why should she doubt him? She was often being told by Cyrus that she wasn't ready, but look at what they had already accomplished. Not many masters could claim to have killed a shade, yet the two of them had with Lepkin's help. They had also hunted down garunda beasts and wylkins. She nodded her head and decided not to argue about his strength.

"If we leave now, the vampire will come after me," Kyra noted thoughtfully. "Cyrus has made that pretty clear. The pattern of attacks on my family and my house seem to confirm that." She didn't mention the nightmares she had been having, but those too seemed to agree with Cyrus' assessment. The vampire was after not only the dagger, but *her* as well. The thought of an undead creature hunting her for the rest of her life was not one she wanted to think on for too long.

Leatherback growled and nodded his head. "Then let him look for us. If he ever finds us, we'll be ready."

Kyra smiled faintly and shook her head doubtful. She knew that Leatherback understood the danger Severin posed. A vampire would live until destroyed, meaning it would hunt them no matter where they went.

"Has Njar seen you today?" Kyra asked. She was eager to change the subject, but also it had just occurred to her that she had not seen the satyr since before the fight with the shade.

Leatherback shook his head. "He must be resting, his injuries were great."

Kyra nodded. She had hoped Njar would be able to give her advice for finding Severin, but that would have to wait.

"What are we hunting?" Leatherback asked.

Kyra shrugged. "Not sure. It's something that kills sheep, horses, and cows."

Leatherback smiled and nodded. "If we are to spend our nights hunting monsters, then why not try to fly north. If I get tired, I will turn back. Maybe we will make it. We can be free."

Kyra opened her mouth to argue, but then she let the words sink in. Freedom was what she wanted most. She was surprised that instead of thinking about revenge for her mother, the first reason to stay that came to her mind was Lepkin. She wasn't entirely sure she could leave him, and certainly not without saying good-bye first.

Even though she was still furious with Linny, she found herself thinking of her roommate as well. She had grown quite fond of Linny too, even despite being spied on by her.

Then, for some reason Kyra couldn't explain, she made up her mind and nodded. "Okay, let's go north. We can take some of your gold here and we can fly until we find a spot that suits us. You can hunt for us, and I can use magic to cook for myself. Let's do it."

Leatherback nodded and gathered a bunch of gold nuggets in the clutches of his rear feet.

"I can go back and get a book, if you like," Kyra offered. "Might be good to take some books for reading."

Leatherback shook his head. "Enough stories," he said.

Kyra was surprised at that. He had always loved her stories. Not only that, but she had loved reading to him. That was how she had first bonded with him while he was still inside the egg. She had read to him every day. Now, without any reason, he was done with it. It felt strange. *Too strange.*

"What about The Moon dragon?" she asked.

Leatherback looked to her with his great big eyes and then he softened. "You can tell the story, as we fly and the stars come out."

"How about I tell it now? After all, we should wait for dark before flying over the northern part of the Middle Kingdom."

Leatherback nodded and laid back down on his gold.

Kyra smiled. At least he wasn't entirely done with stories just yet. She nestled into the crook just behind his foreleg and leaned back against his hard, warm scales. She recounted the story, complete with hand gestures and voices. Leatherback laughed at points, but even then Kyra knew this might be the last time she told him the story. Leatherback was growing up now, and his interests were compelling him forward, to new things.

The treasure was evidence enough of that.

When she finished the story, she looked down at the gold and picked a piece of it up. The hunk of yellow metal was rough, with bits of dirt clinging to it. The gems were likewise rough an unpolished.

Kyra smiled and placed the hunk down. The two waited until the sun dropped below the horizon and the blanket of night began to spread over the sky. Then, they prepared to take flight. Kyra checked that the staff was secure in its holster on the saddle.

The staff was an added guard against Nagar's Blight. Njar had created the entire grove for the aspen's ability to cleanse dark magic from an area. The staff was nowhere near as powerful as the grove, but every layer of protection was more than worth it. Leatherback was her friend, her family even. So, she did everything she could to protect him.

The two of them then launched into the early night sky and began their long trek northward, leaving everything behind.

Her mind raced as the wind rushed about her.

Were they doing the right thing? Was it cowardly to leave while Severin was still roaming about the Middle Kingdom? What would her mother think? Would they even be able to find the northern continents, or would they get lost in the vast expanse between?

Then, as a billowy cloud of silver swallowed them in its cool mist, she forgot all about her cares. She leaned forward and closed her eyes, enjoying the ride as they flew out across the sea for several hours.

She had fallen asleep before they every came to the mountains that marked the northern most border of the continent. Leatherback snorted to wake her. Kyra rubbed her eyes and looked across the carpet of soft clouds to see massive spikes protruding upward for thousands of feet.

"Are we flying low?" she asked.

Leatherback grunted. "No, we are at the same height we were before, still above all the clouds. The mountains are taller."

Kyra held on as Leatherback climbed into the brightening sky. The silvery yellow glow in the east told Kyra that they had flown through the entire night, and now she was just beginning to understand how large the world actually was.

Up and up they went, nearly stopping all forward progress so they could get up above the mountain range. The air grew thin and deathly cold. Though it was the middle of the summer, there were glaciers atop these peaks, and Kyra's skin was turning a light shade of blue.

As they climbed higher into the sky, she gasped for air and her limbs grew weak. She called out to her friend. "Leatherback," she cried. "I can't…"

Darkness closed in around her and she slumped backward, letting go of the saddle entirely.

She woke on the side of a mountain, nestled on a bed of pine boughs and encompassed about by fire.

"I'm sorry," Leatherback said. "When you lost consciousness, I brought us down below the clouds, thinking I could find a way through the mountains at a lower altitude." The dragon looked up to the bright sky and frowned. "I carried you in my mouth for most of the day, but it is no use. We have reached as far as we can go without flying over the top."

Kyra sat up and looked out over the flames surrounding her. The gray stone of the cliff face seemed to mock her pathetic attempt to escape from the Middle Kingdom. It rose all the way up to the clouds, but she knew that the peak was likely thousands of feet beyond where she could see from here.

"Is there no way around these mountains?" Kyra asked.

Leatherback shook his head. "The barrier goes on as far as I can see in either direction. I might be able to fly high enough to go over, but you would not survive. Then, there is no way of knowing whether the sea starts immediately, or if there is by chance a beach of an area I could land upon and rest after passing the mountains. I would need a rest, I'm afraid."

So that was it then. Njar had been right. They were not ready to travel to the north. Worse still, they now had less time to find the village where the livestock were being killed if they wanted to keep the dragon slayers out of their hair.

Kyra put a hand to her face and cried softly. "We have to go back."

"It will be faster going back," Leatherback said. "I can fly lower and get us out of the mountains without needing to walk out. If we leave at dusk, we should arrive back at the grove before morning. We might even have enough time to find whatever is troubling the village you spoke of, if we happen to see it."

Kyra nodded. "We don't have much other choice." She looked around. "I'm hungry."

Leatherback shook his head. "I have only seen trees living up here. No animals at all."

"Fruit? Nuts?" Kyra asked. "Berries?"

Leatherback shook his head and a large rumble sounded from within his stomach.

"I'm sorry," he offered. "I misjudged my abilities."

Kyra smiled. "It's all right. I do that fairly often myself."

Chapter 8

Kyra and Leatherback flew southward as soon as it was reasonably dark enough to do so. They were careful to stay among the shadows afforded them by the thick clouds hanging low in the night sky. The two were silent and alert, scanning all around themselves constantly for any sign of the reported beast.

As they soared high above the ground, Kyra couldn't help but wish that they were hunting more wylkins instead of a winged creature. Wylkins walked upon the ground with two legs, and were easily outmaneuvered by Leatherback. There was a part of her that feared they may be up against another dragon. Despite all of her studies, and even Lepkin telling her that there were no dragons north of Ten Forts, they could be wrong. After all, Leatherback had thus far managed to hide without being discovered. Couldn't an older, wiser dragon do the same?

In all her previous battles, whatever she lacked, Leatherback could usually make up the difference, except for their first encounter with the shade when Cyrus had needed to come to their rescue. If they were hunting another dragon, however, Kyra would have little to offer Leatherback should he be overpowered.

As if he sensed her thoughts, Leatherback turned around and offered her a single wink of his right eye. "Fear not," he said in a whisper.

She smiled back at him and nodded, trying to force her doubts from her mind.

A minute later, they rose up through a thick, moist cloud. Droplets of water collected on her skin only to be whisked away as Leatherback increased his speed and drove them higher into the night.

The crescent moon gave little light as they burst out through the top of the cloud, but the view of the millions of twinkling stars was beyond description. It was as if the lack of moonlight allowed her to see them in clearer detail than ever before. Some were green or blue, while others were red, orange, or yellow. Then there were the thousands and thousands of white stars varying from dim pinpricks barely visible to great stars that hung heavily in the sky and shared their immense light.

The two of them flew above the clouds, passing over the silvery blanket of rolling mist as quickly as a sparrow. Each beat of Leatherback's wings churned the vapors, curling them upward in the dragon's wake.

Then, after several hours of flying and scanning the clouds, there was movement. Something broke through the surface and then smoothly dove through the clouds some four hundred yards ahead of them. Kyra tapped Leatherback's neck, but he had already begun to turn. He had seen the movement as well, and his muscles tensed beneath Kyra as he started into a gliding pattern toward the creature.

It rose again, just breaking the clouds with a horned head and ridged spine before diving down into the mist. An orange burst was seen through the clouds.

"He's attacking something," Kyra said as she heard a roar accompany the strange glow. "Is it a dragon?"

Leatherback snarled. "It is a fire drake, we can handle this easily enough."

Kyra looked at the animal and nodded her agreement. All of her reading about the dragons of Kendualdern had taught them both enough to recognize many different types of dragons and drakes. Killing the drake should be easy enough, given the size difference between it and Leatherback, and it might even give the dragon slayers enough of a dragon-like creature that they might see the body and then return to Ten Forts, satisfied that they had found the monster responsible for causing havoc in the north.

Leatherback rose high into the air, abandoning the smooth glide in order to gain a greater advantage. Kyra leaned forward and gripped his neck, her eyes glued to the clouds below.

The dragon leveled out several hundred feet above the clouds, and then began circling the way an eagle might before diving after its quarry.

Another orange glow appeared along with a roar and the faint sound of bleating sheep.

"We have to strike," Kyra said.

Leatherback didn't respond.

Then, when the drake broke through the clouds again, Leatherback pointed down into the steepest dive Kyra had ever witnessed. She almost screamed at first when she found herself entirely upside-down, but she managed to stifle her fear enough to avoid spoiling their element of surprise. Then, as Leatherback attained unimaginably fast speeds, Kyra found herself struggling to hold onto the saddle. She wound the straps over her wrists, essentially lashing herself to her friend.

The clouds, which before had seemed thick and took several minutes to fly through, parted as Leatherback tore through them in a matter of two seconds. The dark figure of the fire drake loomed another fifty feet below them. It too was in a dive, but not nearly as steep as Leatherback.

An orange glow erupted as the drake let out its fiery breath. One second later, Leatherback slammed into the drake with his chest, snapping the creature's spine as Leatherback wrapped his forelegs around the drake's chest and dug in with his claws.

Kyra gasped at the ferocity with which Leatherback tore the drake apart. She heard the tearing and ripping of sinew and snapping of bones, and then a cloud of warm liquid burst around her as the drake was ripped in half.

Leatherback let out a roar and then tossed the broken halves out to the sides before breaking his dive and soaring out over a flock of terrified sheep.

Kyra was about to chide him for being so loud, for she didn't want any shepherds to see or hear them, but before she could say anything another pair of drakes came in from the sides.

"Watch out!" Kyra shouted.

Leatherback flipped upside down and tucked his wings under his back as he engaged the two new drakes with his claws.

The attackers came in spewing fire and diving for Leatherback's sides. Fortunately, they were less than half of Leatherback's total size, perhaps only twenty feet long or so from nose to tail, and the dragon was easily able to use his legs and claws to block their fangs and claws.

Unfortunately, the drakes had come in so fast that they still impacted Leatherback with tremendous force. Kyra fell to the ground as a sharp tail lashed out and severed the straps holding the saddle in place. A few feet before she landed, she was able to conjure a cushion of air that softened the blow, but she still tumbled across the grassy vale for several yards, the saddle still lashed to her wrists, and received numerous abrasions and bruises before she came to a stop.

A terrible crashing noise was heard over the sound of frantic bleating. Sheep ran in all directions as Leatherback and the two drakes ripped through the grassy dirt as they all came to an abrupt halt.

Leatherback pushed the drakes off and rolled to his feet, fully ready to engage the attackers.

Kyra hurriedly pulled at the straps around her wrists to free herself from the cumbersome saddle. She then reached for her staff, which had miraculously remained intact, and jumped up to go and help her friend.

The hairs on the back of her neck stood on end as she felt something coming from behind. She wheeled around and saw a mess of teeth rushing toward her face. Kyra dove to the side and sent out a lightning bolt. The sudden flash of blue light illuminated the diving body of yet another drake. This one was black in color, its eyes a menacing green that glowed in the night.

It ripped into the grass where she had been standing and then it turned its head toward her and its mouth opened. Kyra barely had time to throw up the ward before a crushing wave of flames issued out from the drake's mouth.

The magical shield crackled and sizzled, but it held strong against the creature's attack, saving Kyra's life. However, the drake seemed undeterred by the barrier. It lunged forward, raking its sharp claws across the magical ward and then biting down on it with tremendous force.

The shield cracked, and then broke apart, dissipating into the air and leaving no barrier between her and the drake. The drake swung its head, knocking into Kyra and sending her back several feet as she lost her grip on her staff and it fell to the ground.

She jumped up quickly, gathering her senses about her as the black drake stepped forward.

Just then, a mangled, bloody form crashed into the drake in front of her. She jumped back at first, but then realized that Leatherback had thrown one of the other drakes. She glanced to him, and saw that he was nearly done with the second attacker as well.

She turned back to the black drake and prepared two spells. In her right hand she gathered enough electrical energy to kill a horse, and in her left hand she formed ice crystals into a spear.

The black drake shoved aside the mangled body and stood on its hind legs. It breathed a spurt of fire into the air and then dropped to all fours and stalked toward Kyra. The young sorceress stood firm and smiled.

"You aren't the only one with powers," she jeered. Kyra let the lightning fly at the beast's neck and face. It snarled ferociously, but seemed unharmed by the spell. It shook its head, curled its upper lip back to reveal its fangs, and then came forward.

She had expected this. That was why she was secretly preparing a spear of ice. She waited patiently, locking eyes with the drake as it charged. Then, it opened its mouth and just as she saw the red spark of fire deep within its throat, she let the spear fly.

The ice soared straight and true, as fast as the lightning had before. The sharp, cold point sailed into the drake's open mouth and then tore through the back of its throat and neck. The drake's eyes shot open wide and it jerked its head to the side. Blood oozed down its neck as the body crashed to the ground two feet in front of Kyra. It twitched a few times, emitting a sound that seemed a mix of a snarl and a squeaking cry. Then it gave up the ghost and was still.

Leatherback was there in an instant. Never one to take chances, he drove his claws through the black drake's chest. Then he turned to Kyra and bent his neck low.

"We must leave."

Kyra nodded, and only then did she realize there was shouting coming from the west. Someone had seen the battle. If they didn't leave now, Leatherback would be discovered. She ran to him, stopping to pick up her staff and then leapt onto his neck and patted him on the side.

Then, just as Leatherback was poised to launch into the air, she screamed and jumped off. Leatherback tensed and prepared for another fight, but then relaxed when Kyra ran toward the fallen saddle and picked it up.

"We can't leave this!" Kyra said.

Leatherback reached around and took it in his mouth, and then they took to flight as quickly as they could, soaring for the clouds and shadows.

Neither one of them knew that it was already too late.

Several witnesses had seen them that night, and not all of them were human.

Hidden in the shadows beneath a copse of twisted oak trees, Severin watched the pair climb higher into the night sky. A wicked smile curled his lips upward, accentuating his long fangs. His trap had worked even better than he had hoped.

Now he needed only to wait for the dragon slayers.

*****

Kyra was already awake in her room by the time the knock came at the door. Given the meeting she had witnessed, she had known to expect the Keeper of Secrets in the morning, only she hadn't been there in the morning, because she and Leatherback had tried to run away. It was only logical that the Keeper of Secrets would try to call upon her again. Linny had been agreeable enough to leave early as well, without asking where she had been the day before, affording Kyra the opportunity to speak as freely and openly as she wished with the stranger.

She opened the door and saw Headmaster Herion looking down at her. His expression was somber, without warmth or mirth.

"Kyra, I bring a visitor. Please," he gestured toward the room and she knew that she was to let them in.

She sat down upon her bed, while Herion moved toward the wall that had recently been repaired and traced a finger over the new stones. A moment after that, a tall, heavily muscled man ducked into the doorway, turning slightly sideways so that his shoulders would fit through the opening. Kyra studied him carefully.

The Keeper of Secrets had not appeared so large from her previous vantage point in the secret room, but now that he was in the same room she was, she could see that he was large enough to make Feberik Orres look average. He stood just under seven feet tall, with shoulders nearly three feet wide. A broad, barrel-like chest puffed his black, silken tunic out to dangle over his much thinner waist.

Feberik was strong and thick, complete with a bit of a gut that protruded out in front of him, but not so with this man. He was all muscles and grit, lean and shapely. His skin was well-tanned, lined with a few scars that she could see. The sleeves on his tunic were made to accommodate his burgeoning muscles, but even with the extra width and a V opening on the sides, the sleeves struggled to hide his bulk. A long, wriggly vein ran from under his sleeve and down his right bicep until it disappeared inside his elbow. As he crossed his arms, his muscles grew taught and pulled at the skin. From the look of him, he might have been the only man she had seen that could beat Feberik in a contest of strength.

"I am a friend," the Keeper said in a low, but soft voice.

Kyra realized that he had caught her staring at his arms and immediately averted her gaze. "I am Kyra Dimwater," she replied.

The man nodded. "Let me look at your eyes," he said.

Kyra turned her face back up to his. The man's green eyes narrowed and stared into her, as if searching for something he had lost a long time ago. As he stared at her, she studied his facial features. The scar under his left eye was intriguing. Jagged and thick, it spoke of a terrible wound and she could only wonder what kind of monster had gotten close enough to deliver such a blow. Like many warriors, he had a rather square jaw. The hair along the sides of his head appeared much brighter in the full light, almost like silver. The hair on top of his head was darker, but also had a fair amount of white in it as well which she had not noticed before. Yet, despite the age suggested by the man's hair, there were no wrinkles upon his face, except for nearly imperceptible creases on either side of his mouth and faint crow's feet near his eyes.

"You think me old?" he asked.

Kyra frowned, afraid that perhaps this man had read her thoughts somehow.

"My name is Mindaugas Reif. I am the Keeper of Secrets."

"He is of the same order as the priests from Valtuu Temple," Headmaster Herion put in quickly as he turned away from studying the patch in the wall. "He and the priests intend to visit your dragon today."

"He isn't *my* dragon," Kyra replied evenly. "He is my friend, but I don't own him."

Mindaugas smiled and let out a short chuckle. "Would you accompany me and the others?" he asked. "I wouldn't go without your knowledge, but it is important that I go and see him."

"Why?" Kyra asked. "The priests see him regularly enough."

Mindaugas turned to the headmaster. "Headmaster Herion, might I have a word with Kyra Dimwater in private?"

Headmaster Herion frowned. He glanced between the two of them for a few moments before finally nodding. "I'll be right outside, if you need me," he told Kyra.

She watched him leave and then Mindaugas pointed to Linny's bed. "Can I sit there?" he asked.

Kyra had to fight the urge to correct his use of the word 'can' and did her best to nod politely.

"I have a special position, given to me many years ago. While I can't tell you all of the details, I can say that I am a friend of dragons. I am a follower of the Old Ways. I long for the return of the Ancients to the middle kingdom." He smiled softly and looked at her with his intense, green eyes. "The priests are here to ensure that Leatherback does not succumb to the taint. This is a fear that I share. I must say that I have not seen or heard of a dragon in the Middle Kingdom during my lifetime that did not ultimately succumb to the terrible curse."

"So you have come to kill him then?" Kyra asked pointedly.

"I can see your patience is running thin, so I will get to the bottom line. No, I haven't come to kill him. All of the reports I have received say that he is pure. He has never shown any signs of aggression toward any of the priests, and they have found no evidence of the taint in him."

"So why did you come?"

Mindaugas smiled. "Partly to see him for myself. I should like to see another pure dragon."

"Another?" Kyra repeated questioningly. "I thought you just said you hadn't heard or seen any other pure dragons."

Mindaugas smiled slyly. "I said I hadn't seen or heard of any *in the Middle Kingdom.*" He paused, letting that sink in for a minute before continuing.

"Where have you seen them?" Kyra asked quickly. Perhaps the Keeper of Secrets knew a place that was safe for dragons. If he worshipped them like the priests of Valtuu Temple, then surely he would want Leatherback to be safe from the blight!

"I have seen only one in my lifetime," he replied. "He was the one who made me what I am now."

What he is now. What was that supposed to mean?

"Can Leatherback go there, wherever the other one is?"

Mindaugas frowned. "No, I'm afraid he cannot."

"Why not?" Kyra demanded, frustrated that the possibility to save her friend wasn't even going to be explored by the man.

"As the Keeper of Secrets, I am sworn to silence on many things. It is part of the job. However, please understand that if it were possible, I would have suggested it myself. I would be more than eager to see your fried safe and protected from the blight."

"Then how did the other dragon stay safe and not succumb to the blight?" Kyra asked pointedly.

"He didn't. I served him faithfully for many years, and then I was forced to put him down when the blight overtook him."

There was pain in his eyes and he had to clear his throat and look away for a few moments before he could speak again.

"I'm sorry," she said.

Mindaugas nodded and then said, "The second reason I came is to see you. There is a prophecy about a young warrior who will overturn Nagar's Blight, and banish it from the Middle Kingdom forever."

"You think that could be me?" she asked. The notion was intriguing, but she didn't fully trust Mindaugas. He had yet to prove himself to her satisfaction.

Mindaugas shrugged. "I'm not sure, but I am sworn to follow any and all leads that might result in finding the chosen one."

"What about me makes you think I could be the one?"

"Because you have a dragon, and you have helped it remain pure," Mindaugas said bluntly.

Kyra shook her head. She had read many legends of chosen heroes, but she had never believed such things could ever be real. "I have help," she explained.

"You mean the satyr and the aspen grove?" Mindaugas replied evenly.

"How did you…" she stopped herself.

Mindaugas pointed toward the door. "First, the priests told me about the satyr and the grove. They could see his imprint, so-to-speak, a magical signature left behind by him. Later on, Headmaster Herion told me about him after he received a letter from Njar just before Caspen Manor was attacked. Don't worry, I am not here to meddle with the satyr. He has not shown himself to be an enemy, and I have no need to make new ones." He laughed then and gently slapped his knee, looking to her as though she should have gotten the joke. "A Keeper of Secrets has no shortage of enemies," he explained after wiping a tear from his right eye.

"I am born of a vampire," Kyra said, interested to see how he would react in front of her. To her surprise, he neither balked nor hesitated.

"I don't care about that," he replied. "A person is judged on their character, not their skin color, religion, or ancestry."

She was shocked. The priests had certainly viewed her differently for the most part. "Not everyone shares that opinion."

Mindaugas nodded and frowned. "Prejudices exist, but they shouldn't. It's as simple as that. As far as I am concerned, I want to see what your desires are, and what kind of person you will become. Let's go and visit your dragon. It would be a good thing for me, and perhaps I can have the priests ease off a bit as well. I have no desire to interfere so long as the dragon is unharmed by the Blight. For all I care, you can hunt shades and vampires until the end of your days. However, if you want to try and make something more of yourself, then perhaps I can convince you to come with me to Valtuu Temple. There is a test I would give to you. It is dangerous, there is no hiding that fact, but if you pass it, you would have even greater abilities than you do now, and you would be able to permanently protect Leatherback from Nagar's Blight."

So, there it was. Mindaugas had found the right words to say, and now Kyra was hooked. She still wondered how Mindaugas might be using her, but now she at least had more incentive to see what this test was all about. The chance of saving Leatherback from the blight was something she couldn't pass up.

"Very well, let's go." Kyra stood up and opened the portal to the sanctuary. "Let me first go and tell him you are coming. The priests can guide you to the grove."

Mindaugas nodded. "Very well," he said.

Kyra used her portal to arrive ahead of the others and tell Leatherback who was coming. To her surprise, he seemed notably less wary about the meeting than she. The large dragon continued to doze, snoring lightly every other breath while Kyra waited for the priests and the Keeper of Secrets to arrive.

To pass the time, the two of them discussed whether Kyra might be able to find good maps and charts in Kuldiga Academy's library to guide them on their journey north when the time came. They spoke for several hours, planning what they would do once they were able.

Kyra even tried to figure out what kinds of spells she would need so they could both pass over the formidable mountain range.

It was late afternoon by the time the others arrived. Warty gestured for the other two priests to hang back while he and Mindaugas approached.

Kyra tapped Leatherback on the side. "They're here," she said.

The dragon opened his eyes and then his head twitched up when he caught sight of the Keeper of Secrets.

"I told you he was big," Kyra commented.

Mindaugas undid his sword belt and left it in the grass before coming all the way into the aspen grove. He was all smiles, beaming like a child might upon receiving a puppy. His arms went out wide and he bowed to Leatherback.

"Shall I start the exam?" Warty asked.

Mindaugas shook his head. "There is no need," he said. "You and the others may leave. This creature is not tainted."

"With all due respect, Keeper, you have not the gift of True Sight."

Mindaugas turned, his smile vanished and his tone grew harder. "You may go."

Kyra glanced to Leatherback, but the dragon was already putting his head back down over his crossed forelegs. She watched as Warty reluctantly left the grove and the other priests joined him on the long walk back.

"So, this is Leatherback," Mindaugas said as he came closer.

Kyra nodded.

"Does he speak yet?"

Leatherback turned his head to regard the Keeper of Secrets. "I speak."

Mindaugas put his right hand up over his heart and laughed. "I knew it!" Mindaugas shouted. He pointed at the dragon and wagged his finger. "I knew your mother," he said.

This caught Kyra by surprise. Surely the man had to be mistaken. Njar hadn't mentioned anything about Mindaugas before, and he had told her all about Leatherback's parents.

"It was only a brief meeting, but I knew her." Mindaugas came up and reached out a hand to Leatherback's long snout, lightly patting the scales next to Leatherback's nostrils.

"You knew his mother?" Kyra asked.

Neither of them heard her. Mindaugas' green eyes were now locked on Leatherback's right eye and the two seemed to be... speaking.

"Leatherback?" Kyra said. No response. She folded her arms, a little affronted that she was being left out of whatever conversation they were having. She started tapping her foot, then she began pacing. Finally, she went over and sat on the rock that Njar often sat upon during his visits. She had no way of knowing exactly how much time had passed, but it felt like hours before Mindaugas finally broke away from Leatherback.

The large man turned back toward Kyra and was wiping tears from his face. "You have a very special friend," he said as he came to lean on the boulder she sat upon. "A very special friend indeed!"

"What did you talk about?" she asked.

"He brought me up to speed on everything that has happened since his hatching."

"Everything?" Kyra asked, glancing nervously back to Leatherback.

Mindaugas nodded. "Don't worry, I am not here to enforce the rules of Kuldiga Academy."

"Oh," Kyra managed to say.

"I also asked for his permission to train you. I told him who I am, and what I am working for."

"Why not just ask me for permission?" Kyra said agitatedly.

"Because I don't want him left in the dark on this any more than I would want you to come against your will," Mindaugas replied. "I will say that it is very important, possibly the most important thing you will ever do. If you are even a little inclined to come with me, then I would urge you to do so."

"What did you say?" Kyra called out to Leatherback.

The dragon smiled and nodded his head. "This is a good man, Kyra," Leatherback replied. "I say we finish hunting the vampire, and then you should go with him."

I should go with him? Kyra repeated in her head. She barely knew the man, but now she was supposed to trust him indefinitely? That didn't make sense.

"He speaks to me in the language of the dragons," Leatherback said. "I wasn't trying to exclude you, it was a sign of trust between him and me."

Kyra listened to her friend and then realized that she already trusted Mindaugas as well. Even if she hadn't, she had always asked for Leatherback to have faith in her and her judgment, which hadn't always worked out well. In light of that fact, she accepted her friend's explanation and decided to go along with it.

"I understand," Kyra said with a smile. At that moment, Mindaugas' words about banishing Nagar's Blight came back to her then, and she knew that Leatherback was right to trust him. She turned to Mindaugas.

"Very well, after we settle the issue with the vampire, then I will come to your temple, if that is so important to the both of you."

Mindaugas smiled. "I will need to leave. There is much for me to prepare back at the temple."

Kyra shook her head. "If I am to do something for you, then why not help us fight the vampire?"

Mindaugas turned serious and his mirth vanished. "It isn't that I don't want to, but there are other matters that will need my attention before I can prepare the temple."

"I thought you said this would be the most important thing I could do with my life, so why risk losing me to a vampire?"

Mindaugas smirked and nodded. "I like your spirit," he said. "The truth is, each Keeper of Secrets is charged with searching for the Champion of Truth, the prophesied hero I spoke of who can destroy Nagar's Blight. Each Keeper before me has had their own idiosyncrasies and particular methods for finding and training candidates. What I will say is this, I have high hopes for you, but if you are killed by a vampire, especially considering you will have the help of a dragon, then you would not pass the Test of Arophim anyway. At the risk of sounding cold, this last fight you have will be a sort of final screening process before I am willing to begin your training."

"That is callous," Kyra said.

Mindaugas nodded. "If you knew the prophecies the way that I do, you would see the wisdom in my methods, though I admit it does seem harsh to the uninitiated."

"Trust him, Kyra," Leatherback said once more.

"I must be off," Mindaugas said before she could respond to her friend. "I am satisfied here, both with him and with you. I will inform the headmaster of your decision to join me after you resolve the matter with the vampire. He hadn't seemed overly fond of the idea, but I expect he will respect your wishes."

"Are there others?" Kyra said before he could start his next sentence.

"Other candidates?" Mindaugas asked.

Kyra nodded.

"I have put forward three candidates in the past. My predecessor found seven, and his predecessor had found four. None of them passed the test."

"Are there other candidates right now?"

Mindaugas stopped and smiled at her. "You have a sharp sense of perception. There is one other I wish to look at, but I have not decided whether to include him as a candidate yet."

"Who?" Kyra pressed.

"A boy, trained and raised by elves before he started studying here."

"Lepkin," Kyra finished for Mindaugas.

The Keeper of Secrets nodded. "I need to interview him still, and I haven't heard as much about him as I have of you, but everything I have heard indicates he may be a worthy candidate."

Kyra smiled and nodded. She liked the idea of training with Lepkin. This way, she would have a friend at Valtuu Temple.

"Until we meet again, Miss Dimwater," Mindaugas said with a bow of his head. He then turned to Leatherback and offered a full, gracious bow. "Take care of her, my friend." Then he turned and left, stopping only for a few moments to pick up his sword before disappearing into the forest.

*****

"Move along Kathair, there is much to be done today," Dengar said after a few moments of surveying the carnage upon the grassy valley before them.

Lepkin hated that Dengar refused to call him by his family name. He had never liked the name, Kathair, and was all too ready to be rid of it. Britner and Foman didn't seem bothered by Lepkin's name preference, but Dengar always used Lepkin's given name, as if it would help remind the apprentice of his station or something.

Perhaps Dengar's insistence on calling him Kathair was why Lepkin ignored the command and stood on the top of the hill overlooking the valley for another few seconds. A silent battle of wills playing out without a direct argument. In any case, his eyes took in the full scene. Lepkin had been trained at the hands of elves before being sent to attend Kuldiga Academy, and he was already an accomplished warrior, tracker, and strategist. Even if Kyra hadn't forewarned him that she and Leatherback would hunt down the winged beasts reported by the shepherd and others, he would have instantly recognized this as the work of a large dragon.

The carrion birds circled above in the sky, apparently too afraid of the corpses to come down and make a meal of them, except for the few who landed near the ruined and broken bodies of what had once been sheep.

Similarly, a small band of men was standing on a hill on the opposite side of the valley. Dengar and the others would surely want to question the possible witnesses, but they would stop at the drake corpses first.

Lepkin hurried to catch up with Foman, a large and menacing warrior with a scar under his left eye. Foman looked down and nodded to Lepkin.

"Tell me what you see," he commanded.

Lepkin squirmed inside. He had hoped they would let him simply observe this time. He didn't want to give them any clues that might point to Leatherback, but on the other hand, he was not sure if they would catch him lying if he withheld information.

They approached the bottom half of a drake first, and Lepkin pointed to it just before covering his nose as the intense odor of sulfur and puss assaulted him. "There are four dead drakes," he started. "This one was ripped in half."

"What could do that?" Foman pressed.

Lepkin replied honestly, "Something much larger."

Foman nodded. "What else can you tell me?"

"This one died first," Lepkin surmised. "My guess is that it was caught unawares by whatever killed it. Then, the other three moved in afterward to attack."

"So we are looking for a fifth monster, very good," Foman said. The large warrior motioned for Lepkin to walk with him until they reached the mangled body of a tan colored drake. "Tell me about this one."

Lepkin bent down and inspected the body. While he noted the many lacerations, depressions in the scales, and blood smears, Dengar and Britner walked up behind him. He sighed, knowing that he was now going to be judged on his findings by all three of them.

"Well?" Dengar pressed impatiently.

"This one was killed by the same creature that killed the first," he said. "These puncture wounds are too large to be caused by a drake of the same size. Whatever killed this one had claws nearly as large as swords." Lepkin then pointed to the blood streaks and then to the torn turf. "The ground has been disturbed here," he said. "As if this drake crashed or was thrown." Lepkin then turned around and pointed to the black drake. "Perhaps the body was thrown at this drake here."

"Perhaps," Britner put in. "Or perhaps this is where the tan drake was tackled."

Lepkin shook his head. "No, look again at the holes in the tan drake's body. There are no corresponding claw marks or tracks along the ground here. I am certain it was thrown to this point."

"Good job so far, now move on to the black one, Kathair," Dengar commanded.

Lepkin shrugged off the use of his name, and the demeaning tone in which it was said, and went to the black drake. His heart jumped into his throat and his mouth fell open as soon as he saw the strange, gaping hole in the drake's throat.

"Something has you surprised?" Dengar asked.

Lepkin then realized that each of the dragon slayers had noticed him staring at the hole. There was no sense in trying to hide his discovery, but perhaps if he spoke quickly he could direct their perception of the wound.

"This was done by magic," Lepkin said as he pointed to the hole. "A magical spear or missile of some sort."

"Are you certain?" Britner asked.

"Some villages have access to wind-lances," Foman put in.

Lepkin didn't take the bait. He knew that none of them thought it could be a wind-lance. The hole was far too large in diameter for that. He shook his head. "No, this was done by a powerful wizard," Lepkin lied. "A master of magic. A wind-lance would not produce a wound this large, and even if it had, there should be evidence of the missile used." Lepkin spun around, making a show of investigating the theory he already knew to be false. "I see no evidence of such a weapon. Nor would I think the villagers would be standing without it if they had one."

"Good work," Dengar said. "So, then, what of these marks?"

Lepkin had already seen the numerous puncture wounds in the black drake's chest. They matched the claw marks in the other corpse. "Those were done by the same beast that killed the first two drakes." Lepkin then studied the wounds closer, noting the peculiar lack of blood around the openings. "My guess is that the magical missile killed this drake, but that the beast who killed the other drakes came to finish the black drake and stabbed him after death."

"Impressive," Britner commented.

"He was trained by the elves," Dengar spat. "I would expect nothing less."

"Now then, what killed them?" Foman asked. He folded his arms over his chest and stared at Lepkin.

The young apprentice shrugged, trying to buy some amount of time. He knew there was only one thing big enough to rip a drake in half, but he didn't want to start a dragon hunt. Somehow, he had to stop the dragon slayers here.

"Whatever it was, it seems as though it was defending the flock," Lepkin said.

"Bah!" Dengar roared as he cuffed Lepkin up the backside of his head. "Dragons don't *protect* anything. They kill, maim, and lay waste to anything that gets in their way. What we have here is a territorial dispute. These drakes wandered into territory claimed by a dragon. The dragon killed them."

Britner nodded and grunted his agreement.

Foman looked away from Lepkin, but only after a disappointed shake of his head, and addressed Dengar. "What of the magic?" he asked as he pointed to the black drake.

Dengar shrugged. "Not sure, but I doubt some wizard could control a dragon. Once the blight takes hold, the true dragon's nature always comes out."

"So…" Foman pressed.

Dengar stuck his chin out at the corpse and said, "Likely the dragon fought with his breath. I've seen a full size dragon rip the top half of a drake's head clean off when the two both spat fire at each other at the same time. The little drakes can't match the pressure and force of the full size monsters. Simple as that."

"Let's go talk to the witnesses, see if we can figure out which way the dragon flew after the skirmish," Britner said.

The dragon slayers all turned and Lepkin let out a small sigh of relief before following. The men knew a dragon was involved, but at least they didn't suspect Kyra.

The men standing on the hill seemed almost as afraid of the dragon slayers as they were of the corpses lying in the grass. They kept staring at the spiky, bladed armor each of the dragon slayers wore and shooting nervous glances to each other.

Dengar had to ask four times about the dragon before one of the men finally had the courage to speak up. His voice was low and deep, but his speech was marred with the drawl common among some of the farmers and shepherds along the western coast. Lepkin had to focus on the man's mouth to fully understand what he said.

"The dragon came outta nowhere, like some sort of demon," he said. "Killed these baby dragons and then flew into the sky."

"Dragons are not demons," Dengar said forcefully. "They are much easier to kill. Now, which way did it fly?"

The man shrugged and turned to the others. They all looked down at the ground, and a couple of them pushed the first man out toward the dragon slayers as if he would be forced to answer if he was the closest one.

They were correct.

Dengar stepped in and placed a hand on the man's shoulder. The man winced and from the look on his face he was debating whether to turn and run.

"Which way did he fly?" Dengar said. "East? West? North? South?"

The man shrugged. "Can't say for sure. He got into the clouds and I never saw him after that."

"How big was he?" Dengar pressed. Lepkin noted that Dengar's fingers began to dig into the man's shoulders a bit.

"Sixty feet long," the man mumbled. "Maybe a bit longer. It was dark! He stood taller than a tree, and could bathe the whole valley in fire!"

Dengar turned to raise an eyebrow at Lepkin. "See, Kathair, the dragon's fire breath is what made that hole."

Lepkin nodded, holding inside the satisfaction of knowing that it was, in fact, Kyra who had made the hole. At his moment, Lepkin felt it was almost a shame *not* to tell Dengar, if only to see the stupefied look on his otherwise smug face. The young apprentice had to turn away as he could feel a mischievous grin busting out despite his best efforts. Once he had it under control, he coughed, cleared his throat, and then turned to listen to the still-stammering man.

"South!" the man squeaked after being pressed yet again for a direction. "It flew south!"

Lepkin's heart skipped and his stomach lurched at the same time. The fool had just said he hadn't seen through the clouds. Yet, when pressed for a direction, he had managed to guess the one direction that was correct.

"You are sure?" Dengar asked.

The man nodded. The others behind him started agreeing as well.

Dengar let the man go and dismissed them all with a wave. "Go tend to what is left of your flocks."

The men were all too eager to comply, nearly stumbling over each other as they left.

"Bait and wait?" Britner asked.

Dengar nodded. "The corpses are here. The sheep are here. Let's see if the dragon returns tonight."

"We can camp under those oak trees over there," Foman put in. "Should hide our presence while affording us a clear view of the valley and the sky around here."

Dengar spat and then offered a single nod. "Let's set up camp." He turned to Lepkin. "Kathair, we have several hours before sundown yet, follow the shepherds and see if you can acquire some food. Bread, meat if they have it, and some ale. Go."

Lepkin nodded without a word and began jogging to the west. The village was another two miles away, but he didn't mind the distance. This would give him time to think and create a plan. Somehow he had to warn Kyra. As he crested up a hill and then started down the other side, he wondered what the penalty might be for getting the dragon slayers drunk and sneaking off.

Chapter 9

The three dragon slayers sat around the fire, some hundred yards away from the copse of oak trees where they had made their camp for the night, stuffing the last morsels of flatbread into their mouths and washing it down with what Dengar had described as water with a hint of fermented grape. Lepkin had been unable to find any ale to bring back to them. All he had to show for his four mile round trip was a single bottle of wine that had been made by one of the village elders' daughters.

Unfortunately, the wine was far too weak to put even one of the dragon slayers into a drunken slumber. So, Lepkin sat on the opposite side of the fire and ate a baked roll that had cubes of fat and spiced meat inside of it. If any of the men noticed that Lepkin had kept the best bread for himself, none of them said anything.

In fact, they hardly spoke at all, except for Dengar's incessant complaints about the wine every time he took a drink. They kept their eyes to the sky, and their conversation short. Each of them was dressed in their full set of armor, with helmets and weapons resting nearby at their sides for easy access. The black steel was a marvel to behold. It seemed to dance and shimmer in the firelight, and yet the spikes and blades protruding from the armor spoke of a fierceness that even Lepkin admired.

Britner caught him staring and smiled. "Telarian steel is the best there is," he said.

Lepkin nodded. "Strong enough to withstand a dragon's flame without melting or warping," he said. "The armor is light enough to afford the wearer maximum flexibility, almost like a suit made of leather padding, but the steel can withstand a dragon's claw, or so they say."

Britner's smile widened. "All that and more," he said. "The spikes and blades even allow us to strike a killing blow in death," he explained. He put his arms out and mimicked a set of jaws, fingers interlinking like long teeth. "A dragon swallows one of us, and we make sure to wriggle all the way down."

"A dragon's final meal," Dengar said. "That is the commitment we will need from you, Kathair," he said, changing the subject slightly. "In order to wear the Telarian steel of our order, you must be willing to sacrifice yourself if necessary."

Lepkin nodded. "You told me a story about Alerik once," he said. "He was able to control a dragon."

Dengar shook his head. "Not control it," he corrected. "Maybe for a time, but not forever. A dragon will always succumb to its true nature. Don't for one instant think it can be any other way. There can only be one winner of this war we are fighting. Either we exterminate the dragons, or they will overrun the Middle Kingdom." Dengar pulled a slim, vicious dagger from a sheath on his side and pointed it directly at Lepkin. "You are either one of us, or you are against us."

"Someone's coming," Foman said quickly.

Dengar closed his mouth and put the dagger away, but he kept his eyes locked on Lepkin.

Does he know? Lepkin wondered. He was still trying to decide whether this was the latest of Dengar's speeches about the honor of dragon slayers, or if it was meant as a threat when the stranger entered their camp.

Unlike the villagers from earlier in the day, he seemed unafraid as he approached the fire and waved. He was holding a guide rope, pulling a mule along which in turn was carrying loads inside of large leather pouches slung over either side. The animal quickly bent its head low to nibble the grass while the stranger came closer to the camp.

"Hello," the stranger said in an easy, smooth voice.

"Can we help you?" Dengar asked. Lepkin noted that none of the dragon slayers moved for their weapons, but Dengar's voice had an edge to it that seemed to denote he was deciding whether the stranger was a threat.

"Oh, I am traveling southward. I saw your fire and thought I might rest with you gentlemen."

"There is a town," Dengar said quickly as he thumbed over his shoulder. "It's only two miles that way."

"Yes, I know. I have stayed there before. I heard of the drakes though, and I wanted to see them for myself." The stranger sighed and looked around. "Looks like I didn't manage to beat the sunset, though. Pity. I will have to look at the creatures in the morning."

"Not often that I meet a villager who *wants* to see drakes," Britner said.

"Ah," the stranger said as he held up a finger. "Allow me to introduce myself. I am Alistair Myn, purveyor of magical items, enchantments, and charms." The silver-haired man bowed low and then pointed to his mule. "Perhaps I could interest you in a charmed rabbit foot? They bring luck."

"If they bring luck, then why is the rabbit so easily hunted down for his foot?" Dengar replied evenly. Foman gave a derisive snort.

Alistair seemed unruffled by the comment. "I never said the rabbit was a lucky animal. The foot is charmed because it enhances luck enchantments. Different parts are good for different things. For example, a rabbit's eye is good for stomach pain, did you know that?"

Dengar waved Alistair off. "Unless you have ale or wine that doesn't taste like wet socks, I am not buying anything."

Alistair smiled. "Oh, but I do have some wine. Can't hardly travel without it!" Alistair turned back to the mule and produced two very large leather skins with what appeared to be badger fur trim. "Tell you what, if I can share the fire, then you can share my drink. Besides, I'll be safer with you in case any other drakes come tonight."

Dengar stretched his hand out and took one of the skins. "Please, share our camp with us."

"Ah, how kind of you to invite me in," Alistair said as he moved to sit next to Dengar.

"What do you want with the drakes?" Foman asked.

"Well, I don't want to give away any trade secrets, gents, but I will say that if a rabbit has many special uses for its body parts, then a drake's body is one thousand times more powerful."

"Well, I hope you already have a drake's foot in hand, for we aren't expecting any more of the small ones tonight," Foman said.

Alistair gave the man a blank look.

"We're hunting a dragon," Dengar said.

Alistair whistled through his teeth and took a deep drink. He then handed the wine skin to Foman and shook his head. "Well, what would it take to buy a dragon's body from you if you kill it?"

Dengar laughed loudly and slapped Alistair on the back. "This one is made of stone and greed! I like him."

The group passed the next hour drinking and swapping stories while Lepkin scanned the skies. While in this particular instance he was happy that the dragon slayers were letting their guard down and allowing themselves to become inebriated, he wondered if this was a routine practice while hunting dragons. If it was, then the men were fools. Lepkin saw nothing sensible about getting drunk with the threat of a dragon looming over them.

Still, he couldn't complain too much since he had hoped for this very scenario. The only trouble was that Alistair did not appear to be drinking as much as the others. All of them would need to fall into a drunken stupor if Lepkin was to escape during the night to warn Kyra.

Lepkin looked to Alistair and the silver-haired man smiled at him. Something about the expression made the hairs on Lepkin's neck stand on end. There was danger behind those curled lips and twinkling eyes. The young apprentice turned to ask Foman about dousing the fire and retiring to their hiding spot in the trees but at that moment, all three of the dragon slayers slumped down and began to snore terribly loudly.

Lepkin drew his brow together and stared at them.

Alistair rose to his feet. "Never mind them, lad," he said in a smooth tone. "I do believe that the dragon will not be returning tonight, but you already know that, don't you?"

Lepkin jumped to his feet, but Alistair was quicker. A strong hand went down and caught Lepkin's sword arm at the wrist while Alistair's other hand seized Lepkin's throat.

A strange, hazy feeling overcame Lepkin and his body relaxed involuntarily.

"That's it, don't fight it," Alistair said. "Just look into my eyes."

Lepkin gazed into the strange, swirling red and purple hues in Alistair's eyes and then he went entirely slack. The young apprentice was only vaguely aware of the fact that Alistair had set him back down into a sitting position.

"I could kill you now," Alistair said.

Lepkin didn't respond. He had been subdued by the man's spell.

"Of course," Alistair went on as if expounding upon some great philosophical lecture, "I wouldn't get nearly as much enjoyment out of that." Alistair looked up to the night sky and took in a breath. He waved his hands at the campfire and the flames died down and turned green, barely offering any light at all. "You and your friends have made quite a mess of things lately, and I intend to repay you for your kindness."

Lepkin nodded dumbly.

"Where is the dragon, boy?" Alistair said.

At the mention of the word dragon, Lepkin's senses fluttered back to him. He sucked in a sobering breath of cool night air and saw Alistair for who he really was. The man kneeling in front of Lepkin was not some merchant peddling magical wares and trinkets. No. It was Severin, the very same vampire who had slain two of Kuldiga Academy's masters only a short time ago. Lepkin fought against sluggish muscles and reached for his sword again.

"Stubborn, I see," Severin commented. "Good. I do tire of killing mindless sheep. It will be fun to watch you and your friends crumble beneath my feet like dried clumps of clay."

Severin gripped Lepkin's arm harder, holding it in place with the sword firmly in its sheath. Lepkin grunted. He wanted to scream and wake the others, but he couldn't find his voice.

"Enough," Severin said harshly. "If you will not tell me where the dragon is, then I shall find out another way."

Severin slapped Lepkin on the forehead with the flat of his palm and the boy instantly fell asleep. The vampire let Lepkin fall to the ground and then he placed his left index and middle fingers against Lepkin's right temple. "Show me where the dragon is," he said. "Show me everything you know about Kyra and her cursed dragon!"

The vampire closed his eyes and sat still for several moments, allowing Lepkin's knowledge to flow into him unfettered. He saw everything. Severin was displeased to see that Lepkin had never been to the dragon's current sanctuary. That would make things a bit more difficult, but he knew he would be able to approximate the beast's location by replaying every memory Lepkin had of Kyra and the dragon.

The vampire saw the original nest where the egg had been found, where Lepkin had hidden it after a battle with a wraith, and followed the boy's memories up until the day before, gathering all of the clues he needed to start his hunt for the dragon's sanctuary. More than that, he saw a secret tunnel inside of Kuldiga Academy that led to a small chamber that had peepholes looking into a secret council room. The vampire smiled wickedly, for some of the boy's memories of Kyra were linked with this tunnel, and by watching these replay, he saw enough of the wizards and their dealings to gain an advantage over them.

A plan began to form within the vile creature's cruel mind. Before, he had been content with destroying these three annoyances, but now he had the chance to do so much more than simply repay Kyra, Lepkin, and Leatherback. He would strike at Kuldiga Academy, and he knew just how he was going to do it.

They would all pay for crossing his path and interfering with his destiny.

Severin looked down to the unconscious boy. "When you wake, you will not remember our special conversation. You will know only that you fell asleep first. The dragon slayers fell asleep afterward, and I will have left in the early morning.

The vampire then pulled his fingers away and let out a soft laugh.

"This is going to be delicious fun," he said to the darkness. The vampire then snapped his fingers. The mule, as well as the drake corpses, all disappeared from the valley. Then he changed into a large bat and flew southward. He had a dragon to find.

Chapter 10

Leatherback went to his favorite pool in the late evening. Kyra had warned him about the dragon slayers after their battle with the fire drakes, but he was certain he had been careful enough to avoid detection. Fish had started to populate the pool that he and Kyra had made from a mountain stream, and though it was never enough to sate his hunger, he couldn't resist a good trout...or twenty.

He slipped into the water on his belly and let the cool liquid envelope his entire body. He swam down to the bottom, stirring up mud and rocks as he went. He snatched a pair of fish straightaway and then settled upon the murky bottom of the pool. He chewed carefully, not letting any water into his gullet while he enjoyed his snack. He had worked on holding his breath for several weeks now, and was fully capable of lying in the cool water comfortably for more than twenty minutes at a time without coming up for air.

Njar and Kyra would likely not want him out of the grove for such long stretches, but the dragon figured that if trips outside the grove to hunt elk, or flying north for hours to slay rogue fire drakes hadn't hurt him, then swimming was likely not going to either.

He closed his eyes and let the water course around his bulk, letting his senses dull to the noise of the brook as he slipped into a near meditative state. Aside from his jewels and precious metals, this pool was one of the most therapeutic things he had found so far.

A fish made the mistake of swimming alongside his cheek.

Leatherback opened his jaws ever so slowly and the fish turned, voluntarily swimming into the dragon's open maw. The jaws shut and Leatherback smiled, enjoying his treat.

He then went back into his calm, near sleeping state at the bottom of the pool, completely unaware of the danger nearby, watching him from above the surface of the water.

*****

Severin smiled. The dragon had not sensed his presence, but then, that was to be expected. What juvenile dragon would ever suspect a humble bat roosting high in a pine tree overlooking the pool of water?

The vampire had spent hours searching for the dragon. He had used Lepkin's memories of the surrounding areas to guide him. When he found this pool, he saw some tell-tale signs, claw marks and the like, that told him he was close. He then continued his search for the dragon's lair only to be frustrated by an enchantment over the whole of the aspen glade. He had been forced to return to the pool and wait for the dragon to come for water. Severin had of course recognized Njar's meddling hand in the magic, but he knew better than to charge in. He had to find a way into the glade that would not trigger the wards and enchantments set by the crafty satyr.

It was one thing to hunt a sorceress, but another thing entirely to trifle with a satyr from Viverandon who had power over the Pools of Fate. The magical, oracle-like waters would surely have alerted Njar to the possibility that Severin would enter the glade, and if he had seen that in any sort of vision, then the satyr would have already prepared the appropriate wards, the kinds best suited for dealing with vampires.

Severin had once seen a rival vampire fall into such a trap. It was several centuries before, and a different satyr controlled the

Pools of Fate then, but the end result was a ghastly affair nonetheless. Issyl the Blooded had been seeking after a fabled creature, one of the last unicorns to roam over the Middle Kingdom but a satyr had laid a trap for Issyl. The vampire had attempted to break into an enchanted grove under the protection of that particular satyr only to find that the moment he stepped through the tree line, sunlight poured all around the grove, despite the fact that it was the middle of the night. Issyl, unable to escape as magical barriers rose between the trees, was burned to a pile of ash.

Severin had no love for Issyl the Blooded, but he still shuddered at the thought of how the vampire had died. It was a terrible way to meet one's end, vampire or not.

Still, Issyl's death had alerted all of the vampire folk to the threat posed by the satyrs and the Pools of Fate. Since that time, no vampire had ever dared tempt a satyr's wrath.

Until now.

Severin used his enhanced sight to watch the dragon lying upon the bottom of the pool. He knew his charms would not be enough to turn the dragon into a thrall, as he had done with the fire drakes. No, this dragon was too powerful, and his mind far too tough for such crude tactics. Even a juvenile dragon was nearly impossible to charm or beguile with illusions. The entire species had always had a natural immunity to such thing. Drakes were controllable because they were not a sub-species, but different altogether, and thus did not have the genetic defenses against magic that dragons had. Severin would have to be subtler, and craftier.

The thought to simply kill the dragon came into his mind, but that was nearly as risky a proposition now as it would have been inside the aspen glade. Even without the satyr's fancy wards and deadly magic, the dragon would be difficult to slay, though certainly not impossible. Severin was not without his own deadly magic.

He stared down into the waters and the furry corners of his bat-mouth curled into a wicked sneer. He was never one to simply kill his prey, not when they had caused him so much grief. First, he would cripple them. Then, he would watch them crawl and limp away, licking their wounds as the realization of just how terribly they had crossed him, and how hopelessly outmatched they were, dawned on them. Then, as hope drained from their eyes, he would finish it.

He let go of the branch he hung from and dropped into the air. He opened his wings, beating fervently to keep from plopping into the water. He landed in the damp earth near the edge of the water. He crawled forward, bent his mouth to the cool liquid, and took a drink. It did nothing to slake his thirst, but that was not why he drank.

As the water went into his body, Severin focused his magic, analyzing the water within him. His magical senses were far more advanced than his physical abilities. He used it to scan and study the water, bits of algae, and small microbes within the water that he had drank. After a few moments, he seized one of the smaller microbes with his mind and straightened, confident he had what he needed. He had a special use in mind for the essence of this tiny organism.

He reflected on how convenient it was that so few understood the many benefits a vampire gained by consuming the life-carrying fluids of another creature. Certainly it sustained and strengthened them, but once he had consumed a being's essence, he could alter his shape to match.

Even now he could still feel the tearing of sinews that had come along with that first transformation. Shapeshifting was a tiring, draining, and precarious process, but after centuries of life as a vampire, Severin had mastered the skill, and now had hundreds of human forms he could assume, most recently increased by the essence of Alistair the wandering trader.

The bat essence he had called upon this day had been one of his first acquisitions. He had been a lowly, despicable creature at that time, unsure of how to grapple with his new-found identity as one of the undead. As he sought for some power to make him something more than a despised and hunted creature, he had hit upon the idea of a bat's essence. It had been foul, to be sure. He remembered how it had felt for his magic to move over and through the essence of the shape he desired, how it had contorted his body and rearranged his very being to become that which he had consumed.

Fortunately, once a shape was attained, it was forever possible to return to that form, without needing to consume additional essences, so only one bat had been required. While he enjoyed human blood, he cared little for animal blood.

Still, even with the numerous forms he had taken, he had never tried one quite as small as this microbe. He had sensed their presence before, but had always chosen to ignore their essence, rather than use his magic to activate it as he was about to now. None of his earlier transformations came close to the agony this one brought him.

He fell to the ground and his bat wings began to shrink back into his body until they were nothing more than leathery stubs. It took all of his strength and will to keep from crying out as a burning sensation ripped through his entire body. Pressure built up on his bones and skin, crushing him into smaller and smaller shapes as the bones and sinews broke and tore. Then, when the squishing had done all it could do, bits of the bat began to dissolve and fade away into nothing.

Severin nearly lost his will to go on, but he focused on his purpose. He called the dagger to his mind and poured himself into that image of the weapon, the key to his ultimate power. All around him it seemed everything was growing to gigantic proportions. What was once only an inch of space between himself and the edge of the water was now perhaps a hundred miles, or so it seemed.

Even the grains of dirt and sand appeared as large as mountains.

Severin nearly became lost in the vastness of his new reality.

Had it not been for his refined magical abilities, he may have languished on the bank forever. The microbe body he inhabited was strange and foreign to him. He felt as fragile as a bubble, yet the minute form was energetic and easy to maneuver.

Using his magic to guide him, he floated up into the air and then down into the water.

He could hear the dragon's heartbeat. It was like a drum that filled everything around him. *Tha-THUMP, tha-THUMP, tha-THUMP!*

He drifted down, using his magic to guide himself to the enormous beast. After several minutes, he slipped into the edge of the dragon's nostril. He had thought to enter the dragon that way, but then realized that even his magic would not likely save such a fragile form from the dragon's breath. So, he darted out from the nostril and made his way along the dragon's snout.

He chose not to enter the beast's mouth. That way presented two problems; fire and acid. No, he was going an altogether different route. He floated to the dragon's closed eye and aimed for the inner corner. He worked his way into the salty tear duct and then drifted until he found a passageway to the dragon's sinus cavity. Knowing he was still dangerously close to the airway through which the dragon spewed his liquid death, Severin hurried to find an entrance into the animal's blood stream.

Once he was in, he noticed how terribly warm the dragon's blood was.

Severin's magic alerted him to a pair of white globs floating toward him. He wasn't sure what they were, but he could sense the threat they posed. The vampire struck out with lightning, searing the two white globs and cutting clean holes through each of them. Unfortunately, the lightning also tore a small opening in the blood vessel.

The dragon lurched upward and the tissue around Severin was pressed in, as if something was pushing on the spot from outside. The heartbeat accelerated, and Severin was sent even quicker toward his target.

In a matter of two or three minutes, for it was very difficult to judge time when confined to such a small form, Severin was dumped into the heart. Working quickly with his magic, he latched onto the inner wall of the smaller chamber. He set wards about himself as more of the white globs appeared and tried to smother him. Whatever they were, they were no match for his magic.

The trap was now set, and he had only to wait for his time to strike.

*****

Njar sat in front of the Pools of Fate, contemplating the vision he had just witnessed. It was less clear than any other he had ever seen before, but he knew for certain that there was danger. Something was about to attack Leatherback. He had to reach the dragon first and shore up what defenses he could.

The satyr limped away, leaning heavily upon his staff. The wounds in his body were nearly healed, thanks to the abundant magic in Viverandon, but the aches and the stiffness were still there. He opened the portal to the aspen grove.

A golden glow ripped through the air and then a silver mist divided the rim of gold until a passageway was made clear before Njar. He limped through, his staff stabbing the ground with each pained step forward. The warm hum of the portal's magic enveloped him as he stepped through. A rush of wind swirled around him, and then he stepped out the other side and into the grove.

He turned to find Leatherback sitting upon his haunches. The dragon's large eyes looked down and regarded the satyr curiously.

"Hello Njar," Leatherback greeted. "Have you healed completely?"

Njar nodded to Leatherback, but didn't respond verbally. He turned and scanned the area around him. None of the wards had been activated, but he could feel a strange presence.

"Has anyone strange come to see you today?" Njar asked.

Leatherback shook his enormous head.

"What about last night or the day before?" Njar pressed.

"I flew with Kyra to hunt down a pack of fire drakes in the north. I also met with the Keeper of Secrets, and the priests from Valtuu Temple, but nobody I would call strange."

Njar's eyes darted to the staff made from the aspen wood. "Did you take that with you?"

Leatherback nodded. "Kyra placed it in the holster herself. She has not forgotten your warning."

Njar nodded. Despite the answers, the satyr couldn't shake the uneasiness he felt. It was almost as if evil eyes were upon him. The satyr turned around in place, ignoring Leatherback as the dragon asked him about his wounds. Seeing nothing but empty forest, Njar turned back to Leatherback and shook his head.

"Something is not right," he said. "Come, bend your head down to me," Njar said.

Leatherback hesitated.

Njar narrowed his golden eyes on the dragon. Had Nagar's Blight found the animal at last?

"Bend down to me," Njar said, more forcefully this time.

Leatherback let out a throaty, short growl, but did as he was told.

Njar reached his hand out and placed it upon Leatherback's forehead. As he called upon the very energy flowing throughout the world of Terramyr, he focused his mind and closed his eyes. He would use the world's energy to scan Leatherback. A green mist rose up from the moist dirt inside the grove, rising until Njar was waist deep in the magical energy.

Leatherback took in a deep breath and seemed to calm, for he became still, allowing himself to be inspected.

Njar followed the energy with his mind, flowing through and around Leatherback. As he made the third round of scans, coursing the energy through the dragon's breast again, he found the source of his worry. There was an impurity inside the dragon's heart, something dark, albeit small and hardly detectable. He pulled back from the dragon and opened his eyes, but did not altogether dismiss the green energy swirling around them. If

Leatherback rejected his treatment, or tried to flee or fight back, Njar would need all of the energy in the glade.

Leatherback opened his eyes and the two studied each other for several moments. The satyr tried to guess what the dragon might be thinking, and for a moment he almost let his fear of the blight control him. Then, he remembered Leatherback's loyalty to Kyra. His hope for the dragon pushed his fear of the blight out of his mind and he smiled and spoke to break the silence.

"Leatherback, there is a dark energy within you," Njar said.

"Is it the blight?" Leatherback asked, fear evident in his usually confident voice.

Njar shrugged and answered honestly. "I cannot tell. If it is the blight, then there is little I can do to purge it from you, but if it is something else, then there may be a way for me to remove it." Njar narrowed his golden eyes and stared at the dragon's scaly breast. "Perhaps even if it is the blight, we may have caught it early enough to pull it out of you. Do you trust me?"

"Will it hurt?" Leatherback asked.

Njar nodded. "It is not terrible, but it will not be pleasant either. I will immerse you in the Pools of Fate. There is a powerful magic there, along with the energy within Viverandon. If this darkness can be cleansed from you, then this is the best way I know to try."

Leatherback nodded. "Very well."

Njar summoned a massive portal that dwarfed the entire glade of aspens and appeared with the roar of thunder. The ground vibrated and heat emanated from the opening along with blinding light. Then, Njar focused the energy of the glade and formed a kind of flexible coating around Leatherback. It wouldn't be enough to cleanse the dragon in any degree, but the energy would prevent any additional outside forces from coming into the dragon's heart.

The satyr then stepped through and motioned for Leatherback to follow him.

The dragon lowered his head and pulled his wings in close to his body, stepping through carefully.

Njar then directed him to the Pools of Fate, which were only a few dragon paces beyond the portal. "Go into the pool, and I will begin the incantation."

The satyr began chanting the ancient phrases taught to him by his predecessor. Green and blue mists rose from the grasses around the pool, gently swirling upward and mingling with each other without mixing together. Next a blanket of golden yellow flew in from the north, covering the sky above them and then stretching down to seal the area like a magical, translucent dome.

Leatherback stepped into the waters and the liquid turned dark blue, and then became a rich purple that stretched out from each of Leatherback's legs as he stepped into the pool. A silver mist rose up from the waters, slithering around Leatherback's body until the dragon was in the middle of the pool, then it faded back down to the surface of the water and spread out over the entire body of water.

"Prepare yourself," Njar warned as he finished the preparatory chants. The air inside the glowing dome became thick and heavy, turning red and letting very little light through. The colored mists swirled in furiously, rising up into the air and then falling down upon Leatherback. The Pools of Fate seemed to fight against the dragon then, shooting water up in steaming geysers and forming limbs of purple water that reached out and struck Leatherback in the side and belly until he dropped into the pool. Njar could hear the creature roaring and yelling, but he paid it no mind. If the darkness was to be cleansed, then this was the only way.

Njar had to continue.

The dragon struggled mightily, managing to pull his head out of the water three times while the liquid wrestled with him. A flash of orange light shot out from the dragon's mouth, flames splatting against the inside of the golden dome and spreading out harmlessly along its inner surface. Then, a great column of purple water poured into Leatherback's mouth and the dragon was pulled under the surface once more.

The silver mist closed over the surface of the water, and then solidified as if it were a living surface of lightning. It buzzed and hummed as flashes of light appeared from within the dark purple depths of the pool.

The green and blue mists also became hard, forming spikes that dangled in the air above the silver surface. Then, one by one the spikes fell, colliding with the silver surface and creating terrible thunder that nearly deafened Njar. As each spike fell, it joined with the silver essence, rather than breaking through. Soon it became a blinking grid of all sorts of colors, and a strange melody began to play out over the Pools of Fate.

The spectacle continued for nearly an hour, until the last of the colored spikes had fallen. Then, the multi-colored surface receded from the water and the darkness cleared. The liquid regained its natural blue state, and Njar was able to see down to Leatherback.

The dragon rose up from the depths, but did not gasp for breath when he emerged. Instead, he shook his head and body, and climbed out onto the opposite bank.

Njar used his powers to scan Leatherback once more, a process that was much easier here, at the Pools of Fate, and found that it had indeed been removed.

"It is gone," Njar spoke.

Leatherback snorted, and then slowly lowered himself to the ground.

"No, my friend, it is best to rest in the aspen grove," Njar said. "Come, I will reopen the portal."

Njar had to lend Leatherback some of his magical energy, but the two were back through the portal and in the aspen grove soon enough. The satyr helped the dragon find a comfortable sleeping position, and then bolstered the wards on the grove once more before returning to Viverandon.

"Sleep well, my friend," Njar said as he slipped back through his portal.

Leatherback didn't answer, for he was already asleep.

Never one to leave things to chance, Njar decided to call upon the Pools of Fate one last time. He had to make sure that the threat had been dealt with.

He moved to the edge of the waters and touched the liquid with his staff. "I have asked much of you today," he said to the pool. "However, I must ask for one last vision, and then I shall let you sleep as well."

The silver mist rose from the water and formed into a ball. Njar watched intently, hoping that this vision would show him he had averted the threat.

Instead, the ball formed into a face, and it laughed at him. The pool turned dark once more, but this time it was void of all color and light. The mist reached out and grabbed the satyr before he could react. It constricted his arms and shook the staff free from his grasp. It picked him up into the air and then slammed him down.

Njar wailed in pain as he felt his legs break.

A tendril of the dark mist quickly gagged him, and then it lifted him upright once more, placing just enough pressure on his legs to cause him terrible pain.

"The great Njar and his Pools of Fate," a smooth voice called out from the direction of the water.

Njar watched in horror as a form rose from the surface of the pool and stepped out to stand near him. Even without seeing Severin's fangs, Njar could feel the danger he was in. His mind raced for a way to fight back, but the mist was squeezing the breath out of him and the pain in his legs broke his focus.

"I'm not going to kill you," Severin said in a whisper, as calm as if they were discussing a simple business matter. "I want you to watch everything that happens to your precious sorceress friend and her dragon."

Njar tried to shake free, but he felt the mist bend his head to the side, exposing his neck.

"Hold still," Severin said. "I just need a portion of your essence, and then I shall imprison you in your cursed Pools of Fate, where you will be able to see only what I show you."

A searing, hot pain ripped through Njar's neck then as the long fangs dove into his flesh. He grew nauseated, and then his head became fuzzy. The satyr all but forgot about the pain in his legs as some of his very essence was pulled from him. Then, as if he were nothing more than a doll stuffed with straw, the mist tossed him into the air toward the middle of the pool. He barely registered the slap of the water as he splashed through the surface. The dark, bitter cold liquid pulled him down into the depths.

The magical pool kept him alive, refusing to allow him such an easy escape as drowning. Instead, the waters became like air for him, and sustained his body while simultaneously seizing hold of it and shackling him to the bottom of the pool.

Then, a light appeared directly above him. A golden sphere showed him two visions. The first was of Severin. The vampire, now finished with Njar and the Pools of Fate, shifted and transformed himself to look exactly like the satyr, and then he turned and walked away in the night, heading for the settlement of Viverandon.

Pain and anguish stabbed at Njar's heart as he realized how badly he had failed his kin folk. He had meant to protect them, but his blind ambition to heal the dragon had let a demon into Viverandon.

He tried to close his eyes, but the waters held them open, forcing him to watch the next vision.

He tried to scream and wrestle himself free as he watched Kyra and Leatherback die at Severin's hands, but the waters kept him silent and still. The golden orb grew then and came closer to Njar's face. It then replayed the two visions over and over, never ceasing.

Chapter 11

Severin, disguised as Njar, looked around the peaceful village and laughed on the inside. The moon was high in the sky, and the satyrs were asleep. The temptation to wreak havoc among them was almost too much to refuse. It would be so easy. He could slip in and out of any home in the form of Viverandon's chief.

Though it was not necessary for him to receive an invitation in order to enter a home, as so many of the superstitious believed, being invited in did allow for the charms and illusions which he conjured to continue functioning at full strength. Sometimes, it even enhanced them, as had been the case with the dragon slayers' camp. None of those poor fools had suspected anything amiss about him.

Still, tarrying here would cost him precious time. In order for the rest of his plan to work, he needed to be back in the Middle Kingdom before dawn.

He walked through the village, taking note of each house he passed. He made a note of the buildings he might like to visit after this ordeal with Kyra, the daughter of Bhaltair, was over. Bringing down the Pools of Fate was a monumental achievement, but he wanted the pleasure of slaying the other satyrs as well. Destroying their sacred village would be a most delicious victory.

The only trouble was finding his way out.

He had heard from others more knowledgeable on the subject that Viverandon was a magical place, existing on the plane of the living within and subject to the flow of time on Terramyr, but not exactly occupying a particular space. It was said that the way in and out was limited for those without precise magic, or special key words gain favor of the great tree, Nonac, which was rumored to guard the gateway to Viverandon.

Severin wanted to travel faster, but he dared not change out of his current form until he was safely out of Viverandon. Fooling a village of satyrs was one thing, but risking being seen transforming and then needing to fight their combined might was quite another. Therefore, he confined himself to walking, though he did not keep up the satyr's limp.

After a while, he came to an enormous tree sitting on the edge of a vast forest. The lowest branch on the gigantic oak tree looked to be six feet in diameter. Even with his understanding of magical creatures, Severin marveled that the tree was able to stand. A single leaf on the tree was half his size.

"So, this is Nonac," the vampire said. He approached the tree and studied it carefully, checking the area for magical wards. Not seeing any, he moved in close and placed his hand upon Nonac's trunk. The oak did not move.

Frustrated, Severin moved to walk around the tree. As he did so, the ground itself shifted and moved along with him. Wherever he went, Nonac stood in his way, refusing to let him pass.

Severin silently berated himself. He should have spent more time with Njar and scanned the satyr's essence for memories and spells. He was debating whether to go back and fish Njar out of the Pools of Fate when another satyr approached.

"Njar, what are you doing out so late?" the white-furred satyr asked.

Severin smiled and spoke in Njar's voice. "Trouble is afoot," he said. "I saw a vision in the Pools of Fate, and have come to test Nonac."

The other satyr nodded grimly. "I have felt a heaviness in the air tonight," he admitted. "You don't think Nonac is sick or weak, do you? She has stood valiantly for thousands of years."

Severin took in a breath and turned back to the tree, then shook his head. "I am not sure." He then turned back to the satyr. "I have tested Nonac for weakness, but something still feels wrong."

"What do you mean?"

Severin shrugged. "Nonac will not open for me," he said, hoping his ruse would get the other to open the gateway.

The white satyr frowned and cocked his head to the side. "But you haven't played the pipes," he said. "You have only been using your hands, and trying to walk around it."

Severin felt the fool now. He had revealed too much. His eyes flickered down to the pipes hanging from the satyr's belt and he nodded with a smile. "No, I have not played my pipes *this time*, but I have played them earlier, and Nonac would not open the way. Of course, I was able to use my portal to leave, but I knew I needed to come back and check on Nonac after I returned." He pointed to the white satyr's pipes. "When was the last time you tried to play the pipes?"

The ruse worked. The white satyr looked down and took his pipes in hand. "Not for a few days, but I could try now if you like."

Severin nodded. "Play, and see if Nonac responds for you."

The satyr played a tune on his pipes and then pressed his forehead to the tree. The tree groaned and lifted itself from the ground, exposing massive roots and pulling dirt up. The taproot was actually two giant roots entwined together. Slowly, they untwisted and opened up to what appeared to be nothing more than the forest beyond. The satyr turned around and shrugged.

Severin rushed forward. He seized the unsuspecting satyr by the throat and the two of them shot through the opening. A great rush of air fought against them, but Severin used his magic to accelerate them through as the tree began to close itself even before Severin had reached the other side.

Rather than dispose of the white satyr on the other side of the portal, Severin transformed back into his vampire form and bit

119

into the satyr's neck. He then used his strength to break the satyr's neck and dropped him down where the tree would fall.

Nonac scraped Severin's foot as it closed behind him, but the vampire had escaped. His breathing slowed as he looked back to the massive tree and sneered. In his left hand he held the white satyr's pipes. Now he knew the tune as well. More than that, he had taken enough essence from the white satyr to be able to find his way back.

Severin laughed as he transformed himself into a large raven and leapt up into the sky.

Viverandon was a dead city. They just didn't know it yet.

Hours later, Severin landed in the same valley where he had found the dragon slayers. With his keen sense of sight, he could see them packing their belongings and preparing to leave. His raven form let out a pleased *ca-caw!*

Oh how he loved these games!

He set down some hundred yards away and then transformed back into the form of Alistair. He thought to conjure the same mule he had before, but then a fun plan entered his mind and he thought better of it. He smiled evilly as he made his way to the campfire glowing in the distance.

As he neared, he could hear them shouting and cursing their luck. Not surprisingly, they blamed the merchant they knew as Alistair for stealing the bodies of the fire drakes. Severin couldn't fault them for that, for they weren't wrong. Still, he delighted in taking offense, even if fairly given, and used the insults to fuel his next performance.

He stormed up to the camp and shouted at them. "You call *me* a buffoon! You should look at yourselves!"

Dengar wheeled around and drew his sword. "Not another move, Alistair, or I'll split you in two!"

"You stole from us!" Foman cut in.

Severin shook his head. "You said you wanted a dragon, well I found him. Whatever I took from you, he did worse to me!"

120

Severin spun around, displaying his empty hands. "He took everything! My mule, my charms, and the fire drake parts I had gathered to use as well. If you idiots had tracked him down, none of this would have happened!"

Dengar rushed forward, but instead of striking Severin, he grabbed him by the collar and pulled him close. "You saw him!"

Severin nodded and pushed back from Dengar. "He's that way!" he said as he pointed in the direction of the aspen grove. "It's nearly a day's journey by foot, but you can find the monster in a grove of aspen trees chewing on my mule's bones!"

Dengar spun around and began barking orders. "We need to set out immediately. Foman, gather our gear. Kathair, go and fetch the horses we stabled in the village. Britner, go with Kathair. Go now!"

Severin smiled as the camp burst into a commotion of action. They paid him no mind as he departed from them toward the north. When he was sufficiently far away, he took to his raven form once more and set out to find suitable shelter. Dawn was coming soon, and he was not about to get caught out in the sun.

*****

Lepkin was running toward the village, easily keeping pace with Britner who was dressed in every piece of his armor except for his helmet. His feet set lithely upon the grassy hills, propelling him forward in the night as his mind raced for answers that his limited wisdom was unable to offer.

If he did nothing, the dragon slayers would reach Leatherback and there would be a battle. Whether Leatherback won or not, the consequences would be dire. Kyra's secret would become known, and the dragon slayers would not offer her any degree of amnesty from her crimes. They would fight through Headmaster Herion, or anyone else if needed, to get to her.

On the other hand, if he betrayed the dragon slayers, he would be dishonored. He might keep Kyra's secret safe, but the dragon slayers would come for him.

Off in the distance, the lights in the village were twinkling, reminding him that he had precious little time to choose. In a moment, he saw his future flash through his mind in both options.

There was only one thing he could do.

He reached out and tripped Britner with his left leg.

The large man fell to the ground and tumbled down the hill.

Lepkin sprinted toward Britner. The dragon slayer cursed Lepkin and pushed up to his hands and knees. A momentary doubt fluttered through Lepkin's mind.

Britner didn't know that the trip was intentional. Lepkin could easily apologize, blame it on the darkness, take a slap or two to the face, and be done with it.

The young boy narrowed his eyes on Britner. No. There was no going back. He leapt in, driving a forceful kick to the back of Britner's head. The man slammed his face into the ground and snarled.

"Kathair!" Britner launched himself up. He was extremely nimble for having all of that armor on. "What's gotten into you?"

Lepkin drew his sword. "I'm sorry," he said.

"What are you going to do with that?" Britner asked.

Lepkin didn't respond. He came in with a sideways chop. Britner blocked it easily with his left arm, allowing the strong Telarian Steel to absorb the shock of the blow.

Lepkin struck again and again, but Britner blocked each attack.

Then, Lepkin heard the terrifying sound of steel scraping against steel. Britner had drawn his sword.

"Explain yourself, and I might let you live," Britner said.

Lepkin fell into his training with the elves in Tualdern. Britner was larger, and more experienced, but Lepkin pushed the fear out of his mind. He was going to win this fight.

He jumped in again, striking and slicing.

Sparks kicked off the two blades every couple of swings, but Britner merely laughed at Lepkin's attacks. Little did the man know that Lepkin was holding back, purposefully allowing his attacks to be slower and predictable.

It was the only way Lepkin was certain he could catch Britner off guard.

Lepkin continued to press his assault at roughly half his actual speed. Then, just as Britner became lazy in his blocks, limply swinging his blade from side to side and laughing as he did so, Lepkin erupted into a fury of action that had the dragon slayer back-pedaling up the hill.

Lepkin swung left, then right, then down at the knee joint, expertly slipping his blade into the flesh behind the slim opening in the armor's joint.

Britner howled with both pain and rage, but Lepkin pulled back, easily avoiding the onslaught of furious chops and swings. Then, Lepkin jumped left and slapped the back of Britner's head with the flat of his blade. Britner stumbled forward, putting his left hand up to the back of his head to check for blood.

That was when Lepkin jumped up and came down hard with the pommel of his sword. He connected with Britner's head with tremendous force, dropping the large warrior to the grass in a heap, face in the dirt and rump up in the air.

Lepkin used his foot to push Britner onto his side. The man was breathing, but his eyes were twitching behind closed lids and his limbs were limp.

"I'm so sorry," Lepkin said once more, then he sheathed his sword and bolted for the village.

When he got to the stable, he prepared his horse and then pulled it out to the side of the stable and hitched it behind a large barn. He then went back to the stable and prepared some lengths of rope which he used to attach dangling sticks and bundles of straw to the tails of the dragon slayers' horses.

"Sorry," Lepkin said before lighting the sticks and straw on fire. He then smacked each horse on the rump and chased them out of the stable toward the coast.

It was a dirty tactic, but he needed every advantage he could get over the others. Besides, he had already dishonored himself with his betrayal of Britner. Scaring a few horses and possibly burning their tails a bit was the least of his worries now.

He rushed back to his horse and then galloped in a wide arc around the valley, heading straight for Kuldiga Academy. With any luck, he would be able to warn Kyra before the dragon slayers reached Leatherback.

Chapter 12

"There he is, right where the old goat said he would be," Foman said as he pointed to the aspen grove.

"How did a dragon that big get this far into the Middle Kingdom without anyone seeing him?" Britner asked, rubbing the hard lump on the back of his head.

"Shut up, both of you. It's time put the beast down. Foman, you go around the back. Britner, you will attack him from the front. I'll come in from the side."

The three dragon slayers pulled their helmets on and checked their weapons. Britner had a sword at his side and a spear made of Telarian Steel in his hands.

Foman carried a large halberd, also made of Telarian Steel.

Dengar was the only one carrying only a sword. Most dragon slayers preferred one long reach weapon, with either a sword or ax for close fighting. Dengar was always one to rush directly into the fray. He traded the comfort of reach for the ability to dance under a dragon's legs and strike at the underbelly, trusting in his armor to protect him from the claws and fangs that were sure to come at him.

Dengar kept his eyes on the looming form just inside the grove. In terms of appearance, this particular dragon was rather dull. Dark brown scales and thick, stubby horns that curled out to the sides and then downward. Dengar had hoped that this would be a fantastic beast with bright green or orange scales, something he could brag about as he hung a scale upon his wall in his room back at Ten Forts.

This dragon was hardly worth his time.

He watched as Britner and Foman moved into position. They made no noise as they moved through the forest. Their black, Telarian Steel armor gave them the appearance of thorned ghosts as they faded away into the trees.

Everything was going smoothly, and then the dragon turned and his massive blue eyes peered through the aspen branches and found Dengar.

"Icadion's beard," Dengar cursed.

The dragon rose to its feet and roared mightily. Dengar rushed in, not wanting the dragon to gain the advantage by leaving the ground. He raced between the bright aspen trees and rolled under the dragon's talons as it swiped at him with its left foreleg.

Britner came in from the side, halberd jabbing at the dragon's haunches while Foman dashed into the grove from the other side.

"Fire!" Foman shouted.

Dengar looked up to see the dragon's head rearing back. The tell-tale glow of red and orange appeared in the back of its throat and then came the hissing roar of flames. Dengar turned and covered his eyes. The searing flames washed over him like a terrible wave, crashing him down to the ground. The Telarian Steel held fast, but it did little to cool the fires as they beat down upon him. The leather padding beneath the armor afforded him some protection, but sweat poured from his body and he found it nearly impossible to breath except in short, quick breaths.

The fire stopped then, with only the lingering flames atop the grass or the nearby trees still burning. Dengar turned to see that Foman had charged in to distract the dragon. The man was jabbing his spear in and out as quick as lightning, but nothing was getting through the monster's scales.

"Watch out!" Britner called.

Too late.

The dragon's tail slammed into Foman and sent him cart-wheeling through the air. He landed hard into an aspen, about half

126

way up the trunk from the ground. The tree split and then the top half fell atop Foman, pinning him to the ground with a sickening *thawump!*

The dragon roared and glanced back at its tail. There were a few crimson gashes, courtesy of Foman's barbed armor.

"You are the dragon slayers," the monster said as it backed away and looked at Dengar.

Dengar paused. This dragon was different from the others he had fought before. It seemed unaffected by the blight. That made it no less lethal, of course, but it was curious to be sure.

"All dragons are enemies of the Middle Kingdom," Dengar stated.

"I am not," the dragon said clearly.

Britner moved in and swung his halberd up into the inside of the dragon's right hip joint. The dragon snarled ferociously and leapt into the air. Dengar watched helplessly as Britner struggled futilely to free his weapon. The blade had bitten into the joint, and was now lodged solidly inside. As the dragon rose higher and higher, Britner's grip began to slip.

The dragon flew up into the air and then shook itself as it dashed forward. Britner was thrown free, and came crashing down to land on a large boulder in the center of the clearing inside the grove of aspens. Sparks flew out from the stone as the armor bit and ground against it. From the way Britner's back arched over the rock and his limbs hung limp, Dengar knew the man was dead.

A moment later a terrible wave of fire came roiling down from above. Dengar darted out to his right, but the dragon matched his every move. The flames found him, and pushed him down into the ground once more.

Just as the heat became so intense that Dengar was about to lose consciousness, a heavy point drove into his back, pinning him to the ground. The flames stopped, and the dragon's rumbling voice was heard close above him.

"Finish it then!" Dengar shouted.

"Who told you where to find me?" the dragon asked.

"What difference does it make, demon?" Dengar spat.

"Someone from the school?" the dragon inquired as he pressed his heavy talon deeper into Dengar's back. The Telarian Steel groaned under the pressure, but it held together enough to prevent the man from being run through.

Dengar was not about to give the dragon any information. "Foman!" he shouted, hoping his other comrade was still alive.

"Was it the boy?" the dragon asked.

Dengar stopped struggling for a moment. "The boy?" he repeated in a whisper.

"The boy who was with you, was he the betrayer?"

Dengar cursed himself. He had thought that Kathair had tripped Britner and run away out of fear. He had never suspected the boy to be in league with the dragon. "You know Kathair?" Dengar spat.

The pressure eased on the man's back. "He did not betray me then?"

"I didn't say that," Dengar said, hoping he might be able to turn the dragon against the traitor.

The pressure lifted then. A moment later, Dengar was rolling across the ground, having been flicked by a large talon. "I can tell by the way you reacted that you had no knowledge of the fact that Lepkin knows me," the dragon said. "Enough of this, I wish for no more blood to be shed."

"You attacked me," Dengar snarled as he pushed up to his feet and scanned the area for his sword.

"A fine accusation coming from the men who were setting an ambush at my home. I did not attack you, I have done no harm!"

Dengar saw his sword, but it was back where the dragon had pinned him. To run for it would mean to run toward the dragon.

The dragon must have noted Dengar's stare, for he placed his right foreleg atop the weapon, concealing it entirely. "No more fighting," the dragon said.

Dengar shook his head. He knew this was simply a trick. Dragons always used tricks. He needed to find a way to make it appear as though he was falling for the dragon's feigned wish for peace. Hopefully that way he could buy himself enough time to formulate a plan.

"A merchant told me where to find you," Dengar said.

"Merchant?" the dragon echoed. "I have not seen any merchants."

"He said you ate his mule."

The dragon shook his massive head. "I have done no such thing. I eat only from the forest, taking elk, deer, and moose as my food. If I am lucky, then I eat fish."

"You expect me to believe that?" Dengar said. His eyes caught a flicker of movement near the broken aspen tree on the opposite side of the clearing in the grove. He didn't focus on it though, for fear of drawing the dragon's attention to it. He smiled at his turn of fortune, for the dragon could not see the smile through the helmet's visor.

Foman was slowly, quietly, extricating himself from under the broken tree and sneaking toward the dragon's rear with his spear. There was hope yet, as long as Dengar could keep the dragon talking.

The large warrior sat down in the grass and held his hands out to the sides as if to show he was giving up. "Tell me then, who ate the sheep to the north?"

"The fire drakes," the dragon answered. "When I heard of them, I went and hunted them down."

"What do you mean you heard of them?" Dengar pressed.

Foman was closer now, almost within range to strike.

The dragon seemed to frown. "I have a friend who told me about the attacks. I was afraid that you would go north, looking for dragons, and that you might eventually find me. I thought perhaps if I killed the drakes for you, then you would stop hunting for a larger dragon."

"How did you know of us?" Dengar asked. Then, he put a finger in the air. "Wait, it was Kathair, wasn't it? He told you we were here. Tell me, dragon, how long have you been in league with the boy? Did he demand part of your treasure to keep your secret?"

"He took nothing from me," the dragon said.

An instant later he roared terribly and spun about.

As soon as Dengar saw his sword was uncovered once more, he leapt up and sprinted for it. He managed to pick it up and jump out of the way just before the dragon had fully spun around, placing a back foot down where the sword had been.

Dengar looked up and saw the black spear sticking out from an area near the underside of the dragon's tail. He smiled wider and went to work on the dragon's leg that had just come down. He hacked with all of his strength, his sword biting into the scales on the inside of the leg and breaking them apart to slash the skin underneath. A spray of blood shot out and the dragon roared again.

Then the leg went up, coiling near the dragon's underbelly and poised to strike. Dengar jumped to his left, but the dragon adjusted his aim and the clawed foot came back with tremendous force.

As a child, Dengar had once been kicked by a horse in the stomach. That incident had left him injured for days with terrible pain and a near-permanent dent in his abdomen.

This was much worse.

The talons connected first, driving into Dengar and lifting him off his feet. Then the force of the full foot slammed him a half-moment later and all the air in his lungs was suddenly gone, replaced by a burning desire for breath that he could not regain. The ground below him seemed to fall away as he flew up in an arc over the aspen trees at the edge of the clearing. He hadn't reached the apex of his flight before slamming into an exceptionally tall tree.

After the ringing in his ears cleared and his vision came back to him, he realized he had not fallen to the ground after hitting the tree. Instead, his barbs and blades on his armor had hung him on the tree. As the tree swayed under his weight, he watched the scene unfold below.

Foman was terribly outmatched.

Dengar couldn't understand it. As a trio, they had defeated several other dragons together. The battles had been hard, but never as one-sided as it was in this case. Foman put up a valiant effort, cutting and slicing with his sword as the dragon parried and danced around him.

Then came the blood-curdling scream. The dragon, having learned his lesson about the barbs on the armor, used a single talon to deliver the death blow. He came in over the top and drove his talon down through the neck joint where the armor was weakest. Foman crumpled to the ground and then the dragon turned back to regard Dengar.

"We will never stop," Dengar said as the dragon leapt up into the air and hovered in front of him, beating his leathery wings and bobbing slightly up and down.

"Then there can be no peace for us," the dragon replied.

Dengar's breathing came harder now. Even if the dragon did nothing, he knew he was done for. He could feel the blood gurgling up with each exhalation. The coppery taste filled his mouth and the odor laced his nostrils. He tried to protest when the dragon gripped his helmet between two talons, but he had not the strength to lift his arms.

"I will make this quick," the dragon promised.

"I will see you in Hammenfein," Dengar swore as his helmet came off.

The last thing the man saw was a talon screaming toward his neck.

*****

Lepkin's legs and lungs ached terribly by the time he arrived at Kuldiga Academy. His horse had put a leg down a gopher hole sometime during the night and snapped its leg, leaving him to run the rest of the way on foot.

He could only hope that somehow he would reach Kyra before the dragon slayers found Leatherback. He rushed through the hallways, up the stairs, and sprinted for the door to Kyra's room. The sun was only barely starting to show above the horizon, so with any luck she was still inside.

He slammed into the door and nearly took it from its hinges.

Linny shrieked and pulled her blanket up over her nightgown, while Kyra turned and seemed ready to blast Lepkin with a spell. The young apprentice held up his hand and slumped to his knees, gasping for breath.

"Leatherback...the dragon slayers..."

Kyra's rage melted instantly, replaced by concern and fear. She rushed to Lepkin and bent down to meet his eyes. "They found him?"

Lepkin nodded. "Warn... Leatherback." He huffed and panted, the air burning his lungs.

Kyra opened a portal and then grabbed Lepkin's hand and dragged him through.

They dropped into the clearing and were met by a terrible sight.

Many of the trees had been charred, or altogether burnt, and there were three bodies in the area. Leatherback was lying on the far side of the clearing, tending a series of gashes and puncture wounds in his foot.

"Leatherback!" Kyra screamed. She ran toward him.

Lepkin hung back, still doubled over and struggling to regain his breath. He held a hand up to try and signal that he needed a moment, but he collapsed on the ground, gasping horribly. After several minutes, he managed to resume a kneeling position and surveyed the scene.

As he had feared, he was too late.

Kyra shouted something, but Lepkin was too busy looking at the broken bodies of his former trainers to hear it.

A moment later, he was pinned to the ground, one of Leatherback's talons on either side of his neck.

"What have you done?"

"I didn't do anything," Lepkin said, suddenly finding his voice again. "A merchant came to our camp, and told the dragon slayers where to find you. I tried to stop them by scaring the horses away, and I tried to warn Kyra."

"Leatherback, stop!" Kyra shouted. "Lepkin is not our enemy."

The dragon pulled his talons back and let Lepkin up.

"Thank you," Lepkin offered. "I promise I did the best I could to prevent them from discovering you. My horse broke its leg in the night, otherwise I would have been able to warn you first."

"Where are the other horses?" Kyra asked.

"I ate them," Leatherback said with a derisive snort.

"We have to get these bodies out of here," Kyra said. "We have to move to a new place."

Leatherback shook his head. "It isn't that simple," he admitted. "They will never stop now. I have killed dragon slayers. More will come. I will never be safe where they can find me."

"What do we do?" Kyra asked. She turned to Lepkin, but he only shrugged. "Where is Njar?" she went on. "He should have seen this! He should be here!"

Leatherback nodded. "I will go to Viverandon. You two will return to Kuldiga Academy."

"We have to hide the bodies," Kyra said again.

Leatherback shook his head. "You must tell the truth," he said. "Tell Headmaster Herion that I acted in self-defense. Tell him that I did try to offer peace. I tried to explain it to the humans, but they would not listen."

Lepkin noticed the venomous tone with which Leatherback had spoken the word *humans* and shivers ran down his spine. There was no coming back from something like this. Kyra may not see it, but Lepkin knew that the group was about to split and go its separate ways.

"Njar can keep me safe from the blight, and no dragon slayer will find me in Viverandon," Leatherback said. "I will be there. When you have found the clues you need to fight the vampire, then come for us, and we will help you."

Kyra began to cry. "What about reading stories at night? Who will…" Kyra's words trailed off.

Leatherback bent his head down to her and softly nuzzled her with his snout. "This is the way it must be now, for it will be too dangerous. Imagine what would have happened if they had found out our secret, but come for you first," Leatherback said. "It is better this way. We will both be safe."

Kyra threw her arms around Leatherback's snout and leaned onto him. "Take me with you," she said.

Lepkin stood there, watching as the two of them struggled with their good-bye. For the first time, no words of comfort came to his mind.

Leatherback pulled away from Kyra and then looked at Lepkin. "You will guard her."

Lepkin nodded. "Always."

The dragon offered a half-smile and then leapt into the air, ignoring Kyra's pleas for him to wait.

Lepkin moved in and she collapsed into his chest, crying softly as Leatherback disappeared into the clouds above, possibly leaving the Middle Kingdom forever.

Chapter 13

Linny left her room as soon as she could get dressed. She was concerned for Kyra, but there wasn't anything she could do for her. So, trying to think of a way she might be able to cheer her friend up, as well as help smooth things over for having followed her into the tunnel, she decided to go into the field to the south of the school grounds and pick wild flowers.

It was something she had done for her mother whenever she had felt sad. She smiled then as she remembered her mother as she was before she had gotten sick. The two of them had often gone out to pick flowers. As the tears threatened to well up in her eyes, she focused on thoughts of Kyra and the dragon instead.

She must have walked a mile away from campus before she finally found a patch of bluebells and daisies that seemed good enough to pick for Kyra. She waded through the tall grass and flowers, searching only for the best specimens to take back with her. Whenever she found an ideal flower, she would pick it near the base, leaving long stems, and then she tucked them into the crook of her left arm.

As she was picking flowers, a middle-aged woman approached from further down the small road leading to the south. Linny didn't see her until she was only a few feet away. The sight of seeing someone else out here who wasn't obviously part of Kuldiga Academy startled her, but the fact that it was a woman put her at ease quickly.

"Hello, dear," the woman said in a soft voice. Her brown eyes sparkled beneath her auburn hair. Her facial features were angular, but not gaunt, giving her a striking appearance. Her lips were full and bright red, and they stretched into a wide smile revealing exquisitely white teeth.

Linny's teeth had never been white. At her best they had been a dull gray, sometimes yellow, but never sparkling, shining white.

"Out picking flowers are we?" the lady asked.

Linny nodded.

"Sorry, where are my manners?" the lady said. "I am Miss Freen. I sometimes come to pay a visit to my alma mater and speak with Lady Priscilla, do you know her?"

Linny shook her head.

"No matter," the lady said. "Say, would you like an apple?" Miss Freen pulled a large, green apple from a basket that Linny hadn't noticed before. "I have three, and that's more than I need. Here, you take one."

Linny took the proffered apple and smiled at Miss Freen. "Thank you," she said sincerely.

"Green apples are my favorite," Miss Freen said. "Most people prefer the sweet red or yellow apples, but I like the ones that have a sour bite to them. They're my absolute favorite!"

"Mine too!" Linny replied.

Miss Freen smiled and nodded. "Excellent, well, you have a wonderful day, dear. I am sure we will meet again."

Linny waved good-bye as Miss Freen walked away.

The girl then continued picking flowers, taking bites of her apple as she went along.

*****

Miss Freen walked around a large bend beyond the grassy field where Linny was picking wild flowers. When she was certain she could no longer be seen, she turned and walked straight into the forest to the right of the road.

She was breathing heavily now, and pain was rolling over her body. She no sooner reached the shade of a large oak tree than she transformed back into her true form.

Severin stood there, hunched over and grunting at the stinging burns. Over the last century he had perfected his magic in order to walk in the open during the daytime, but despite his best efforts it was nearly impossible to be out for long.

His fortune was that Linny had come out before the sun was fully above the horizon. Early morning was dangerous, but not nearly as perilous as mid-day. He examined his smoking burns and shook his head. He would have to wait until he was back in his lair before he would be able to heal those. For now, he would have to make his way back to the small fox den he had taken from its previous owner after leaving the bumbling dragon slayers.

In order to escape the deadly rays of the sun, he transformed himself into a fox and hurried through the forest, careful to use the more shady pathways to avoid excessive damage to his body. Swords and arrows were hardly a menace to him, but the light of the sun was a most troublesome foe, and the burns required much magic to heal.

Even so, Severin was certain he had made the right choice. He could still scarcely believe his fortune when he had discovered Linny in Lepkin's memories. A third child who knew the secret of the dragon. She was the perfect target for this assault. This would allow him access to Kyra and her friend without tailing them directly. It was perfect.

More than that, the spell he had put into the apple, and the monsters it would summon, was sure to strike the girl down.

Before this day ended, Kyra would lose another friend.

Severin smiled wide and laughed aloud.

Oh, how he loved playing with his prey.

*****

After returning to Kuldiga Academy, Kyra and Lepkin had tried to speak with Headmaster Herion about what had happened.

What they had hoped would be an understanding discussion leading to some sort of peaceful resolution turned into the worst four hours of their lives.

Herion had them separated into rooms in the basement and interrogated them at length about Leatherback, the dragon slayers, and the fire drakes. There had been no hint of mercy in his voice.

When the ordeal was over, he had simply told the two to return to their rooms and not to leave again until he came for them after dinner.

They both had understood there would be a secret meeting about them and Leatherback, and so rather than obey, they made their way directly to the hidden chamber behind the walls of the Headmaster's secret meeting room.

They had found Linny already in the sitting room below their eavesdropping spot, arranging flowers on the table and trying to put on a good smile and ask how they were doing.

"Why are you here again?" Kyra asked incredulously.

"No, I wasn't here to snoop," Linny said. "Look, I was trying to get flowers for you. I know it's been a hard day, and I was trying to make up for snooping before."

"No," Kyra said with a shake of her head.

Lepkin grabbed her arm and turned her back to him. She was startled by the force he used, but caught off guard by the pained look in his eyes.

"Enough fighting," he said. "We have few friends as it is. Let's try and be nice to the ones we have. She looks up to you."

"So what should I do? Should I just forgive her for snooping and then let her come along and see what it is we are about to do?"

Lepkin nodded. "Yes." There was no boyish grin. No hint of mirth in his tone. His sad eyes glanced to Linny and he offered the other girl a smile. He let go of Kyra's arm and walked past her. "Everything is fine, Linny, thanks for the flowers. That was thoughtful of you."

"I can go," Linny said.

"No," Lepkin replied quickly. "Come, I want to show you something, but you have to promise to be quiet as a mouse."

"Um…"

Kyra turned around and forced a smile. Maybe Lepkin was right. She had been too hard on Linny. She wasn't really mad at her. After all, Lepkin and she had met under similar circumstances when he found her out in the woods on the way to Leatherback's first nest.

"It's all right," Kyra said. "Join us. You already know about Leatherback, so you may as well see what the others think of him."

"The others?" Linny repeated.

Lepkin grabbed the bookcase and smoothly swiveled it out to the side, revealing the ladder going up into their special spot where they eavesdropped on the others.

"Come on," Lepkin whispered as he placed a finger to his mouth.

The three of them were climbing the ladder leading to the secret area from which they could eavesdrop on the meeting Headmaster Herion was certain to call to order.

They got into position and waited quietly. Kyra tried to offer Linny a reassuring smile, but the girl would look away quickly. As Kyra watched Linny uncomfortably fidget with her fingers, she noticed that the girl's right eye was twitching, as though she had suddenly developed a tick. She was about to ask her if she felt all right, but then the lock on the door clicked and scraped.

The door opened and a tall, blonde woman with an athletic build came in first and sat down near the opposite side from where Herion usually sat. Kyra scrunched up her nose as she tried to figure out who the woman was, but she was sure she had never seen her before. Feberik Orres came in after her, a grim expression on his face. Master Fenn was the next person to enter the room. Warty, the leader of the trio of priests from Valtuu Temple came in after him. He was alone this time. He stopped mid-step and seemed to look right at Kyra as she peered through the slim crack in the wall she always used to spy on the meetings.

She held her breath, but the priest moved along to sit with his back to the wall without saying a word.

Finally, Headmaster Herion came in, walking alongside none other than Mindaugas Reif, the Keeper of Secrets.

"You all know why you are here," Herion said without any of the pomp such a meeting might normally require. "Our worst fears have come to play out in a small grove not too far from here."

Feberik and the blonde woman exchanged glances.

"Another attack?" Feberik asked.

Herion waved his hand furiously. "That's right, you don't know yet. I just informed Master Fenn, but now I will need to let you in on the secret as well."

Kyra's heart skipped. Herion was going to tell them all about Leatherback, and there was nothing she could do to stop him. Her hands trembled as Headmaster Herion told them everything he knew about Leatherback, and Kyra's dealings with him. She glanced to Lepkin, who was glued to his peephole and sitting there with his mouth open, casually shaking his head every other second as if wishing Herion would stop talking. She couldn't see Linny's reactions because her view was now blocked by Lepkin. Kyra closed her eyes, willing the meeting to stop, but Herion continued until he had expounded upon every incident up until the fight with the dragon slayers.

The adults in the room all remained still and unmoving, listening intently to everything Headmaster Herion said. Master Fenn's face was red with anger, but at least he held his tongue. Kyra couldn't see the expression on Feberik's face, for his back was to her, but she saw him tapping his heel and had to guess that he was getting fairly upset.

"This isn't as bad as it sounds," Mindaugas spoke when Herion had concluded his account of Leatherback's life to this point.

"Not as bad as it sounds?" Herion shot back, fire in his eyes. "There is no way to conceal this! Villagers have claimed seeing dragons, and now three dragon slayers are dead! Whether they attacked him first or not makes no never mind to their order."

"Headmaster Herion, please, we can reason through this," Mindaugas said. "They will not charge you with anything. It is not your duty to slay dragons, it is theirs. Even if Leatherback was hiding close to the school, what harm is that? There is nothing they can hang around your neck."

"No," Herion said as he shook his head. "Listen to me. I know Commander Tillamon. He is a hard man. He will look to hold someone accountable. There have been several reported sightings of dragons lately. Albeit they were all false reports, they were reported to the dragon slayers nonetheless. Furthermore, as protocol dictates, the three dragon slayers who were here made sure to forward those reports onward. Commander Tillamon already has the reports. He knows that I know of the reports as well."

"Then he will conclude that you have helped with the investigation and that the dragon slayers were sloppy in their execution," Mindaugas countered. "Surely I can put in a word and reason with the commander."

"No," Herion said. "Leatherback was too close to the school. The priests have been reported as living here the past several months. Tillamon will put it all together. He is a smart man. I should know, for I trained here at the same time he did."

"The priests are under my stewardship and control," Mindaugas countered. I have them up here because of the reported sightings. I will speak on their behalf and say we have found no dragons terrorizing the countryside, for that much is true."

Herion slammed a hand on the table and walked away from his chair for a moment. He was facing the other wall and shaking a hand out to the side as if arguing with himself. Then he turned and spoke again. "Leatherback lived too close to the school. Tillamon will figure it out. It will gnaw at him until he starts a full investigation. He'll realize that a dragon large enough to slay three of his men is one that could not hide in the Middle Kingdom without help. He will be looking for someone to blame." Herion threw his hands in the air dismissively. "You all know the story of Yageston. They had a juvenile dragon there for several years. They hid him in the mountains in the east. Then, when the dragon turned evil it wiped out three villages to the north before the dragon slayers put it down. There was no evidence pointing to Yageston then, but Tillamon figured it out. He led an inquisition and rounded up every single citizen involved and had them put to death for treason." Herion shook his head and moved back to his seat, flopping down angrily. "I don't have to remind you that harboring a dragon is illegal, do I?"

Mindaugas sighed impatiently. "This group here, sitting around the table, is a special unit run by the king. You act in his name. Send to him for help. Surely he could intervene."

"Not without divulging the existence of the group," Herion said. "Between that revelation and the fact that we as a group would be seen as harboring a dragon, it would be enough for Tillamon to charge us with treason. He would launch an investigation like the one in Yageston. The dragon slayers will come and demand full control of Kuldiga Academy. They will not stop until the dragon is found."

"I have seen their inquisitions before," the blond woman said. "A village far to the south was once rumored to have harbored a dragon egg. The dragon slayers found out about their involvement and they put every man, woman, and child into stocks and chains until they had gotten their confessions. They punished everyone who had knowledge of the egg, either by execution or sending them to work in the mines, and then they slew the dragon egg as well."

"Yes, I am familiar with the history of Oridell," Mindaugas said flatly. "Surely, you cannot believe they will interrogate everyone in the school. That is madness."

"Those who join the order are not known for forgiveness," Herion said. "We played a dangerous game, and now we have lost. The best we can do now is plan how to handle it, and make a pact between those of us present today to take the truth to our graves."

Master Fenn rose from his chair and took in a breath. "It gives me no pleasure to say this," he began, "but I must formally demand that Headmaster Herion step down from his position as headmaster."

"Now hold on a minute!" Feberik bellowed. "We can beat this, but we all have to stick together."

"No, Feberik," Herion said. "Master Fenn is correct. The only way we have a chance at appeasing the dragon slayers is if I resign from Kuldiga Academy."

Feberik slammed a fist on the table and started to say something, but Mindaugas silenced the man with his own booming voice. "Be silent!" he thundered.

Feberik bristled, but settled into his chair with his arms folded and no more than an angry huff coming out of him.

"What we must remember is that the dragon slayers will come to us for answers. They will want to know how this could have happened. Tillamon will want to know who is responsible. If I play the part well, then my punishment will likely be an early retirement in the countryside and a private stripping of my title. But if we do not unite on this, and make sure there are no loose ends for Tillamon to pull at, then we could risk much more than our school. If the full extent of our covert activities come to light, then there are nobles now who would use that information to revolt against the king. Worse than that, if Tillamon suspected this group of treason for harboring the dragon, then he might side with the dissenting nobles." Headmaster Herion stammered then and shook his head. He sighed and his chin quavered. After a moment, he cleared his throat and began to speak again. "When the dragon slayers come to you and want to know what has transpired here, I expect you to tell them the truth."

"I am not telling them anything," Feberik snarled.

Mindaugas shot him a disapproving look, but Feberik only shrugged and shook his head.

"The *truth*," Herion started, "is that *I* am a bungling old fool past my prime. While I have helped the dragon slayers to the best of my abilities, including hunting monsters such as the wylkins and the fire drakes. *I* was unable to find the dragon's lair, despite the fact that it was so close to the school. Because I was not vigilant enough to spot the danger so close to our doors, I am unfit for the office I hold. Therefore, I must step down, for I am no longer competent enough to be the headmaster." Herion pointed to Master Fenn.

Master Fenn nodded and held up a brown leather book. "I am holding Headmaster Herion's journal. This book, written in his own hand, details the investigations into the many reports about mysterious creatures in the surrounding countryside. It outlines his plans, and what he and the dragon slayers did to find the reported dragon. While it shows he meant well, it also displays his lack of competent strategy, and his slothfulness in doing all he could have done to have the countryside searched. It shows where he directed the dragon slayers to, which conveniently leaves out the area where the dragon was ultimately found. The journal also explains how the headmaster defeated the shade, and the fire drakes."

"This is ludicrous; you can't take the blame for any of these things, you will be entirely discredited!" Feberik said.

Herion sighed loudly and shook his head. "Sometimes a leader must fall upon his sword in order to preserve the plans already put into motion. If we all stick to this plan, then this group can carry on its work and Tillamon will not see a need to press an investigation. The task you will be charged with is securing Kuldiga Academy. Whatever happens to me, the vampire must never be permitted to enter these walls and attack our students. Feberik, I will expect you to protect Kyra Dimwater."

"You know you don't have to ask me to do that," Feberik said.

Herion nodded. "Lady Arkyn, I will need you to keep an eye on the dragon slayers. We must ensure they never get wind of Kyra's involvement. She has already done so much, and may yet do many more great things."

The blond woman nodded. "I have always wanted to spy on the dragon slayers, it will be an honor."

Herion gestured to Mindaugas. "You will take her after the vampire is dealt with."

Mindaugas nodded. "She has agreed to come with me afterward."

Herion shook his head. "No, I want you to listen. I am *telling* you to take her as soon as the vampire is dealt with. I do not want the dragon slayers to be around her any longer than necessary."

Mindaugas frowned, but nodded his agreement. "What of the boy?" he asked. "I had intended to ask him as well."

Herion shook his head. "Kathair will need to go with the dragon slayers. He has already been formally apprenticed to their order, and their commander will want to bring him back to their headquarters for debriefing. If you have further interest in the boy, I'm afraid you will need to make arrangements with Commander Tillamon. If you were to pull him right away it might raise questions. Besides, Kyra is the better of the two candidates."

"I thought you didn't believe in the prophecy," Mindaugas said.

Herion frowned and sat down. "I don't, but if you are looking for the best, then Kyra is the one you want."

"I will not be able to lie to my brothers," Warty said. "Even if I were to try, they will see the truth in my aura. I will not be able to hide it."

Mindaugas cut in. "I will send them back to Valtuu Temple," he said. "They will obey my command."

"What of Leatherback?" Warty asked.

Herion shrugged. "Let us hope that he stays away from the Middle Kingdom. We can no longer offer him any amount of protection. To do so would risk the wrath of the dragon slayers. It has to end here." Herion then pointed to Master Fenn. "Master Fenn is the senior most instructor of sorcery at Kuldiga Academy. I believe it only right that you should declare him the new headmaster."

Fenn nodded. "We will convene a proper meeting of all the instructors after the dragon slayers have accepted Headmaster Herion's resignation. As protocol dictates, I will be the interim headmaster until that meeting. Even with the investigation that is sure to come, I'm certain the appointment process can be successfully concluded before the upcoming academic year."

"It is imperative that Fenn become the headmaster," Herion said. "The headmaster has always traditionally been responsible for leading not only the school, but *these* meetings as well. Fenn is close to the king, and will not lead you astray. Put your trust in him, and serve as faithfully for him as you would for me."

Kyra was having a hard time absorbing everything she was seeing and hearing. To think that Herion was willing to sacrifice so much in order to protect *her*. Now she understood his anger from earlier. She felt ashamed for failing him.

Just then Linny screamed so loudly that she jumped up from her spot.

A pair of imps had descended upon her, clawing and biting at her face. They were slightly larger than the ones Cyrus had summoned to train Kyra with. They were maybe two feet tall, with leathery wings as wide as the imps were tall. They had fiery red eyes and sharp fangs and claws. Linny was on her back, swatting helplessly at the creatures.

Before Kyra could think through the ramifications of her actions, she sent a pair of lightning bolts out to strike the imps. One was hit in the chest and flew into the wall. The second dodged easily.

Lepkin was up in an instant, punching the second imp and knocking it to the floor. He then tried to stomp on it, but the imp launched a fireball at Lepkin that set his shoe ablaze and caused him to stagger backward into the wall.

Kyra moved in, but then the entire wall facing the secret room came crumbling down.

The imps were seized by purple cords of magic and pulled into the meeting room, where Master Fenn quickly banished them to a different plane.

Kyra looked to each of the stern sets of eyes in the room and her stomach hit the floor.

"It would appear that we have guests," Mindaugas said with a grimace on his face.

Herion stood nearest to them, jaw clenched and body trembling with rage.

The only sound any of them could hear was Linny's soft sobs as she picked herself up with Lepkin's help and began to dust herself off.

"I'm sorry," Linny said. "I don't know where they came from. I'm so sorry."

Herion shook his head. "You think you're sorry now? Just wait. I will show you the meaning of the word sorry." He turned to Master Fenn. "You will come with me. The rest of you are dismissed." He turned back to Kyra then and glared at her. "You three are coming with me."

Kyra shook her head. She turned and summoned her portal. "Come on," she shouted to Lepkin and Linny as she leapt through. A magical cord wrapped around her right ankle. She struggled to reach the other side of her portal as Herion shouted at her and angrily tugged on the magical cord.

Kyra turned to see Lepkin running forward. He pulled his sword and came down hard on the magical cord. There was an explosion of light, and Kyra went hurtling through the portal to land on the grass in the aspen grove. The portal closed before she could see what had happened to Lepkin. She had intended for all of them to escape, but now she was here and they were back at the academy.

She pushed up to her feet and a familiar voice called out to her.

"Difficult day?" Cyrus asked.

She poised herself, ready to fight back if he tried anything, but he simply held his hands up in the air and shook his head.

"I am not here to trouble you," he said. "I am here to help."

"How could you help?"

Cyrus smiled. "The dagger," he said. "With the grove partially destroyed, and the dragon slayers that are soon to come looking to avenge their fallen, there is only one option to save your friend."

"He is safe," Kyra said as she shook her head. "He is in Viverandon."

Cyrus sighed. "That will not keep him safe forever. Nagar's Blight can still reach him there, and you know it."

"We'll fly to the north!" Kyra shouted.

"He is injured," Cyrus said. "I heard what you told Headmaster Herion about the dragon's wounds. He will not have the strength to cross an ocean for some time."

Kyra tried to think of something else, but her mind was blank. She didn't have any other ideas.

"Don't fret," Cyrus said in a smooth tone. "Listen. If we get the dagger, we can help him."

"How can the dagger help?"

Cyrus smiled. "I told you, the dagger has powers. What we need to do is get Leatherback to a different plane of existence. We have to move him out of the Blight's reach."

"Another plane of existence? Like the astral plane? Can you do that?" Kyra asked.

Cyrus frowned. "No."

"But the dagger can?"

Cyrus shook his head. "The dagger has its power based in Hammenfein. It can't open the way to the astral plane, as it is beyond its grasp, but it could open one of the lesser dominions of Hammenfein."

"That would send him to Khefir and Hatmul," Kyra argued. "I can't do that."

"There are many dominions of Hammenfein," Cyrus said. "We can find one wherein he can hide. Then, when he is strong enough, we can open the way and you can fly to the north."

Kyra shook her head. "But doesn't Hatmul despise dragons? I have read that ever since the first Great War, he has blamed all dragons for his father's downfall. It is in the histories of Roegudok Hall. Hatmul is the reason the first dragon prince became the One who could enter the mountain. He attacked the nest of the

148

Ancients. If we send Leatherback into Hammenfein, then we are sealing his doom."

Cyrus shook his head emphatically. "We will have to figure that out as we go," he said. "But it is the only plane we might be able to access that can save him. First, we need that dagger."

"I don't know where it is," Kyra said honestly.

"Let's go back to the academy. We'll sleep on it for tonight, and then you and I can resume our search in the morning."

Kyra nodded. "I shouldn't have run away like that, I was just…"

Cyrus moved to her and wrapped an arm around her shoulders. "It's all right, I am sure we can smooth this over."

"Wait, how did you know I would be here?" Kyra asked.

Cyrus looked down and gave her a wink. "Herion had ordered me to watch your room, but you never came back. I figured you had come here. I was almost about to give up when I saw your portal." He smiled and gave her a light squeeze on the shoulder. "Come, let's get you back to your room."

Chapter 14

Cyrus was all too eager to be awake the following day. He stood in an upper floor window overlooking the courtyard. The way things were falling out was simply delicious. When he had returned to the school with Kyra, Janik had been positively gushing with information.

The first thing that he told him was that Linny was being expelled. In addition to being caught snooping in the school, but Herion had taken a closer look at her registration documents in order to prepare to send her home and found them to be forgeries.

When he confronted her with the discovery, Linny had confessed to being a low-born girl and told Herion where she had obtained the papers.

The second bit of information was that Lady Priscilla was arriving today to see her husband, along with their newborn. Cyrus had heard plenty about the imps that had attacked Linny. Even more fortunately, Headmaster Herion had found Linny tainted with dark magic, apparently the work of Severin according to Herion. The imps had been a pair of the vampire's familiars. It set the stage perfectly.

Feberik Orres was escorting Linny out that morning. She was to use the carriage that Lady Priscilla was arriving in. Cyrus couldn't have been more pleased with things had he planned the events himself.

He watched and waited as the morning dew burned away under the increasing gaze of the watchful sun. Feberik and Linny came out into the courtyard and walked to the middle of the round, dirt drive in front of the stables. Cyrus studied the girl. Even from this distance, he could see her hanging head and almost taste her sadness.

Janik had been all too happy about finally ridding the school of his illegitimate half-sister, but Cyrus saw great potential in the young lady. All he had to do was play the next few minutes just right.

He prepared the summoning spell and then waited for Lady Priscilla's carriage to arrive. It was drawn in quickly by two gray draught horses, bouncing and bumping over the dips and holes and splashing in puddles left by the brief storm last night.

Then, just as the carriage circled around to a stop and the doors were opened to allow Lady Priscilla and her baby to exit, Cyrus finished casting his summoning spell.

Two wylkins appeared in a puff of black smoke, snarling and growling ferociously.

Cyrus laughed to himself as Linny screamed and ran away.

Lady Priscilla quickly reached around her baby with one arm to retrieve her wand, but Cyrus quickly cast a dispel charm that rendered her magic useless.

Feberik predictably rose to the occasion like the noble gentleman he was. He had not been carrying his sword, for he had carried Linny's trunk out to the carriage, but that did not stop him from jumping into action. Improvising in a most dashing way, he used the luggage in his arms to intercept the first beast. Cyrus smiled as the first wylkin was slammed to the ground with a massive blow to the head that splintered the trunk apart and sprayed clothes all over the monster and the grass and dirt nearby.

Lady Priscilla shrieked and cried out for help as the second wylkin came for her.

Feberik was there in an instant, drawing the beast's attention. Despite his large size, the warrior was surprisingly spry and agile on his feet. He ducked under a hooked swipe, then leapt to the

151

side as the wylkin came in with his three tails. The spikes missed the large warrior who was quick to answer the monster with a savage left hook to its face. The wylkin stumbled backward and crashed into the carriage.

The horses reared up and bolted away, dragging the carriage with them.

"Behind me!" Feberik shouted to Lady Priscilla. The woman quickly ran around Feberik and held her baby close as she sprinted for the open door.

The first wylkin jumped to its feet and sprinted after Lady Priscilla, but Feberik bent down and picked up something that from Cyrus' vantage point looked like a good-sized stone.

A gray streak shot across the courtyard and a moment later the first wylkin grunted as its head jerked to the side violently and then it fell to the grass. Its body twitched, but it did not get up again.

The second wylkin was rising again, but Feberik was already charging it. He started off with a massive front kick to the wylkin's chest. The bipedal monster swung out with its massive, sharp hooks, but caught only the front of Feberik's shirt. Feberik then pressed the attack. A left hook to the face. A quick shot to the body. A kick to the wylkin's right knee. Then he jumped back to avoid the wylkin's hooks and tails once more before lunging in to finish the fight with one terrible punch to the creature's throat.

The wylkin coughed and sputtered, staggering to the side as its knees lost their strength and it fell to the ground.

Feberik moved in slowly, wary of the deadly hooks on the ends of the wylkin's arms. Then, he lashed out and kicked the beast in the ribs. Even Cyrus cringed as the snapping bones echoed off the walls of the courtyard. The wylkin collapsed and gave up the ghost.

At that precise moment, Master Fenn and Headmaster Herion were charging into the courtyard.

Cyrus didn't hear the particulars, but he heard enough to get the idea. Master Fenn was accusing Linny of attracting the wylkins with her dark magic. The carriage was brought back by the driver and the girl was being roughly gathered up and placed into the carriage. Then, Master Fenn was hugging his wife and child before going and throwing his arms around Feberik in an embrace of gratitude.

"That ought to earn Feberik some points," Cyrus said, pleased with his work.

He watched until the courtyard was clear. Feberik and the others went back inside after Herion burned the wylkin bodies. Linny was hastily driven away in the carriage by herself.

"Now for the next part of the plan," Cyrus said to himself. He closed his eyes and then transported himself to the carriage without the use of a portal.

Linny jumped when he appeared beside her, but he stifled her with a hand to her mouth and then gave her a serious look that told her to keep quiet.

"I can help you, but you must remain quiet."

Linny nodded.

"You know I am Kyra's instructor, right?"

Linny nodded again.

"Do you still want to learn magic?"

Linny shook her head.

Cyrus smiled and pulled his hand away from her mouth. He then reached down and held her hand, closed his eyes, and the two of them disappeared from the carriage.

A moment later, the two of them were standing in the middle of a forest.

"Where are we?" Linny asked. "Why have you brought me here?"

"You have a secret," Cyrus said slyly.

Linny looked nervous. Her eyes darted to the trees around them and her lip quivered just slightly. "What do you mean?"

Cyrus held up a hand. "I mean your name is not Linny Ravia of Nortwyn Abbey."

Linny frowned. "That isn't a secret, at least, it's not a secret anymore," she replied. "Headmaster Herion already figured out the papers were faked."

"Ah, but does he know your true heritage?" Cyrus asked.

The girl folded her arms and her face grew red. "Listen, I don't have to explain myself to you! Just leave me alone!"

Cyrus laughed. "If that is what you want, then I will, but first I want you to listen to me explain *who* you really are."

"I am Eleanor Hughes," she said quickly. "I was born in the slums of…"

"No," Cyrus said loudly. "You are the daughter of a nobleman. That is fact. Moreover, I know who your father is."

"I have no father!" Eleanor shouted.

Cyrus bent down so that his eyes were level with hers. "Give me two minutes. Once you have heard what I have to say, if wish to go back to the slums, then I will honor that. However, you deserve to know the truth before you decide."

Eleanor's face was still red, but she closed her mouth and arched a brow as her blue eyes stared back at him expectantly.

"You share the same father as Janik and Feberik Orres."

"Impossible!"

Cyrus held a finger to her mouth. "Not only is it possible, but Janik is the one who told me. He told me of how your father wished to send you a portion of his wealth upon his death. Your name, and that of your mother, was written in the will, did you know that?"

Eleanor shook her head.

"However, Janik hid that fact, and cheated you out of your due inheritance. More than that, he was the one who went to great lengths to get Herion to inspect your documents. Neither Kyra nor Kathair are being expelled, so why are you being kicked out?" Cyrus waved his arm out to the side to emphasize his rhetoric. "I'll tell you why, it's because Janik didn't want his half-sister taking honor away from his family."

"Why are you telling me this?" Eleanor said with tears forming in her eyes.

"Because, in this world, men will take from you anything you cannot hold and protect for yourself. They will rob you, cheat you, and lie to you. You have to learn to make your own way if you are

154

to survive." Cyrus then pulled her ebony and opal wand out from the folds of his robe.

"Headmaster Herion took that from me, how did you get it?" Eleanor asked.

Cyrus smiled and held it out for her. "I took it back from Janik, after he took it from Herion," he lied. The truth was he had asked Herion for it after Linny was expelled. Herion had little problem giving a wand to an instructor of magic, but that version would not engender the hatred he was trying to build within Eleanor. "Also, you should know that the portion of wealth intended for your mother and you was used in the dowry to buy Kyra's hand in marriage."

Eleanor frowned and took the wand in her hands. She turned it over for a minute and then shook her head. "Kyra wouldn't have known about that," she said. "She told me she doesn't even like Feberik."

Cyrus smiled and put on the best version of an empathetic face he could muster. "I know, but I bring it up because it was Janik's decision. He and Feberik have taken so much from you, I don't want them to steal away your future too."

"What do you mean?"

Cyrus smiled and stood up fully. "I have friends who can teach you magic. You can keep your wand, the wand your mother bought for you, and train until you are strong enough to forge your own future." He turned and gestured to a tree nearby. "I can introduce you now, or I can return you to the carriage bound for the slums. Which will it be?"

Eleanor thought for a moment and then looked at her wand. "Are they good people?"

Cyrus shrugged. "They will be good to you," he told her. "Learn from them, and you will finally have the power and future your mother and father wanted you to have. You will no longer have to ask anyone for scraps to eat. You will have a bed all your own, and a home to belong to. Moreover, you will not have to use a fake name. You will be Eleanor Hughes."

Eleanor nodded. "I would like that."

Cyrus smiled wide. "One more thing, you will not be able to see Kyra again," he said. "From this point, you will walk separate paths."

Eleanor nodded, albeit slower and less enthusiastic this time. "I understand," she said.

Cyrus motioned for her to follow him. He conjured a leather bag and seized the top. The bag heaved and writhed as the contents inside squirmed.

The two of them moved next to a basin resting upon a stone.

"This is the beginning of a new life for you," Cyrus said. He could see the girl was nervous, but he was sure he had her convinced enough to follow through now.

Scanning the woods around them, Cyrus made sure they were alone before pouring the bag out into the basin. A nine inch long cucumber slug slammed down and slimed its way to the bottom of the bowl where it encountered a deep pile of powdery ash and recoiled against the substance. Next came a sheep's eye, a spider's egg sack, a snake head, and a lizard's tail.

He waved his hand over the basin and spoke. "As the day is eaten by the night, the darkness is the truest keeper of the light." Cyrus spat into the ashes and they began to glow. "Darkest night, reveal your face and let me partake of your light."

Green flame reached through the ashes, enveloping the slug and the other offerings in the basin. The slug shriveled, but did not char. Instead, the offering simply absorbed into the ash as the flames grew taller. A pale, wrinkled face peered out at them from the flames for only a moment before vanishing again.

The oak tree beyond the basin began to swell, doubling, then tripling in size. A knot slid into the center and slowly dilated. The tree groaned and creaked at the effort. Finally a mountainous mass emerged up from the dirt and joined to the back of the mutated oak tree.

Cyrus ran his hand through the flaming ashes in the basin. The flames licked and tickled his arm, but he remained unharmed. His fingers sifted through the ash until he found the round, gelatinous mass. He pulled it from the basin and walked to the tree. He reached forward and deposited the black, smoldering mass into the dilated knothole. The tree closed around his forearm like a mouth, sucking the blackened ooze from Cyrus' palm and only releasing his arm when all of the slime was cleaned from his skin.

The tree emitted a low, rumbling groan. The knot swelled again until it was large enough for them to pass through.

"Come on," Cyrus said as he reached back for Eleanor's hand. He could see the hesitation in her eyes, but there was something else as well. Curiosity. He smiled when she stepped forward and put her hand in his. "It's not far from here," he told her.

Ethereal green flames hovered in the air before Cyrus' face. The inside of the oak smelled like freshly chipped wood, but it resembled stone in its appearance. The magical cave descended steeply into the ground. Cyrus held Eleanor's hand with his right hand and steadied himself with his left hand as they passed through the tree-like cave entrance and moved into an earthen tunnel.

The hovering green flame floated before them still, lighting their way as they descended deeper and deeper into the ground.

At last, they came to a great chamber. A pair of underground rivers flanked them as they stepped out from the tunnel and into the chamber. The glowing, azure rivers converged in the center of the great hall, forming a living pool of light. In the center of this pool, upon an island of stone, was a woman next to a cauldron, periodically glancing to a podium which held a large tome. Beyond the woman a young girl about Eleanor's age sat behind a desk of stone on a chair made of mammoth bones, stirring a solution in a beaker.

The woman looked up from the cauldron and smiled at them. "Cyrus, it is good to see you."

"And you, Sister Hairen," Cyrus said. They walked toward the edge of the stone platform, stopping a couple of paces away from where it gave way to the ever flowing rivers pouring into the pool. "I have brought a friend who is looking for a home, and for training in magic," Cyrus said.

"Well, bring her here, let me take a look at her," Hairen said.

"They are witches," Eleanor said in a hushed tone to Cyrus.

"They will help you, when all others would kick you to the slums. Be careful you do not judge them too harshly before getting to know them. Otherwise, you will be no better than the likes of Janik, who sees only an inconvenience, an embarrassment, a stray orphan not fit to make a place for herself at the same school as the girl whose dowry was purchased with your inheritance."

Eleanor looked at her feet, and Cyrus knew he had hit a nerve. He summoned a bridge of floating stones and led Eleanor across.

"This is Eleanor Hughes," Cyrus said as he pulled her forward to present her to Hairen. "She has quite a gift, but her powers are raw and unrefined."

"Ah, yes, I can see the gift inside of her," Hairen said as she bent down and placed a hand on Eleanor's forehead. The witch smiled at Eleanor. "You are welcome to live with us. I am Hairen, and I conduct the training here."

The younger girl had left the mammoth bone chair and came up beside Hairen. She smiled shyly and clasped her hands in front of her blue dress.

"My name is Merriam, come, I can show you our room."

Cyrus let go of Eleanor's hand and the two young girls disappeared down a side corridor of stone. After they left, Cyrus turned to Hairen and smiled. "I told you I had found a good candidate."

Hairen smiled coyly. "Yes, that you have. You think you can keep bringing recruits for the coven?"

Cyrus laughed. "Well, let's say I have an agent in place at the academy who can handle these operations without drawing too much attention to himself. Not only can he screen the nobles, but he will have access to information about other promising prospects as well. I should imagine you will have several new witches and warlocks running about these halls soon enough."

Hairen groaned with pleasure. "It will be good to have the halls filled with strength once more," she said. "The Order of the All-seeing Eye has all but forgotten about me."

"I would never do such a thing," Cyrus replied quickly.

"Then you have my allegiance as promised," Hairen said. "Shall I address you as High Patriarch now?" Hairen teased as she reached out to play with the front of Cyrus' robes.

Cyrus shook his head and gently pushed Hairen's hand away. "I still have the other warlocks to deal with, but I can assure you the time is nigh at hand."

"I shall look forward to it," Hairen said.

"See that you do not lose this one," Cyrus said, nodding toward the cave. "Eleanor has a lot of potential. It would be a shame to let a fine catch go."

Chapter 15

Kyra was lying awake on her bed. She hadn't slept at all as Cyrus had suggested. Instead, she had tossed and turned, unable to sleep. Everything seemed to be crumbling around her. Leatherback was gone, perhaps unable to ever return. She was no closer to finding Severin, or the dagger for that matter. The fact that Linny had been packed out of the room before she had returned was on her mind as well.

Nothing was certain anymore. She found herself wondering whether she should forget about the dagger and go to find Leatherback, but then she knew that wouldn't work. The vampire would come for her no matter how far she ran.

As she was deep in her thoughts, she heard a scream come from somewhere outside. She recognized the voice as Linny's She didn't have a window, so she ran to her door. She knew there was a room down the hall that overlooked the courtyard. Kyra ripped open the door only to find Janik barring the way.

"Sorry, Kyra, but I am not supposed to let you out until your instructor comes to get you."

"But that's Linny," she argued.

Janik grabbed Kyra's shoulders and forced her back into her room. For a man with a crippled hand and leg, he was certainly much stronger than she would have guessed.

"Please let me go!"

Janik shook his head. "Feberik is with Linny, if she is in danger, he can take care of her."

"Please!" Kyra repeated.

"Stay put!" Janik bellowed as he shoved her back toward her bed. He then pulled the door closed once more and Kyra heard the metal tumblers of the lock clicking into place.

Kyra tried to open a portal to the courtyard, but Herion had put an enchantment on her room that kept her from casting any spells. When the portal failed, she tried to cast her own dispelling charms to counter Herion's enchantment, but those failed miserably.

Kyra was left to wonder what was happening without any way of helping her friend.

She beat her fists on the wall, slamming the newly replaced bricks and stones that the two of them had labored for the better part of a day setting into place after their magical mishap with fireballs. With each strike she hoped beyond reason that the wall would crumble and allow her to reach her friend, but it held strong and refused to yield to her.

It was maybe an hour before a knock came at her door. She heard some low mumbling, and then a key was inserted into the lock. When the door opened, Cyrus was standing there, smiling at her.

"Linny?" Kyra said.

"A pair of wylkins came to the school, but never fear, Feberik put them down rather easily. Linny is safe and on her way home."

"Where is Lepkin?" Kyra asked.

Cyrus frowned. "Packing, I believe. I think he will be leaving the school in a few days. Don't worry, though, you'll have time to say farewell."

Kyra nodded and smoothed out the front of her black skirt. "And the dagger?"

Cyrus smiled wide. "I'm still working on that, but in the meantime I have some more spells you need to practice that will be helpful against the vampire."

Kyra nodded and rose to her feet. She followed her instructor through the hallways, but they all felt empty somehow. It was as if losing her friends had turned the whole campus hollow and cold. When they finally arrived at the classroom, she moved to sit in a desk, and could hardly focus on any dispel charms as Cyrus began the lesson with smaller illusions to warm up.

After several rounds of her half-hearted attempts to discern which of three golden eggs on Cyrus' desk was real, the wizard sighed loudly and moved to sit in the desk next to hers.

"You aren't the only person to lose someone close to you," Cyrus said pointedly. "You certainly won't be the last either."

Kyra looked at him and drew her brow in tight. "But I haven't lost just *someone*," she replied. "I've lost *everyone*."

Cyrus frowned and nodded thoughtfully, but he remained silent and allowed her to speak her mind.

"I lost my own future when my father sold my hand in marriage," she began. "I know that is how things are done in the Middle Kingdom, but that isn't what I want. I want to choose for myself. I want to *be* myself."

"From what I understand, you have cancelled your wedding to Feberik Orres," Cyrus put in.

Kyra shrugged. "He won't officially cancel it," she replied. "I have tried to make him do it, but he won't. He's stubborn that way. The best I can do is threaten him that if he forces me to go through with it I'll blast him in his sleep."

Cyrus chuckled, but then quickly composed himself and wiped the smile from his face when she shot him a disapproving look.

"I lost my mother," she said then. "She was murdered by that shade. And for what? A dagger?"

"The dagger has enormous powers," Cyrus reminded her. "It can open portals into Hammenfein."

"I don't care," Kyra said. "Then, my father disowns me because of something that is not my fault, nor my doing. On top of this, I make three friends in all the world and now they are either gone, or are about to be sent away. Leatherback is in

162

Viverandon, Linny has been sent home, but nobody will tell me where her home is, and Lepkin is about to be sent to Ten Forts to join the dragon slayers. I'll never see him again!"

She hadn't noticed it, but in her anger she had stood up and begun to pace back and forth. Lightning was crackling from her fingertips and her hands were shaking. She turned around and directed her glaring rage at Cyrus.

"You say everyone loses someone, well, I have lost *everyone!* Who have *you* ever lost?"

Cyrus balked at that and then turned away from her. Kyra stepped toward him, angry enough to want to have a witness to her wrath. However, when she yelled at him to look at her, she saw tears in his eyes.

She had never seen him cry before. Actually, he had only ever worn two expressions that she could remember. There was the stoic, stone-faced instructor who trained with draconian methods most instructors would abhor as far too dangerous to be used in a classroom, and then there was the smug, self-assured smile that accompanied his arrogant side when he caught her with one of his lessons wrapped up in a terribly annoying riddle that she was forced to unpack.

Now he was actively crying.

Tears rolled down his wrinkled cheeks and his voice cracked when he began to speak. "I lost my family," he began with difficulty. "My wife shared the same name your parents gave you. My daughter had a similar spunk and spirit about her as you have, though I dare say she was more beautiful."

Kyra took a step back and slowly found her seat.

"They were killed, taken from me while I was away. They were *my* everything, and I would have done anything to save them. So, I know how you are feeling."

Kyra stared at him dumbly. Her mouth opened three different times to say something, but the words never found their way out.

"I would do anything now to bring them back," Cyrus said. "But, no matter how hard I look for it, that kind of magic eludes me."

Kyra began to cry as well, though now it was only partly because of her pain. The two of them sat in silence for a long while. Kyra was the first to clear her head. She stood up, and then reached out to take Cyrus' hand.

"Come on," she said. "Let's get back to training."

Cyrus didn't come with her at first, but as she continued to pull him up, he nodded and reached up to wipe the tears from his face. Within a matter of moments, the sadness was gone from his eyes, replaced by the stoic, determined wizard she had always known.

"Let's find that dagger," Kyra said. "For your family, and for mine. Let's find the dagger and then kill that vampire."

Cyrus nodded. "For our families," he said. "First things first, you have to be able to defeat his illusions. He won't come at you with a frontal assault. He'll play mind games first."

"Hit me," Kyra said.

Cyrus clapped his hands and the room went pitch black.

For the remainder of the day Kyra spent her time dispelling illusions, banishing summoned imps and battling creatures for whom she didn't know the names. By the time the lessons were over, she and Cyrus were both breathing heavily. She had gained a few new bruises and a couple of cuts, but she felt invigorated, as if she had reached a new level.

As she walked toward the door, Cyrus called out to her.

"I think my daughter would have gotten along well with you, Kyra Dimwater," he said.

Kyra turned back and smiled. "I'm sure of it," she replied.

"I know I am not family, but you could think of me as an uncle, if you wished."

Kyra smiled wider and nodded. "I would be honored."

Cyrus smiled back at her, but it was not his arrogant smile. It was a genuine, proud smile. "I would be the one who is honored," he said with a bow.

Kyra left the room and closed the door behind her.

Chapter 16

After being caught in the secret chamber, Lepkin had been left in his room with the door locked. A guard was posted outside his door to keep him in, but Lepkin was not about to spend his remaining time locked up inside a cell like a prisoner.

Headmaster Herion had informed him that he was going directly to Ten Forts. Before, the plan had been to send him after the dragon slayers sent replacements up to Kuldiga Academy, but now it seemed Herion was all too eager to be rid of him.

The idea had come to Lepkin while lying on his bed that if Herion had sent two masters out to the vampire's lair, then there must be notes or a letter somewhere that explained how to get to the lair. If that was the case, then Lepkin had to find that information and give it to Kyra. With any luck, she could sneak away from the academy, find Leatherback, and attack the vampire before the dragon slayers ever arrived. After all, Ten Forts was hundreds of miles to the south. It would take a long time for them to arrive, and that might be enough of a head start that Kyra could be well on her way out of the Middle Kingdom with Leatherback.

He couldn't leave by the door, but then, he didn't need to. There was a small window at the top of his wall. It was only a little more than a foot and a half tall, but it was much wider. If he could pull himself through it, then he could get back to Herion's office.

The grate in the laundry was likely sealed by now, but Lepkin knew another way to access the tunnel that would lead to Herion's office.

He quietly pulled his mattress from his bed and placed it on the floor near the door. Next, he pulled a large wardrobe over, laying it down on the mattress to act as a barrier in case someone wanted to enter his room. Then he tipped his bed on its end and used the frame to climb up and access the window. He pulled a knife and worked at the edges of the wood frame, cutting away at the seam. It was arduous, painstaking work, but after nearly an hour he had the glass free of its frame without breaking any of it and risking the guard outside his door hearing him.

He sheathed the knife and then pulled himself up. He stuck his hands through the opening and then spread them to either side of the outer wall as he wriggled and wiggled his way through until he was half-in and half-out of the window.

He looked down and realized the one flaw to his plan. There was no ledge below him to grab or stand on. He was dangling from a window on the fifth floor of the northeastern tower. A fall from here would either kill him, or it would cripple him permanently.

Lepkin arched his back and craned his head around to look up. He smiled when he saw the sloped roof jutting out over him. He then turned to look around the outside of the tower to the south. It would be a longshot, but there was a ledge jutting out from a window the same height as his along the eastern wall facing the courtyard. If he could grab hold of the edge of the roof and then make his way to the wall, he could drop to the other window. From there, he could either break in, or he could climb further along the wall as the stones there appeared to protrude more, allowing for finger holds.

He pulled himself back into his room, and then turned around so that his stomach faced the ceiling, then he went back through the window. He pulled and wiggled until he was sitting in the open window, his legs hanging inside his room and his torso close to the outer wall as he stretched upward. He grunted when he realized he was about three inches short of grasping the outer edge of the roof. He would have to stand up to make it.

Carefully, he shifted to his right, pulling one leg through until his foot reached the window. Then, gripping the upper portion of the window opening with his hands, he pressed himself up with his right leg while keeping his left leg stiff and pulling it up and through the opening.

Soon he was standing fully upright, his hands gripping a wooden beam that ran along the eaves above him and out to the edge of the roof. He slid his hands along the wood slowly, doing his best to maintain his balance.

He just grazed the outer edge of the roof when his left foot slipped. He tried to catch himself, but his weight pulled him out and away from the wall. Lepkin knew he had a quickly diminishing chance of reaching his hand hold. He pushed off with his right leg, jumping up and out.

His hands groped and grasped at the roof. He managed to find a lip to grab and held fast as his body swung in the air, dangling high above the ground. Lepkin looked down and breathed a quick sigh of relief. Then he looked toward the eastern wall. From this vantage point higher up, he saw that the smart plan was not to drop to the other window. Doing so would be too great a risk. Instead, he should pull himself up over the lip of the roof, and then scale along it around the tower to drop down onto the eastern wall's roof, which was only six or seven feet below the bottom of the tower's sloped roof.

He looked up and muscled his way up and over the edge of the roof. Pulling himself up was not nearly so hard as changing the motion when his chest and stomach cleared the roof to finish pressing himself up. His muscles shook and quivered, but he was able to scramble onto the roof without slipping down to his doom.

Suddenly he became extremely thankful for the exercises the elves had made him do in his younger years, and he vowed that if he ever trained an apprentice, he would make the boy focus on pull-ups.

He crawled up and then spider-walked around the sloped roof until he was sure he was above the eastern wall. Fortunately, since each of the four walls housed many rooms and several corridors on the inside, the landing area he was shooting for was easily forty feet or more in width. He needed only to drop quietly enough to not cause alarm inside the building.

Lepkin slowly slid to the edge of the roof, then he gripped the same lip he had used to climb up onto the roof and lowered himself to full extension before dropping safely onto the roof of the eastern wall.

He took in a few breaths, thankful that everything had gone as well as it had, and a little embarrassed at how foolish he had been in assuming this would be an easy task to accomplish. Then he ran along the roof toward the southern end. His feet made hardly any sound with each step, for the elves had taught him how to run lightly as well as quickly.

As he neared the south-eastern corner, he stopped and looked out into the courtyard. The sun was going down, but he still wanted to be sure no one had spotted him.

The area below was entirely clear.

He smiled to himself and then ran across the southern portion of the building. He knew that if he could get to the south-western tower, he would be able to make it to Herion's office.

Before long, he was lowering himself over the outer wall and down to a window, which had fortunately been left open. Dropping down to it was not nearly as treacherous as climbing out of his room window had been. He found himself entering a small classroom. The walls were lined with jars filled with various animal parts and organs suspended in a blue-green liquid. Occasionally there was an illustrated diagram of a dissected organ on the wall as well.

"Healers," Lepkin said to himself as he realized what kind of classroom he was in. He moved to the door and opened it carefully. He hadn't come all this way to bump into someone in the hallway.

After seeing that the corridors were clear, he darted across the hall and down the stairs. He knew of one more room that had a small pipe-like tunnel that would lead him where he needed to go.

As he reached the bottom floor of the academy, he peered carefully around the corner, inspecting the area for any movement. A long ways off down the hall to his left he saw a pair of women walking and talking together. He left the stairs and went to the right, quick-stepping to the first door on his right. He pulled at the bronze knob, twisting as he did so.

Lepkin slipped into a janitorial closet and took in a deep breath. He had found this tunnel after exploring the offshoot tunnels deeper in the bowels of the academy. That particular day had ended when he had nearly reached the large grate in the stone basin at his feet. He had been maybe ten or fifteen feet in the tunnel still when Janik had entered the closet and dumped a large bucket filled with gallons of dirty mop water. The ensuing slide back down the tunnel left him cold, wet, and smelly.

This time, however, there would be no mop water. Or, so he hoped.

He moved to the grate and pulled on it.

It didn't budge.

Lepkin frowned and pulled again.

He sighed and shook his head. He could have sworn that the grate had moved before when Janik poured the water in. The grate had been loose, he knew it.

"Herion must have had all the grates fixed," Lepkin surmised. He then looked to his right and searched through the tools. There were two mops, a pair of brooms, and a shovel. Lepkin couldn't guess as to why a janitor would need a shovel inside the academy. He could only suppose that anything too messy for the broom or mop must needs be removed with the shovel. He tried not to think about the fact that such waste was likely tossed down the same tunnel he intended to go into.

He took the shovel in hand and began tapping around the grate. *Ting, ting, ting, tapuk!* He smiled as he found a weak spot. He leaned the shovel against the wall and went back to the door. He checked down the hall and saw that the pair of women was gone. Then, he went around the opposite corner to check the other corridor. No one there either.

Good. No one will hear me.

Lepkin hurried back into the janitorial closet and locked the door behind himself by sliding a broomstick over the doorknob and wedging it across the doorway. Then, he grabbed the shovel in hand and lifted it over his head for a strike. He brought it down hard.

CLANG!

The shaft vibrated in his hand. He hit the spot again, and then a third time before a large section of stone chipped away. Lepkin smiled and reached down to tug on the side of the grate. It wiggled a bit, but was not fully free. Lepkin struck the same area four more time, and then the grate popped up on one side. He pulled the metal grate out of the basin and set it to the side.

He lowered himself into the slanting drain, careful not to catch himself on the jagged edges along the rim that he had created by busting the grate out. Then he gave a push and let the slippery moss and mold along the bottom of the drain do the work for him.

He shot downward at a slight angle for nearly fifty feet, and then he leveled out and slid another few yards before his momentum stopped. He got up onto his hands and knees and crawled the remaining fifty yards to the junction.

He stood up in a small, rectangular chamber that he had been in several times before. In each side of the chamber there were additional tunnels. The one on his right led back to his secret chamber with the table and the bookcase. He bent down and looked through it, but this time he saw only darkness.

Herion must have ordered someone to fill that tunnel in.

The drain to his left was similar to the one he had just used. It led up to another drain in one of the smaller kitchens. The shaft was large enough for him to crawl through, but the grate over the opening was much smaller, perhaps only as big around as a pumpkin. Then, there was the tunnel on the opposite side. He had never explored that one. It sloped downward to what Lepkin could only assume was a great underground pit for waste. He always meant to explore that last tunnel someday, but after the incident with Janik's mop water, Lepkin always feared that someone might unleash water from somewhere and sweep him away forever.

Lepkin brushed his hands off and looked up. He smiled when he saw his chosen handholds in the jutting rocks above him. This was what he had come here for. He climbed up the wall of the chamber and then squeezed into a space that went straight up. It was narrow enough that once he was out of the junction chamber below, he could push his back against the wall behind him and scoot upward with his hands and knees. It was essentially like crawling again, only this time if he slipped, he would end up with a lot more than just a face full of moldy water.

Up he went, about thirty feet or so, before he found the ledge he was looking for. He reached out with his right hand and pulled himself into a chute that ran horizontally. It gave him a chance to rest his knees a bit. He wormed his way through for about twenty feet and then the chute turned upward again. This time, it was wide enough that he used one hand and one foot on either side, using a kind of half-jump to propel himself vertically for another twenty feet. At the top, the chute opened up into a large, square area with beams of wood running parallel to each other across it and smaller poles crossing underneath the beams. The poles held wooden panels in place in the ceiling above Headmaster Herion's office.

It had been an accidental discovery the first time, but once Kathair had found it, he had often returned to this spot. Just lying on the beams above the wooden panels was close enough for him to hear any discussion in the office. Some of the conversations had been horribly boring, but many had been quite informative. Between his time in the secret wall adjoining Herion's secret meeting room, and eavesdropping in Herion's office, Lepkin had learned more about the Middle Kingdom than he had in all of his years before, and that included when he had studied with the elves of Tualdern.

He snaked out onto the nearest beam, careful to move slowly and silently. He didn't hear any talking from below, but there was no way to be sure the room was empty until he removed a ceiling panel. For all he knew, Headmaster Herion might be sitting in the office reading, as he was often wont to do.

Fortunately, as Kathair reached down to pull up his favorite panel which rested above a sturdy bookshelf that reached up all the way to the ceiling and had an actual ladder that he could drop down to, he found the office to be empty.

He maneuvered himself through the open panel and lowered himself down until he was hanging by his hands at arm's length, and then he dropped to the bookshelf. He scurried down the ladder and went for the mahogany desk a few feet away. He had been in the office several times, so he already knew his way around fairly well. He had even stolen Herion's journal before, so he was certain he could find what he was looking for.

He pulled the right drawer out first and rummaged through the two small books in there. One was an old journal, the other was a ledger of some sort for the school. Below them were a few papers, letters mostly. Lepkin scanned through them, but was disappointed to find that they were from nobles. Some were donation pledges, and others were about various apprentices at the academy.

Lepkin shoved them back into the drawer and then closed it as he moved on to the next one. He found a small bottle filled with brandy and a snifter beside it. He pulled the drawer out farther, but found nothing else besides a pair of white napkins. He closed the drawer and moved to the bottom drawer. This one was locked.

It had always been locked.

Not wanting to fail in what might be his final chance to help Kyra, he took a step back and then kicked the front of the drawer. The wood cracked, but didn't entirely succumb to Lepkin's strike. He hit it once more, putting all of his weight behind his kick this time. The wood split and squeaked as the small nails were yanked out around the edges and the wood went into the large drawer. Lepkin pulled his foot back with some effort, and then bent down to put his hand into the drawer.

There was mostly empty space. He reached deeper, and then his fingers touched upon some papers. He seized them and pulled them free of the drawer.

The first was a letter from the king. Lepkin scanned it quickly and saw that it had to do with the secret group Herion had been leading. His eyes moved along the page faster, hoping it would talk about an assignment to attack the vampire, but it didn't. It was mostly speaking of organizational matters, and was frankly useless to Lepkin.

He tossed the letter aside and then moved on to the next letter in the stack. He scanned through four more letters before he found the one he needed.

This particular letter was dated several months ago. It was signed with the drawing of a bird instead of a name, but it claimed to know the location of Severin's lair.

Lepkin read through it quickly, and saw that the letter indeed described the very port town he had seen through Herion's magic when Master Baird and Lady Stirling had tried to subdue the vampire.

He smiled and folded the letter until he could fit it into his left shoe. He then turned and moved to put the thick stack of letters back into the broken drawer when a heavy envelope slipped out and fell upon the floor. Lepkin stuffed the letters into the drawer and then reached down for the envelope. He recognized the wax seal along the back and noticed that it was unbroken.

"What could the elves of Tualdern wanted to say to you, Headmaster Herion?" Lepkin asked aloud. He turned the envelope over in his hand and nodded when he saw the handwriting. He knew exactly who had sent the letter. Underneath the addressee portion, he saw the words 'regarding Kathair's history,' and he squinted at the envelope.

My history? He knew his own history well enough, and it was not so remarkable. The things he had forgotten of his home had been taught to him by his guardians in Tualdern. There was nothing mysterious about him. Certainly nothing important enough to send in a letter like this.

Or was there?

Curiosity got the better of him.

Lepkin stood up and turned the envelope over once more. He slipped his finger under the flap and slid it toward the wax seal. It took a bit of effort, but the seal broke and the flap lifted backward. Lepkin unfolded the envelope completely and stared at the visible portion of the folded letter in his hands. It was thick enough that Lepkin guessed there were several pages there.

On the top of this paper were the following instructions.

This letter is to be given to Kathair Lepkin upon his graduation.

Kathair drew his brow in tight, confused as to what could be so important. He unfolded the letter and began to read the first few lines of the letter aloud.

"Master Kathair Lepkin, my friend, I must first apologize to you. I have held several secrets from you in your youth. It is not normally in my nature to do so, but in your case I had to make an exception. I hope that by the time you receive this letter, you will have the wisdom to understand why I did what I did. I will not presume to ask your forgiveness, but trust that I had your best interest at heart.

"Your history is complicated by your specific lineage and homeland. The strife and troubles your family persevered through, and the sacrifices of others made on your behalf must be unfolded to you now. Nothing is as you thought it was."

The door opened and Lepkin's breath caught in his throat. He looked up to see Headmaster Herion.

The old wizard looked down to the pile of papers and he sighed heavily. "Oh, you should not be reading that."

Lepkin didn't think. He gripped the letter tightly and ran past Herion.

"Kathair, come back!"

Lepkin was sprinting down the hall as fast as he could. He turned at the first stairway but crashed into the solid bulk of Feberik Orres as the large warrior was coming up the steps.

"Easy there," Feberik said as he reached out and grabbed Lepkin by the arm.

"Let me go!" Lepkin shouted.

Herion was there in an instant. "Hold him still, Feberik."

Lepkin felt a surge of heat as the papers in his hand ignited. He yelled in pain and let the flaming pages of the letter fall to the floor. As they floated down, his eyes caught a single portion of a sentence as flames ate their way to it from all sides of the paper.

...their murder.

Lepkin stopped struggling and fixed his eyes on those two words. His mind raced. His parents had been murdered? That isn't what he remembered. Who would have done that? Why?

He looked up to Herion with rage in his eyes and a fire burning in his heart. "My parents were murdered?" he asked.

Herion held a hand up in the air to quiet the boy. "Kathair, there is a lot to your history that is best left in the shadows for now."

"You burned the letter!" Lepkin screamed. "I have a right to know!"

"Kathair, it isn't as simple as you believe it to be."

Lepkin was done listening. He lashed out with his right leg and kicked Headmaster Herion in the groin, hard. The wizard snorted and grimaced as he fell to his knees.

Lepkin felt Feberik squeeze his wrist so hard it felt as though his hand might pop off, but he was not about to back down. He turned and tried to kick Feberik as well, but the large man moved his knee out to block Lepkin. The young apprentice then lashed out with blinding speed and slapped his hand over Feberik's left ear.

The large man grunted and leaned his head to the side.

Lepkin then jabbed a finger in the man's eye.

Feberik let go and put both hands over his eye. "I'll crush you for that!" Feberik snarled.

Lepkin then went in and put all of his rage into a kick that struck its target this time. Feberik moaned and doubled over. Then, Lepkin leapt down the stairs and ran as fast as he could for Kyra's room, stuffing the tears down inside. First he would help Kyra, then he would find a way to uncover the mystery of his past.

*****

Kyra had just managed to slip into her nightgown when there was a strange thud on the other side of her door.

"Janik?" Kyra called out.

A key slipped into the door and unlocked it. The door opened, but it was not Janik who stood there. It was Lepkin, out of breath and all red in the face. Behind him, Janik was slumped over in his chair.

"You hit him?" Kyra asked incredulously.

"I don't have much time." Lepkin entered the room and shut the door behind himself. He locked it quickly and then left the key inside. "I have the vampire's location." Lepkin bent down to his shoe and pulled a folded piece of paper out.

Kyra looked at him strangely, narrowing her eyes. She had never seen him like this before. Sure, he had been excited at times, but this was something far more than that. "You hit Janik," she said.

Lepkin nodded and stepped closer. "He would have stopped me from seeing you if I hadn't," he said. "I had to do it."

"What has gotten into you," Kyra said, ignoring the folded note in his hand.

"I..." Lepkin shook his head and looked to the floor. "It doesn't matter. Here, you have to take this. They are sending me away in the morning. I won't be able to go with you, but I had to give this to you. Herion had the vampire's location written down on this piece of paper. It's a letter from—"

Someone grabbed the door and tugged on it furiously.

"Open the door!"

Kyra recognized the voice as that of Master Fenn.

She turned to obey, but Lepkin grabbed her by both arms and pulled her away from the door and toward Linny's old bed.

"Listen to me," he said. "This will give you what you need. Follow the letter and take Leatherback. Finish this, once and for all."

The intensity in his voice was nothing compared to his tempestuous blue eyes. They swirled a mix of anger and grief. "What happened?" she asked.

She never got her answer.

The door fell to the floor amidst a swirl of smoke and sparks.

Master Fenn stepped into the room, his eyes burning and fixing quickly on Lepkin. "Unhand her!" Fenn shouted. He lifted his hand and Lepkin was magically tossed into the wall at his back on the other side of Linny's old bed.

"Don't hurt him!" Kyra shouted. "He meant me no harm!"

"He has already attacked Herion, Feberik, and Janik," Master Fenn said coldly. "I don't rightly care what his future intentions are; I am here for what he has already done."

Kyra stopped cold and looked back to Lepkin. He opened his hand and let the folded paper fall between the bed and the wall.

"Finish it," Lepkin struggled to say.

Master Fenn whispered something and the two of them disappeared in a puff of gray smoke, leaving Kyra alone in her room. She glanced to the broken door and saw Janik beginning to stir. The man put his good hand to the back of his head and then looked to Kyra. His eyes rested on her for a moment, and then he looked to the door lying on the floor.

"I'm not fixing that," he grumbled. "Herion asked me to sit outside your door and prevent you from leaving your room. He didn't say anything about your friend Kathair coming and whacking me while I took a nap." He made a show of rubbing his head some more and then he stood up. "I'm done. Let Cyrus or Herion watch your room. This is getting to be far too troublesome for me."

With that, the crippled janitor limped down the hallway and disappeared.

Kyra lifted the door and propped it precariously back into place. Though it was by no means a sturdy barrier, it would at least afford her some semblance of privacy. She moved to Linny's old bed and pulled it out from the wall. She reached around and felt for the folded paper Lepkin had brought. She found a paper and pulled it up, but it was not the folded paper Lepkin had dropped. It was an old letter from her mother.

Kyra smiled. She realized the letter must have fallen by the wall around the time Linny had been sent to room with her. She had shifted some of her things then to make space for her roommate, so it wasn't at all surprising that one of her mother's old letters might be lost there by the bed. She placed it on the bed and then reached back down for Lepkin's paper.

She found it and brought it up as well and began to unfold it. She read the letter and felt a mix of joy and sadness at the same time. This would lead her to Severin's lair. Lepkin had come through for her once more. Where she and Cyrus had failed to figure out how to find the dagger and lure the vampire to them, Lepkin had found the vampire. Now she could bring the fight to Severin.

Then again, that might not end so well.

She remembered watching Master Baird and Lady Stirling die at Severin's hands. Surely they had been preparing for the fight, yet they were no match for Severin.

Kyra wasn't even sure she could find Leatherback again. She had only traveled to Viverandon through Njar's portals. She had no way of finding the place herself. She also couldn't sit and wait in the aspen grove for Njar to come for her. The grove was damaged now, and news of the dragon slayers' deaths was sure to spread.

178

If Severin wanted to lay a trap for her, he could easily wait at the grove himself now that its location was no longer secret.

She looked at the bottom of the letter, wondering who might have signed it with the drawing of a bird instead of a name. Was it another agent in Herion's special group, or was it some other spy?

She dropped the letter and picked up her mother's letter. She let her eyes course over the page as she rubbed her mother's signature with her right hand.

"If only you were here," she said. "You would know what I should do." She stared at the letter as though it would answer her if she watched it long enough. She smiled after a few moments and brought it up to her lips and kissed it. "I miss you," she said.

As she pulled the letter away, a violet shimmer ran across the paper. Kyra nearly froze. With all her work with Cyrus, she now realized there was a charm on the letter.

She sat up straight and held the letter eagerly in both hands. Kyra spoke the words of an incantation that dispelled magical charms, but it didn't work. She tried again, but still nothing happened. Holding the letter up over her head, she tilted the paper this way and that, watching the faint shimmering color flash before her.

"What are you hiding?" she asked the paper. She then tried to focus on the charm. She tried every method to dispel it that Cyrus had taught her, but nothing worked. She became so frustrated that she growled and shook the letter. "Show me!" she snarled.

The young sorceress scoured her mind for ideas, but she had tried everything she knew. She had used everything Cyrus had taught her to dispel the charm.

Then, something else came to her mind.

She jumped up and went to her bed. She bent down and reached under the frame. She had almost forgotten about the present her mother had slipped into her bag before she came to Kuldiga Academy.

She retrieved the book from its hiding place and opened the front cover. Once more she read the note her mother had sent along with the book, now tucked lovingly inside the cover.

My Darling Kyra, As promised, here is the first of so many letters, you will not be able to endure them. I know that you are worried about your studies this year being less than you might have hoped. When you feel yourself in need of a stretch, have a look at the spells which you will find here. Be careful not to let your professors find you with this book; they will most certainly disapprove.
Love,
Your Mother

Kyra began flipping through the pages. She had been so bent on solving her mother's murder, and swept up in the events that happened so quickly after finding Leatherback's egg, that she had hardly opened this book while here. In fact, she had nearly forgotten about it altogether.

She turned the pages quickly, barely scanning the headings of various spells and incantations before moving on through the book. She was nearly half way through the book before she saw a hand drawn symbol at the top of a page.

It was a small heart, drawn in her mother's hand.

Kyra began to feel not only excitement, but great joy swell up inside her when she read the title of the spell on that page. "The Stalwart Letter," Kyra read aloud. "This is a simple, yet highly effective spell used to conceal written messages from prying eyes and ensure that only the intended recipient can ever read it."

Kyra devoured the instructions for the spell and then held the charmed letter in front of her. The instructions to work the charm were far simpler than she had hoped, but therein lay the genius of the spell, for giving the simple gesture and pass phrase was the only way the charm could ever be opened.

Kyra had already unwittingly figured out the gesture when she had kissed the letter. The missing phrase she now knew from the book her mother had given her.

She brought the letter to her lips and kissed it gently. Then she said, "Speak, for the friend is listening."

The violet shimmer glowed brighter now, and the ink on the paper was wiped away, erasing the letter that had been written on the paper before. In the previous letter's place, a new message was written as if by an invisible pen with fiery ink. The bright spot flourished along the paper, matching her mother's handwriting exactly and leaving a new, plainly legible letter for her.

> *My Dearest Kyra,*
>
> *If you are reading these words, then you have figured out the true reason I gave you the book. As I write these words, I fear for our safety. There is a great evil that hunts us. Hopefully, I will manage to defeat the monsters that hunt us before you ever figure out how to open this letter. But, if I fail in this endeavor, you should know that I have a plan that might work for you, but it will be dangerous.*
>
> *There is a dagger, hidden in our home, that commands great power. I have only now come to have a modest understanding of its true capabilities and origin. I have kept it because it is one of few weapons that can kill a vampire as easily as a dagger might slay a normal human being.*
>
> *For this plan to work, you will need to succeed where I have failed. You must find a book written by Archmage Durit entitled, Arts of the Soul Thief. Find that book, and then follow the instructions you will find in my other letter, which is waiting for you in my desk drawer at home.*
>
> *With all the love and hope I possess,*
> *Your Mother*

Kyra could hardly breathe. Cyrus had that very book! She stood up, about to run down the hall to the classroom and grab it, but she stopped before taking a single step. The last time she had tried to read from that book, she had been trapped in a nightmare by a terrible spell. Kyra figured it best to leave reading that book until tomorrow, when Cyrus could ensure her safety. She had no desire to fall prey to those terrible nightmares again.

However, if she was careful, she could get to her home tonight and retrieve the final letter from her mother.

Kyra grabbed her blue dress and slipped it over her nightgown, not wanting to take the time to fully change clothes. She then moved the broken door to the side and stepped into the hallway.

Herion had cursed her room so that she could not summon portals, but there was no longer anyone outside of her room to stop her from doing so somewhere else.

She walked part way down the hall and then opened a glowing portal. Through the hole in space, she could see her mother's library. Her heart jumped with both joy and grief at the sight of the books strewn about the floor. She had always hoped her father would have cleaned the room and put it back in order.

Kyra stepped through and looked around the library as the portal disappeared. There was a layer of dust on everything, giving the room a gray and lonely appearance accentuated by the stale air. In the far corner was a dead, brown fern that had once been a vibrant and green plant.

She looked to the door leading to the hallway and thought, just for a moment, to go back into her old room, or into her mother's room. She took in a deep breath and decided that regardless of the memories created in this manor, it was no longer her home.

Padding quietly to the overturned desk, she wondered whether the letter would still be there for her to find. She shuffled through books and papers that had fallen on the floor nearby, but saw nothing of interest addressed to her. She then went to the desk and found one of the drawers still in place. She slid it out and found a single piece of paper. The only words written on it were 'Dearest Kyra.'

She kissed the paper and spoke the phrase, but nothing happened. Kyra sighed and let the paper fall to the ground as she reached into the drawer, feeling around for anything else.

Her fingers fell upon an envelope. She pulled it out and hastily removed the letter inside. This one was fairly generic, asking how Kyra liked her classes and whether she had made many friends. It even asked whether Kyra had been able to get along with Lady Priscilla despite the instructor's insistence to use wands. Kyra laughed at that one, wondering what her mother would think of the fact that Kyra had actually gotten into a duel with Lady Priscilla and ended up knocking the instructor into a wall. Kyra then finished the letter and smiled. Her mother had always been a crafty one. She kissed it and spoke the special phrase.

The letter disappeared and new words appeared on the paper, telling her all that she should do next.

It took several minutes to read all of the instructions, for the words filled not only the entire page, but when she reached the bottom of the paper, the words would vanish to make room for the message to continue on the same piece of paper. This happened four times, turning a single page into a three and a half page letter filled with instructions.

When she finished, she folded the letter and placed it back into the drawer. She closed the drawer and spoke the words the letter had instructed her to say as she tapped the drawer three times. When Kyra pulled the drawer out once more, a red book was inside where the letter had been.

She didn't open the book, for the letter had already told her not to look for the dagger inside. Kyra had to take the book to a special altar in the forest to the north. Only there could she retrieve the dagger from where her mother had hidden it.

All she needed now was the book from Cyrus, and not a small amount of luck.

Chapter 17

Kyra woke early the next morning. Despite the difficulty she had had in calming herself after returning to her room the previous night, and the time she had spent tossing and turning as she contemplated how Lepkin might be punished for the efforts he had taken to bring her the letter, her excitement gave her more than enough energy to prepare for the day as though she had comfortably slept the whole night through.

She concealed the red book in her satchel, sandwiching it between two other text books just in case someone were to look through her things. Bolting down the hall, she nearly bumped into one of the staffers on her way to the laundry room with an armload of sheets.

"Sorry!" Kyra offered over her shoulder as she continued running to her classroom. She was so fast that she didn't even hear what the lady had said in response, but she didn't care. She finally had everything figured out, and she was so close to avenging her mother.

She burst into the classroom and her mirth disappeared quickly.

Master Fenn was in the room, speaking in hushed tones with Cyrus.

Cyrus saw her, and motioned with his head for Kyra to take a seat.

Master Fenn turned around and peered down his nose at her for a few moments, making her squirm on the inside.

"As I was saying," Fenn said as he turned back to Cyrus, "Kathair Lepkin has been sent away during the night. That should help you keep an eye on your student a bit better, as the two of them always seemed to get into trouble together."

"Might I remind you," Cyrus began, "Kyra has not only gotten into trouble, but she has killed a shade and hunted beasts that normally a man of your station should be out hunting."

Kyra smirked and took great joy in watching Master Fenn bristle at the comment.

"I know very well what she has done," Master Fenn said. "What *neither of you* know is that I have been out hunting creatures of the night. In the same time that Kyra has been here at the academy, I have dispatched four wraiths, a garunda beast, and a wylkin as well as a shadowfiend. You would do well not to question my abilities, or my zeal in carrying out the tasks given to me."

That surprised Kyra very much. She had not been aware of that many creatures nearby. In fact, she had honestly thought that she and Leatherback had hunted everything down themselves.

Master Fenn turned around and glared at her. "Surprised?" he asked. "Let's just say that there were meetings you and your friends didn't eavesdrop on and leave it at that."

Kyra nodded silently.

"Also, I should note that these types of incidents have increased tremendously since your arrival."

Was he trying to make her feel guilty? Surely he had to know that none of these things were her fault. The creatures were looking for the dagger, but she had nothing to do with taking the weapon.

"I think that's enough," Cyrus put in quickly. "I'll take your suggestions under advisement, but there is no reason to saddle her with the blame."

"Cyrus, you should be careful," Master Fenn said over his shoulder, his eyes still fixed on Kyra. "I will be the headmaster here very soon. The dragon slayers will be here within a short time as well. I would tread lightly if I were you." He then turned around and offered his hand, as if a handshake would smooth everything over once more.

Cyrus shook the man's hand and then Master Fenn left the classroom.

When the door was closed, Kyra asked, "What did he want?"

Cyrus smiled. "It started amicably enough," he replied. "He had come to inform me that he wanted me to accompany you while you hunted Severin."

"The coward should come himself," Kyra said angrily.

Cyrus shook his head. "He is not as coarse as he would have you believe," Cyrus said. "Apparently, the Keeper of Secrets has set up a few rules for you. Chief among them is the fact that if you are to be considered as a candidate for the Test of Arophim, then you must defeat the vampire either by yourself, or with the dragon for help. All other masters have been forbidden from helping you. The Keeper of Secrets says it is the only way he will accept your candidacy. As such, Master Fenn is bound by the Keeper's wishes in this instance."

"But you aren't?" Kyra asked skeptically.

"I would be, but I am not technically a titled noble. I am not known as 'Master Cyrus,' so it is a kind of legal technicality that would allow me to work with you."

"Why would Master Fenn care?"

"That is my point," Cyrus replied evenly. "Despite his callous, sometimes hurtful display, he does care about you and this school very much."

"*Sometimes hurtful?*" Kyra spat sarcastically.

Cyrus smiled and shrugged. "Come, are you ready for the day's lesson?"

Kyra then forgot all about Master Fenn and let the widest smile she had ever worn stretch her face. "Actually, I came to read *Arts of the Soul Thief* again."

Cyrus eyed her suspiciously. "What for?"

"I think I may know where the dagger is. I found a note from my mother, and she gave me a passage to read from the book. I think it has the last piece of the puzzle."

Cyrus' mouth fell open. "Where did you find the letter?"

"It was a magical letter. I received it a long time ago, but it had been written with a spell on it concealing the true message."

"And you happened to find the right letter with this special charm?" Cyrus asked skeptically, folding his arms across his chest.

Kyra nodded. "It wasn't just one letter. Every letter she sent had the same message on it once I knew how to open the charm." After returning to her room, Kyra had searched all the other letters from her mother for additional clues. She had found only the same initial message behind each charm, but it had served to put her mind at ease, knowing she hadn't missed any important clues.

"Remarkable," Cyrus said. He stroked his bearded chin and then shook his head. "I would have thought that if your mother had any leads, she would have followed them through herself."

"She did," Kyra said. "But, the one lead she couldn't follow was written in the book. She never had a copy of it."

Cyrus nodded. "Not surprising. There are only two copies in existence that I am aware of. Too bad we didn't know that was the last piece to the puzzle. I could have provided that long ago!" Cyrus wheeled around and went for his bookcase. He took the book in hand and then walked back to Kyra. "If it was your mother's clue, then you should have the honor of reading it."

Kyra smiled and held her hands out, but stopped short of taking the book. "Could you check it first?" she asked. "Last time didn't go so well."

Cyrus smiled knowingly and pulled the book back a bit. "I have already cleared it of the wards and traps that were placed upon it. Don't worry, you will not be caught in nightmares again, I assure you." He extended his arm once more, holding the book out for her to take.

She nodded, but couldn't keep the butterflies from forming in her stomach as she reached a trembling hand out to take the book. She opened it slowly, and read through the first page, half expecting herself to be sucked back into that terrible nightmare. After finishing the first page, she let out a breath that she hadn't even realized she had been holding in anticipation. The book was safe now.

Kyra set it on her desk and eagerly flipped through the pages until she found the passage her mother had spoken of in her letter. She read it eagerly, devouring each detail. Her heart was pounding inside of her now as she realized how delicate this plan was. One misstep would mean disaster, and dying at Severin's hand was not necessarily the worst option that occurred to her while reading what it was she needed to do.

After reading it through for a third time, she closed the book and slipped it into her book bag. "I may need to refresh myself once or twice more," she told Cyrus.

The man was sitting at his chair behind his desk, eagerly leaning forward and watching her. "Well?" he asked.

"I think we can do this," Kyra replied. "It should work. We should be able to get the dagger tonight."

"Gods be praised!" Cyrus said as he slapped his hand down on his desk. He struck the surface with such force, the setting of the ring which he wore on that hand cracked under the impact and a strange, orange spark shot off of the metal as the stone become dislodged and fell away, but he didn't notice. He was jumping in the air and dancing around his chair as if he were a much, much younger man.

Kyra did notice, however. As the emerald from the ring rolled across the desk, Cyrus changed a little before her eyes. It was as if his image was blurred by a film of running water, or smoke perhaps. His features blurred, as if a burst of heat had caused the air before him to waver.

Kyra leapt up from her desk and hooked the strap of her book bag over her shoulder. Something was very wrong. "Who are you?" she asked.

Cyrus turned around. Confusion was on his blurred face.

Kyra cast a dispelling enchantment that she had been working on with Cyrus, and then the truth was revealed.

The old, long bearded wizard melted away to reveal a man with dark hair, maybe in his late thirties or early forties. Kyra's mouth hung open and she shook her head as she stumbled away from her desk and back toward the door.

Cyrus looked down at himself and then his eyes found the broken ring.

"Kyra, wait, listen!" Cyrus begged.

Kyra shook her head and turned to run for the door.

WHOOSH!

Cyrus was now standing in front of the door, one hand on the knob and the other out toward Kyra, gesturing for her to stop.

"You must listen!" he said emphatically.

"You deceived me!" Kyra replied. "Who are you? Where is Cyrus?"

"I am Cyrus," he said. "I am the same I have always been. I was the man who saved your mother with Janik those sixteen years ago. I am the same who has been here, teaching you."

Kyra shook her head. "Why the disguise then? Who are you, really?" A terrible thought ran through her head then as she put the pieces together. Cyrus had gone to save her mother, but maybe it hadn't really been her mother he had been after. "You wanted the dagger," Kyra said as she pointed a finger at the man. "You went to where my mother was held captive to find the dagger, didn't you?"

The man's face turned from one of worry to something colder. "Kyra, what did you read? Tell me the last clue, I am begging you."

Kyra shook her head. She stuck her hand into her book bag and prepared a fire spell to consume the books just in case the pretender tried anything. "Why do you want the dagger?"

"Give me the book," Cyrus said with his eyes fixed on her bag. "I can help raise your mother from the dead, I swear."

Tears of anger came to Kyra's eyes. "No," she said.

"Give me the book!" Cyrus shouted.

A blast of air rushed toward Kyra, but she had already put up a ward before it struck her. She quickly prepared a few more spells and cast them. She knew she couldn't likely beat Cyrus in a fair fight. She would have to use her wits.

"GIVE ME THE BOOK!" Cyrus boomed as he sent a series of lightning bolts at Kyra. The first two slammed into the ward, cracking the shield as the continuing gust of wind ripped and pulled at the magical shield. The next three bolts went through the crack and slammed into Kyra. She went flying across the room and crashed into the bookcase so hard that two of the shelves broke and books went everywhere.

Cyrus advanced so quickly that Kyra had no time to move. A black web extended from his left hand, grabbing her and pinning her back up against the wall as he yanked the book bag free from her.

Kyra let tears of anger and grief roll down her face.

"Headmaster Herion once told me that illusions work best when they play off of others' emotions, or show them what they already expect to see," Kyra said softly. "I guess he was right."

Cyrus looked up and his mouth fell open as he realized his mistake. He dispelled the fake image of Kyra and then spun around to locate where she really was.

Kyra was standing on the opposite side of the room, next to an open portal. She had created an illusion of herself to see what Cyrus would do if she refused to give him the book. Now that she knew who he really was, she was ready to do the rest alone, and ensure that neither Severin nor Cyrus would ever get the dagger.

"Kyra, wait!"

Kyra stepped through the portal and was gone.

*****

Cyrus sat in the room for over an hour, replaying everything in his mind. He kept staring at the fragments of the broken ring and shaking his head. Without the ring given to him by the

190

warlocks, he would be hard-pressed to fool Kyra again, let alone Master Fenn.

He had no way to know where Kyra had gone when she teleported away. Possibly to the aspen grove, or perhaps back to Caspen Manor. In any case, he already knew he could not fight her for the dagger. Despite his otherwise cold heart, he had grown fond of her. He hadn't lied when he had told her that she reminded him of his own daughter. Then there was the fact that she had the same name as his late wife.

No, he couldn't fight her for the dagger.

The only option was to wait. Perhaps someday he could steal it back from her, but that would require hiding in wait for a long time. He cursed himself for messing this opportunity up so badly. He was so close to the dagger just a short while ago, and now he had little chance of recovering it in the near future.

Kyra would find it first. The hunt would start anew for Cyrus now.

He rose to his feet and brushed himself off. He took the dislodged emerald in hand and then flicked it across the room. There was only one option available to him now.

He rebuilt his illusion, taking on the form of Cyrus once again. It wouldn't fool Kyra, but it would work on those he needed to deal with now.

He spoke an incantation and a dark cloud of fog formed on the other side of his desk. As the fog cleared, Janik was standing there.

"I really don't like that," Janik said. "I could have been anywhere, doing anything."

Cyrus was not in the mood for arguing with his servant. He snapped his fingers and Janik's mouth was closed so that the man could not speak. "Listen, and hear me well, for I have little time. Kyra broke my illusion. She knows I am not Cyrus."

Janik's eyes went wide.

"Don't worry, she doesn't know you have anything to do with me. She will believe you if you pretend to be surprised as well. What I want you to do is tell Master Fenn about my deception.

Blame my presence for the monsters that have come recently. Then, send Feberik out to hunt me down. Tell them that you last saw me fleeing to the south after I had fought with Kyra. That way, when she returns, she will see you as an ally. She will continue to trust you on some level, even if she doesn't become a close friend." Cyrus took in a breath and folded his arms. "From time to time, I will send you instructions. As per your oath, I expect you to follow them exactly. Continue to serve me well and I will grant you two boons. The first is I will eventually give you some measure of magical abilities. The second, is I will help ensure Feberik becomes headmaster here after Master Fenn. Do you understand?"

Janik nodded.

Cyrus then loosed the man's mouth and Janik reached up with his good hand to rub his jaw.

"That is all."

"Where is Kyra now?" Janik asked.

"She is going to hunt the vampire. If she lives, then I would not cross her if I were you."

Janik nodded. "I will do what I can to gain her trust. How exactly shall I inform Master Fenn about you?"

Cyrus thought for a moment and then nodded once he had the answer. "Tell them you were in the hallway and heard shouting between me and Kyra. You then heard a large commotion, like furniture being tossed around and spells cast at each other. You burst into the room, but Kyra was already gone and you found only a stranger in the room. Tell Fenn that you confronted me and found out that I was masquerading as Cyrus, but, due to your handicap, I escaped. If you look around, you will find pieces of my emerald ring. Show that to Fenn. It will be enough evidence, I am sure."

Janik nodded. "And where will you go now?"

"I have some associates I need to meet with."

Chapter 18

Cyrus walked through the stone corridors down to the antechamber outside the warlocks' inner sanctum. He watched the door on the other side of the room for some time. They were making him wait longer than usual, it seemed.

Finally one of them came out and approached the stone table in the center of the antechamber. Cyrus watched him and smiled when the warlock sat across from him.

"I was told you had urgent news for the order," the warlock said.

Cyrus smiled. He was done with pretenses and games. Now that a warlock had come out to see him, he had everything he needed. His right hand slid a long, slim, but deadly dagger out from the folds of his robes beneath the table.

"I have come to tell you of the developments that have occurred lately. Surely you can sense the vampire has come into the Middle Kingdom."

The warlock nodded. "Yes, he—"

Cyrus snapped out with a flash of his hand, driving the dagger through the warlock's left temple and slamming his head down onto the stone table. Quickly, he pulled the amulet off of the warlock's neck. He left the dagger in the corpse though, for from here on out he would not need it.

He rose from his seat and his body began to stretch and shift. He called upon his magic to strengthen himself. His muscles grew denser, his skin hardened, and even his bones became thicker and fortified.

Cyrus walked to the door on the opposite side of the chamber and held up the amulet he had taken from the warlock. A slight shimmer of silver crossed over the door and then it opened to him.

He walked in and followed the hallway straight into the inner sanctum. At the first fork, he turned right. The last time he had been led through the hallways, he had memorized each and every tunnel he passed by, as well as the passages that led into the council chamber.

Down this hallway were two doors. He opened the first one and found a warlock hunched over a work bench with his back facing the door. He lifted up a beaker filled with dark brown liquid and studied it.

Cyrus raised his hand and sent a single, silent bolt of black lightning through the air. The energy blasted through the warlock's back and left scorch marks on the wall where it had burst through. The warlock fell to the floor. His beaker burst open and smoke rose from the floor as the liquid spread out, hissing, along the stone.

Cyrus then turned to the next door and opened it. Inside he found not a warlock, but a young brown-haired woman dressed in meager clothes. He knew immediately that she was a servant to the others. Unfortunately, that meant she was bound by a wizard's oath the same way Janik was bound to him. Sparing her life would only result in her attacking him at some point in the future.

She stood and was about to shout out a warning, but Cyrus lifted his left hand and made a gripping motion with it. The young woman clutched and clawed at an invisible force around her neck as her body was lifted from the ground and her face grew red. She kicked her legs against the spell, but it was no use. She was dead within moments, and her lifeless body was left to slump on the cold floor.

There were four warlocks left.

Cyrus left the short hallway and continued on his way until he came to another side tunnel. He followed this one and found four people in what appeared to be a kitchen complete with stone ovens and a large fire pit. A young boy was slicing venison at the far bench, while three women were scurrying about gathering pots and various vegetables.

Opting for silence rather than a large, fantastic spectacle, Cyrus used his magic to animate four kitchen knives. The instruments all levitated silently, and then darted out for their respective targets. None of the victims made more than a small groan before they fell lifeless before him.

"Such a waste," Cyrus commented dryly. "I should have let them finish the meal first."

He turned and continued along through the tunnels, making sure to stalk through each and every side passage and exterminate each of the servants he found.

Then, as he made his way toward the council chamber, another warlock came at him from the other end of the hall. Cyrus raised his hand, but the other warlock was able to call out a warning before Cyrus could end his life.

A flash of yellow streaked by Cyrus, glancing off his magical ward and blasting into the stone wall nearby. He answered the warlock by summoning large vines that broke through the walls and seized the warlock around each limb. A fifth vine came in from the ceiling and snaked into the warlock's mouth. The warlock wriggled and fought to get free, but Cyrus only strengthened the vines as he approached the warlock.

The warlock's neck widened as the vine made its way down into the man, and then there was a sudden jerk as the vine stabbed out from inside the warlock's chest, blood dripping to the floor as the vine continued to grow out from the man and curl around his dead body.

Cyrus waved his hand and the vines disappeared altogether, dropping the corpse with a *thump*!

The air grew heavy then and Cyrus could feel the hairs on his arms standing on end. The others had heard the warning, and they were raising their defenses. Cyrus hesitated as a great mess of tangled lightning streaked across the hallway, effectively filling the entire tunnel. The sizzling, crackling energy then coursed down the tunnel toward him.

Cyrus bent down and took the amulet from the dead warlock. He had long ago done his research, and knew how to beat the order's standard defenses.

He stood back from the corpse and placed the amulets he had taken over his neck, and stood motionless. The amulet would be able to save him, but only if he remained entirely still as the energy passed through the corridor.

The blue lightning disintegrated the dead warlock's body, but passed over Cyrus with hardly more than a slight tickling sensation. The energy went to the end of the corridor, and then doubled in strength as it formed a magical barrier to any other would-be intruders.

Cyrus then crept down toward the council chamber as quietly as his leather boots would allow. When he reached the sealed door, he found several wards and traps covering it. He walked back ten yards and then carved a fist-sized stone from the wall with a magical beam of energy. Satisfied that the stone was large enough to trip the wards, he hurled it at the door.

A tremendous explosion rocked the hallway as smoke and bits of debris filled the immediate area. A wave of flame rolled out from the council room and blasted into the wall opposite the door. This was followed by several spears made of ice, and finally a lightning storm and a second explosion.

"A bit much," Cyrus commented wryly as he stepped through the smoking mess to find the final three warlocks standing inside the council room. "Tell me, did you see this coming?"

The warlocks glanced to each other.

Cyrus smiled. "And that is why you are now being deposed. You have squandered your gift." He sent a rather powerful gale toward the warlock on the left side of the table. Even with his ward, the warlock was thrown into the back wall, where he snapped his neck.

"You have betrayed us!" the gray haired warlock said.

Cyrus sent a bolt of lightning.

The gray-haired warlock summoned a shield of stone and deflected it.

The warlock on the right conjured a large, green snake that coiled and hissed atop the table. Cyrus laughed and dispelled the snake with a snap of his fingers.

The warlock on the right yelled and ran forward, shouting the words to a transformation spell as he advanced. Cyrus sent a spear of light at the man, but missed as the body transformed into that of a large, six-legged wolf. Cyrus prepared another spell, but the gray-haired warlock sent a whirlwind at him that sent him flying out the door.

He crashed upon the floor, but his hardened skin and strengthened sinews absorbed the blow without so much as a bruise to show for it. Cyrus moved to stand, but he was not fast enough to avoid the wolf. The creature landed on him hard and began clawing and biting. The front-most pair of legs managed to tear through Cyrus' robes and gash his chest, but Cyrus ignored the pain, reached out, and clamped the wolf's mouth shut.

Cyrus focused on a single spell, calling a blazing ball of energy into his hands. The wolf fought furiously, but Cyrus sent the ball of energy into the wolf's head. The animal's neck whipped back and a gray and black ring exploded out from its head. There were no abrasions or cuts on the wolf, but the animal was dead. Cyrus had put the energy directly into the transformed warlock's brain.

He pushed the corpse to the side and stood up. He jerked his head to the side, cracking his neck, and then he rolled his shoulders and rubbed a hand over his chest. The gashes in his skin healed instantly, leaving only ripped clothing and some dried blood behind.

Another whirlwind was already coming for him, but Cyrus deflected it with a much stronger force of air that pushed the whirlwind back into the council chamber and toward the final warlock.

The gray-haired warlock then unleashed lightning at the ceiling as Cyrus made his way back into the chamber. Stones dislodged and fell, but Cyrus created a spherical shell around himself and the debris bounced off harmlessly.

"Who are you?" the gray-haired warlock demanded. "You are not Cyrus the wizard."

"No," Cyrus replied, "I am not." He moved into the chamber confidently, letting his shell protect him from glaring lightning, intense flames, and magical arrows that the last warlock hurled at him. Then, as he got close to the gray-haired warlock, the sphere pushed the man up into the wall and held him there, pinned as though he was squished between two boulders.

"Why," the gray-haired warlock asked.

Cyrus pouted his lip and raised his brows as he shrugged. "Why not?" He then dispelled his spherical shell and the gray-haired warlock fell to the ground and stumbled toward him. Cyrus slammed his magic-hardened fist into the warlock's face. The warlock flew back into the wall and slid down the stone to land on his rump. Cyrus then bent down and put his thumb to the warlock's forehead. "Don't be angry, I will make this coven stronger than it has ever been before."

"You?" the warlock asked breathlessly.

Cyrus nodded and the energy grew in his thumb until a fiery orb glowed in front of the warlock's forehead. "Me," Cyrus confirmed. The red orb shot into the warlock's head and the man's eyes went black as night. The warlock's head then slumped to the side, and the coven was no more.

Cyrus stood up and took in a breath as he looked around the council chamber. He moved to the table and placed his hand on the chief seat. It would be good to have his own coven. There would be minimized running around for him now. He would recruit others to do the work for him. Hairen would help him find capable witches and warlocks to see into the future to give him an advantage over his foes. One way or another, he would have the dagger, and then he would finally have what he sought.

Chapter 19

After Kyra had escaped from Cyrus, she spent the entire day prepping the plan exactly the way her mother had instructed her to do. It had neither been pleasant, nor easy. Now she was in the middle of a forest deep in the mountains to the west of Caspen Manor, and the full moon was rising high in the night sky.

She rubbed a fresh gash in her left arm, wishing she had spent a little more time learning healing spells. Her mother's plan had no place for any additional players, so she had decided to forego getting Leatherback before setting everything up. With a couple of fresh wounds and a stiff spine, she now thought that perhaps that had been a mistake.

Then again, her mother's plan seemed to be her best line of attack.

For now, she had to focus on getting the dagger.

She trudged up the mountainside, following the clues her mother had spoken of in the long letter in her old library. Faint blue dots lit up under the moon, showing the way to the altar.

Her only hope was that the vampire had not already found the altar.

Everything would be for naught if he was waiting for her.

Kyra moved through the pine trees and up the mountain, scanning the area around her while she followed the dots. At one point she saw a bear meandering through the woods, but it didn't seem interested in her, so she continued along on her way. She couldn't afford to use any magic until she reached the altar. It would attract too much attention.

It took her another ninety minutes to reach the right clearing, which sat upon the top of a small bluff overlooking the heavily wooded hills and mountains around her. The moon hung large in the sky, giving her all the light she needed to see by. In the center of the clearing was a stone altar. The perfect cube stood three feet tall, with an intricately carved design lining the sides. The top was flat and void of any pattern, though there was a large crack in the right-hand side that broke through the cube and scarred one of its sides, reaching half-way down to the dirt below.

Dry pine needles crunched under her feet as she approached the altar. She set her book bag, which now had a fresh blood stain on one side, down at her feet and took in a couple of breaths. She pulled out Arts of the Soul Thief one more time, and read through everything there that her mother had instructed her to learn. Then she focused on all of the instructions in the letter.

Her heart was beating harder, and her stomach was twisted in knots. Without Leatherback, she felt so extremely vulnerable. Her eyes darted up to the woods around her, as if she expected the vampire to emerge, laughing at her as he had in her nightmares.

"You can do this," Kyra told herself.

She took in one final breath, and then bent down to retrieve the red book. She placed it on the altar, and then set her right hand down upon the book. A thin, green mist appeared over the book. It swirled outward and then fell into the altar as she watched.

Her fingers trembling, she opened the book to the correct page and read the words she had been told to read.

"Web of fate and silk of destiny, bring back the suspended offering, and release it to me. Habera bon'des derion, cul hemeth."

The book began to glow, and then it hovered up into the air as green mist stretched out from the book and enveloped her hand and forearm, lifting her along with the book.

A bright yellow column of light connected the book to the altar, and the green mist receded from Kyra, allowing her to drop down and pull her arm back.

The book then snapped shut and a flash of blue light erupted from the altar, coursing high into the sky. The red book turned black, and then it opened once more and a large, curved dagger with rubies in the hilt emerged from it. It continued to grow before her as the book shrank away into nothingness. Soon, there was only the blue light dancing atop the altar and bathing the floating dagger in its glow.

Kyra smiled and reached out for the weapon.

She took it in her hand and felt a strange power flow from it. It coursed through her arm and filled her whole body with an added strength that she had not expected. Her eyes were fixed on the smooth, shining blade. One of the rubies began to glow, and then the altar went dark.

"You can feel it now, can't you?" a smooth voice called out from the edge of the forest. "There is a power in that weapon, isn't there?"

Kyra looked up and saw Njar emerge from the tree line. "Where have you been?" she asked accusingly.

"The vampire attacked me in Viverandon," he said.

Kyra's eyes went wide. "Is Leatherback all right?"

Njar nodded, limping into the clearing and leaning upon his staff. "I believe he is, but I haven't seen him since he returned to the aspen grove."

Kyra had already suspected, but now the illusion was clear to her. "Is Njar dead?" she asked pointedly.

Njar laughed heartily and shook his head. The form turned into that of a tall man with fangs and long, braided silver hair kept neatly with red bows. "No, he is not dead, though he may wish he were," Severin answered. "You can feel the dagger calling to you, can't you?"

Kyra looked to the weapon and gave a slight nod. She couldn't deny that she felt its power, and longed to have it for herself.

"If you are wondering why your mother could not feel it, it is because you have the blood of a vampire running through your veins, and she does not."

Kyra felt the rage swell up inside her at the mention of her mother. "You killed her," she hissed.

"A mortal's life is never a long affair, though it need not be the case with you."

"I will never join you," Kyra said.

Severin laughed. "No, I hadn't expected you would, but just to be clear, I never wanted you to join me. You might make a good servant, but honestly your actions of the last year have proven you to be a little too free-spirited."

"How did you find me?" Kyra asked. "You must have been close by to come so soon after the beacon lit the sky."

Severin pointed to the gash in her arm. "I can smell your blood from a very long way away. It is the same way that wraith found you in your dragon's nest." The vampire looked up to the sky then as a great shadow crossed over the moon. "Ah, your dragon has come to rescue you."

Kyra didn't look up. She knew that Leatherback was not here. It was only an illusion she had cast in the hopes of gaining the upper hand with a distraction.

A great and terrible roar thundered through the air and flames lit up the sky.

Severin laughed and waved his hand. The shadow over the clearing disappeared. "Please, don't waste your time with illusions for my sake. I am far beyond your skill." He smiled at her, his evil fangs shining in the night. "You should ask that boyfriend of yours what my magic is like," Severin said.

"Boyfriend?" Kyra echoed.

Severin chuckled softly and stepped closer to her. "Oh, that's right, you don't know that Kathair Lepkin has feelings for you. Sorry, did I spoil the surprise?"

"How do you know of him?"

"I may have met him and his dragon slayer tutors, though I must say they turned out to be far less effectual than I had hoped.

I led them all straight to your precious Leatherback, but they couldn't even bring him down. Pity, really, because I will not make his death a quick one."

"Let him go, and I will give you the dagger," Kyra said. "All I want is peace. Let us go and we will not trouble you anymore."

Severin laughed and shook his head. "I will have the dagger anyway. You have nothing of value to trade with me."

Kyra knew she had to make her move. The vampire was walking toward her, and she would be no more of a match for his powers than she was for Cyrus. She raised the dagger into the air and then plunged it down to the altar.

"Kung ger'ah sik'en du heth!" she shouted. The dagger glowed with an ethereal silver color as it tore through the stone and the altar split apart. A great thunder rumbled through the mountain and the very ground shook and groaned in protest.

A moment later, something sharp tore through her right shoulder and she was flung back from the altar to land ten yards away on the ground. She moaned in agony as smoke and blood issued out from her nearly severed arm.

"You should have brought your dragon," Severin hissed.

Kyra tried to stand, but screamed in pain with any movement as it only worsened the pain in her arm.

"What were you thinking, facing off against a vampire alone?"

Severin stepped toward the stubby core of the altar and reached for the dagger. His hands clasped around the hilt and the rubies began to glow bright and hot.

"I can feel its power!" Severin shouted. "With this, I shall have dominion over all of—"

The remainder of the altar turned black as the void then, and a silvery shimmer glistened across it. Severin looked down and tried to pull the dagger free, but found that not only was it lodged in the stone, but he was stuck to it.

"What is happening?" Severin asked as his knees went weak and he fell in front of the dagger.

A great, black and silver line appeared in the air near the altar, slicing a vertical gash in the very fabric of space. Thunder rumbled all around and lightning shot out as bony fingers reached out from inside the line and pressed it open into a widening portal.

"What is this?" Severin shouted.

Kyra smiled. The plan had worked. "I had to give the dagger some of my energy," she said through her pain. Severin turned and looked at her incredulously. "That was the only way I could open the rift."

"The rift?" Severin repeated.

The portal opened wide enough for a skeletal figure to step through. He was wearing black, tattered robes, and had glowing yellow eyes shining from his skull.

"You have eluded me for a long time, Severin," the figure said.

"Khefir," Severin whispered. "You can't be here," he protested. "You were banished from the Middle Kingdom!"

The skeleton laughed aloud, its loose jaw clicking and clacking with each movement. "Archmage Durit may have found a way to keep me from this land, but you have unwittingly brought me back."

Severin shook his head and tried again to pull himself free from the dagger. "No, it isn't possible!"

Khefir turned and pointed to Kyra.

She watched as a pale yellow spark lifted from the bony finger and floated over to land in her ghastly wound. She cried out in pain as the stinging magic repaired her arm, growing new tissue and sealing the skin over it.

"Kyra Dimwater, you have come through with your end of the bargain, and now I shall come through with mine," Khefir said.

"You made a deal with a devil?" Severin spat.

Kyra pushed up from the ground and walked over to the vampire. "This altar was built by my ancestors. You see, the Dimwater line has only been practicing noble magic for a few generations. Before that, we were a line of necromancers and dark sorcerers, and we went by the name Noctumbra. When we changed our ways, we built this altar over that of our ancestors. It is one of the last few vestiges of dark magic in the Middle Kingdom. The spell I cast took some of my energy, and then plunged it through the newer altar and down to the ancient one, where it could mix with the underworld and invite Khefir back to this plane in the Middle Kingdom."

Severin held his mouth open in terror, shaking violently.

"When you seized the dagger, it drained some of your power as well, giving the magic an additional boost."

Khefir reached out with a bony hand and gripped the back of Severin's neck. "Part of the deal was that I would get your undead soul. There shall be no more escaping death for you."

"What?! No!"

A black mist formed around Severin's form and a great wind whirled around them. Kyra couldn't see what was happening, but she heard Severin's tormented screams. Then, the mist vanished and a jumble of bones fell into a heap where Severin had once been. In Khefir's hand was a chain made of gold. The fiery links extended out like a leash, and wrapped around the spirit form of a man that looked much like Severin had in his physical form.

"Khallak!" Khefir called out.

A trio of large, red-skinned orcs came out from the portal and knelt before Khefir.

"Take Severin down to the lower levels of Hammenfein. I shall meet up with him shortly, and then he shall begin to have a taste of his everlasting torment for his crimes in this world."

The three orcs rose and took hold of the chain, and then they dragged the kicking and screaming spirit into the abyss.

Khefir then took a few steps toward Kyra and gestured toward the dagger with a bony index finger. "As per our agreement, the dagger is yours. Now that I may come to the Middle Kingdom and collect the souls of the wicked once more, you have made my work much easier."

"Remember what you owe me," Kyra said proudly.

Khefir nodded. "I will not allow Hatmul entry into the Middle Kingdom," he promised with a nod. "While I am permitted to collect the wicked souls, he would torment the living, and I agree

205

that he should not be allowed to do so. Man torments himself enough as it is."

"And…" Kyra pressed.

Khefir laughed, but it was not the menacing sound he had emitted while laughing at Severin. "I have prepared a place for your friend, Leatherback. I will protect him from Hatmul, as my brother would surely enslave him, but I have a dominion of Hammenfein where Leatherback can aid my orc generals in fighting demons that do not yield to the order of Terramyr."

"Well then, I suppose for a deal with a devil, this is likely as good as it could have gone," she said as she put her hand out to shake Khefir's.

"You could have died," Khefir pointed out. "It was very foolish to tempt the vampire as you did." Khefir pointed to her newly-healed shoulder. "He could have killed you if his aim had been a bit better—or"

"Or if my ward had been a bit weaker," Kyra corrected.

"Nevertheless, as soon as he touched the dagger, I would have had my prize."

"And I still would have had mine as well," Kyra said truthfully. "You are bound to your promise whether I am alive or dead."

Khefir nodded. "You were willing to sacrifice much for your friend, and for that, I do hope you can destroy the blight that afflicts the Middle Kingdom. When you have done so, come back to this spot and I shall return your friend to you."

Kyra nodded with a smile.

"One more thing," Khefir said as he started away for the portal. "I have collected millions of souls since the first Great War. I know the wicked from the good. You may have vampire blood in your body, but your heart is as pure as they come on this world. Fare well, young sorceress, and take comfort that if you continue as you are now, despite what others may fear in you, I shall not come to collect your soul when your life reaches its end."

Kyra smiled as a tear rolled down her cheek. It was ironic that priests feared her while one of the rulers of Hammenfein so revered her, but the words were good to hear nonetheless.

She watched the large god disappear back through his black portal and then she took the dagger in hand. Now, she had to find Leatherback.

Chapter 20

Kyra managed to reach the coastline by early morning. She didn't have a boat, but she knew how to find Leatherback's mountain on an island in the sea. She traveled by way of a magical platform she summoned using one of the spells in the book her mother had given her. It was not as fast as flying through the air, but it was much faster than any boat she might have been able to pilot by herself.

She reached the island by late afternoon.

She climbed up the eastern slope and then navigated her way around the west face of the slope where Leatherback's mine was. To her dismay, the dragon was not there.

To pass the time, she gathered fruits and cooked some fish from the mountain stream. She built a fire and waited long into the night, but Leatherback didn't come.

She had no way of finding Viverandon, and she didn't want to risk being caught at the aspen grove, so she waited on Leatherback's island. She stayed there, making do with what food she could find for three days before she heard the familiar beats of Leatherback's wings.

The shadow he cast over the mountainside was a welcome sight as well, filling her with joy. She called out to him loudly, waving her arms.

Leatherback dropped down, a smile on his face.

"I was looking for you," he said. "I searched our pond, but you were not there. I couldn't go to the school either."

Kyra frowned. "Well, why didn't you have Njar use the Pools of Fate to find me?"

"Njar is missing, and the Pools of Fate no longer work, they are cursed."

"Cursed?" Kyra repeated.

Leatherback nodded. "I have been looking for him as well, but I can't find him."

Kyra took it all in. This was supposed to be a happy victory. She had not expected to be caught off guard by something like this. "Does anyone know where Njar went?"

Leatherback shook his head. "He was with me last, and then he went to Viverandon. There was another satyr that was killed underneath Nonac, the great tree that guards the way into Viverandon. The others fear that Njar is dead."

Kyra felt a pit form in her stomach. She had thought that Severin was lying when he had spoken of Njar. Now she realized how wrong she had been to assume that. If the Pools of Fate were now cursed, and Njar was missing, then he was either killed by Severin, or imprisoned somewhere.

"Why have you come here?" Leatherback asked, pulling her from her thoughts.

Kyra produced the dagger. "Severin the vampire is dead."

Leatherback roared and shot fire into the sky as he jumped up and whirled around happily. "When can we make the journey north?"

Kyra shook her head. "I can't make that journey yet. I still have to find the right spells to help us get over the mountains."

Leatherback frowned. "I have to go. Without the Pools of Fate, I have no protection."

Kyra shook her head and smiled softly as she reached out and stroked Leatherback's snout. "Actually, there is a place where you will be safe." She raised the dagger up for him to see it. "You can go there while I train harder and prepare for our journey to the north."

"Where will I be?" Leatherback asked.

"It is a place between Iverglendar and Hammenfein," she replied. "But, Nagar's Blight cannot reach you there."

"Will it be safe?" he asked, suddenly sounding much smaller than he really was.

Kyra nodded. "I made an arrangement that will keep you safe. There will be others with you, orcs that are sworn to fight for Khefir in the afterlife. They fight against demons and other things in Iverglendar and some planes of Hammenfein."

"Dragons?" Leatherback asked.

Kyra shook her head. "No, the demons are kind of like the wylkins and garunda beasts we have already fought. There shouldn't be anything down there that will give you any trouble, especially with an army of orcs beside you."

"I don't like orcs," Leatherback snorted.

Kyra laughed. "You haven't met any orcs," she said.

"Will I be able to fly and see the sky?"

Kyra frowned. "You can fly, but the sky there is red and filled with thick clouds. There is light, but it is not the same as here."

Leatherback snorted and a puff of smoke issued out from his nose. "You will come for me soon?"

"As soon as I am able to travel to the north with you, I will come."

Leatherback nodded. "Will you come with me now?"

Kyra shook her head. "There some more things I must do here. Lepkin and Njar both need my help, I think. I will find them, and I will continue to train. I will come to you as soon as I can, I promise."

"I would help them too," Leatherback said.

"It is not safe for you to stay on this plane," Kyra said softly.

The dragon nodded and then moved in close to nuzzle her with his snout. "Before I go, will you tell me the story of the Moon Dragon one more time?"

Kyra smiled and threw her arms around Leatherback's snout and let a couple of tears fall onto her friend as she leaned in for the best hug she could manage.

"There is always time for one more story, my dragon-friend," she said.

About the Author

Sam Ferguson is a fairly average guy.
That's it.
No, really, that's it.
Oh- you are actually reading this?

Well… the truth is that Sam is a very *lucky* guy. He juggles work in such a way that he makes sure to spend enough time with his loving wife and five sons. He is blessed to be writing full time now. In his spare time he is an avid powerlifter, and competes from time to time.

He spent nearly five years serving as a U.S. Diplomat and absolutely loved the experience, but decided to move back home. Outside of the U.S. he has lived in Latvia, Hungary, and Armenia. He speaks Russian, Hungarian, and Armenian. (He used to speak some Latvian too, but he has no one to practice with anymore…)

He has a a large, happy dog.
He plays the Elder Scrolls series.
His favorite superhero is Wolverine, but Batman is a close second.
If the kids go to bed at a reasonable hour, he will cuddle up with his wife to watch Scrubs reruns, the Big Bang Theory, Castle, and Burn Notice.
See, really just an average guy after all.

If you enjoyed this book, then join Sam Ferguson's Facebook page, sign up for alerts on his Amazon page where we would encourage you to leave reviews on the books you have read, or you can follow Sam on his author blog:

www.talesfromterramyr.com/

and on his weight lifting blog:

www.steeldads.blogspot.com

Other Books by Sam Ferguson

The Sorceress of Aspenwood Series

The Dragon's Champion Series

The Wealth of Kings

The Netherworld Gate Series

The Dragons of Kendualdern series

The Fur Trader

The Haymaker Adventures

Other Books by Dragon Scale Publishing

The Protector of Esparia by Lisa M. Wilson

Kingdom of Denall Series by Eric Buffington:

The Troven

Secrets at the Keep

The Changing

Tales of the NoWhere and NeverWhen by Jason Hauser

Wisp the Wayfinder

Puck the Pathwinder

Also available exclusively on the

Dragon Scale website:

Tharzule's Tome of Wishes by Malinda Smiley

Orcs and Elves by Bethan Owen